The Shadow Road

BOOK FOUR

The Shadow Road

THE WARLOCKS OF TALVERDIN

K.V. Johansen

ORCA BOOK PUBLISHERS

Library and Archives Canada Cataloguing in Publication

Johansen, K. V. (Krista V.), 1968-
The shadow road / written by K.V. Johansen.

(The warlocks of Talverdin ; 4)
ISBN 978-1-55469-165-4

I. Title. II. Series: Johansen, K. V. (Krista V.), 1968- .
Warlocks of Talverdin ; 4.
PS8569.O2676S53 2010   jC813'.54   C2009-907265-3

First published in the United States 2010
Library of Congress Control Number: 2009942220

Summary: In Book Four of the Warlocks of Talverdin series, half human
warlock Nethin is abducted and forced to use his formidable powers to open the shadow
road, an action that may have terrible consequences beyond anyone's imagining.

*Orca Book Publishers is dedicated to preserving the environment and has printed this book
on paper certified by the Forest Stewardship Council.*

Orca Book Publishers gratefully acknowledges the support for its publishing
programs provided by the following agencies: the Government of Canada through the
Canada Book Fund and the Canada Council for the Arts, and the Province of British
Columbia through the BC Arts Council and the Book Publishing Tax Credit.

Cover artwork by Cathy Maclean
Cover design by Teresa Bubela

ORCA BOOK PUBLISHERS   ORCA BOOK PUBLISHERS
PO Box 5626, STN. B   PO Box 468
VICTORIA, BC CANADA   CUSTER, WA USA
V8R 6S4   98240-0468

www.orcabook.com
Printed and bound in Canada.
Printed on 100% recycled paper.
13 12 11 10 • 4 3 2 1

To Karla and Mike, in return for restful days by the lake.

✤ CONTENTS ✤

Continued…

PART TWO

�֍ ✖ ✖

Here follows "The History of the Shadow Road," thought to have been written by Nethin'kiro Rukiar, based on his own experiences and those of others—if we can believe his tale to be true. This manuscript is said to have been taken from the secret archives of Greyrock Castle, though the Princes of the Freemarch of Greyrock, descendants of Hermengilde'lana, deny to this day that such archives even exist. But do we dare dismiss the tale as untrue?

ISLAND OF
ESWILAND

coronation shrine
gulf of
shai
R.shai
Dralla
the fens
talverdin
oakhold
River senna
kanifglin
sennamor castle
GREYROCK
RIVER KOR
south branch
cragroyal
hayonwey
the westwood
RIVER BELDAIN
R. roshing
eswy-dunmorra
talverdin mountains
RIVER ESTA
river narra
RENSEY
RIVER DORTHA
n
w   e
s
to hallasbourg,
[hallaland], hallsia,
ronish empire, etc.
0   50   100 miles

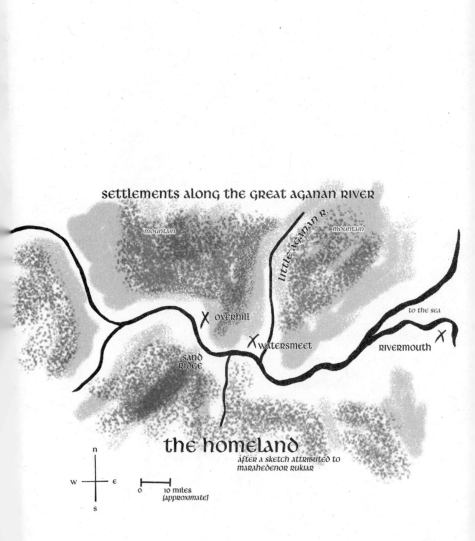

settlements along the great aganan river

mountain

little aganan r.

mountain

to the sea

X overhill

X watersmeet

RIVERMOUTH

SAND
RIDGE

the homeland

after a sketch attributed to
marahedenor rukiar

n

w ——— e

s

0 — 10 miles
[approximate]

Part One

Chapter One

Nethin: The Coffin

Late spring, end of Fuallin-month

I surfaced, struggling, from a well of dreams in which I had floated for time out of mind, drowning, with nightmare creatures surrounding me, pawing me, claws and slimy frog fingers on my skin. In the nightmares, the monsters were my own family, their faces horribly distorted by expressions of hatred and hunger.

Waking did not end the nightmare. The darkness was nearly absolute. Only the faintest pattern of light floated like stars above my eyes. Fireflies? No. My head pounded, and a foul stench in the air made my heart race. Not fireflies. A ceiling of wood pressed close above my nose, light seeping through a pattern of tiny holes. I did not need that faint light to see by. The wood held its own soft glow, the night-colors any true Nightwalker could see in the most absolute darkness. And I was a true Nightwalker, no matter what some people—my great-grandfather in particular—had said. For me, and for all Nightwalkers, darkness held faint, elusive colors, pearl and velvet. This wood was new and golden red, streaked like marble.

The cloying well of nightmare pulled me down again. I was on one of Korian'lana's ships, sailing to the human empire he had discovered, West Overseas. The deck was bucking and heaving, and my father lurched towards me, eyes glowing in the darkness. "Human mongrel," the thing said, but it was not my father who said that. Never my father.

Other wakings followed, as nightmarish as the dreams. Voices. Hands. Blazing light, blinding my eyes. Pale, dark-eyed faces. Broth, salt and slippery with barley. Water. Occasional visits to roadside bushes, staggering, half-carried, arms and legs stabbing with pain. I was ill, I realized. Yes, of course, but why this camp by the roadside? I had dreamed of ships, but all I saw were boxy wagons, one draped in dusty lavender palls as though it carried the dead, and a coach with the twin blue trout of House Langen on its door. Hefty Eswyn-bred draft mules stood nose-down where someone had spilled feed out onto the grass for them. It must have been the feeling of movement that made me dream of ships...

Someone pressed a cup to my lips. Not broth. I was so thirsty I drank, and then choked and spat at the taste, remembering it from other hazy wakings. But they held my nose and tipped it into me when I gasped, so it was swallow or choke. Bitter. My stomach heaved, and the voices shouted at one another. A woman sang a spell, hands on my shoulders.

Then the nightmares came back, worse than the worst of the fever dreams during that illness that had carried off both my sisters and half the other children of the castle, the year I was four. Perhaps I was still four and dying of the black fever. Perhaps my mother—who had put all the strength of her own young life into her witchcraft healing, trying to save us—lay dead upon my bed. I was wrapped in the reek of rotting flesh, the smell remembered from a crow found dead in the woods, buzzing with flies. I had thought my mother dead, seeing her sleeping beside me, pale and frail, on my first clear-headed waking as the black fever left me. Perhaps all my life since was a hallucination, a wish only, and I was about to die and join the older sisters who had gone before me.

Panic made me try to sit up. I discovered I was too weak to do so. Just as well, or I would probably have bashed my head and knocked myself out again. But I could think, I realized. I was not dreaming. I was...very ill, yes. But I still lived, and it was years since that plague had raged through Talverdin. I was older now than my eldest sister had been. My mother was alive, though never strong, and I was...I was...

In a coffin. I smelled of death, of rotting flesh. Dots of light danced before my face. The night-colors of wood...

I screamed, though it came out only a harsh rattle of breath. I was sealed inside a coffin, lying on a thin cushion of quilted wool, bare wood walls inches from my shoulders, flat lid of boards over my face. I tore my fingers raw, thumped feet and ankles to throbbing, before any sort of reason could make itself heard again.

I was not dead; of course I was not dead. The light was shining through air holes. I was not buried alive. I was... Why wasn't I getting out of this?

✠ Chapter Two ✠

Nethin: Sitting by the River

The previous autumn, Mullin-month

The past fall there had been an…incident. That was how I thought of it. I had lost my temper, not just badly, stupidly, but hysterically. It had seemed so important then. Everything, for months, had seemed to be flying to pieces inside me. In the dark of the night I had wondered if I were going mad. Some said my mother was mad, and a murderer, though I could not believe it. But in those moods of utter misery, I wondered: What if this roiling temper and moodiness was a sign of that evil growing in me?

I couldn't seem to control my feelings. Everything blew up into anger or shaming private tears. I didn't want to see my friends, not that I had many. I didn't want to study. I didn't want to ride. I escaped into books, long tales of human knights on desperate quests, but too often, in the Eswyn ones, the evil abductors of the knights' ladies or the betrayers of the kingdom turned out to be warlocks, so in the end they only made me angrier within myself. And the Talverdine tales were desperate, tragic stories of escape into Talverdin, the characters pursued by murderous humans, or myths and legends of the sort my father studied. Hearing them torn apart in the search for deeper historical truths at the breakfast table had long ago drained them of any romance, so far as I was concerned.

So I decided to go away somewhere, anywhere, as if that would help. Since I couldn't escape into stories and verse, I would escape by leaving home, as if I could leave my self behind and find a new one. I decided to travel alone, to stay with my human cousins in the Fens of Dunmorra. The journey would be an adventure, a chance to work out things in my head, a chance to talk to my human uncle-by-marriage about the fears I had in the night. Uncle Korby would not turn around and talk about me to my parents, as I feared his wife, my mother's sister Robin, would. My mother and her sister were very close, and my mother worried about me, her only surviving child, with the fierceness and devotion of a mother cougar.

But my father said no. I was not old enough to go off traveling on my own without even a man-at-arms to look after me, especially not across the human kingdom, which might be an ally and a friend but still held too many people who hated and feared Nightwalkers.

I do not look in the least like a Nightwalker, and I was ashamed of that, so perhaps that was why I screamed at my father that I was never allowed to do anything on my own (so hideously, embarrassingly childish that I squirmed remembering it, even locked in a coffin). I wasn't made of glass, I screamed, no matter what my mother thought. And hadn't she been an outlaw in the forest when she was little older than me? Hadn't the prince and the baroness crossed the breadth of Eswiland alone, hunted by Chancellor Arvol's men, when they were my age? I stalked out of my father's study and slammed the door.

And the door exploded into flying splinters, deadly arrows that left me and my father bleeding on opposite sides of the ruin. Quills of old oak pinned a precious rare manuscript to my father's writing desk, and my father's big white and orange tomcat, Samzon, was alive only because the beast had, moments before, fled out the window to the roofs below to get away from the shouting. The footstool where the placid cat had been sleeping was in worse shape than the irreplaceable parchment pages. Since his cat and his son had both survived, my father was most put out about the damaged manuscript.

At the time, though, he said nothing about that. He made sure neither of us had any wounds requiring stitching, told me to wipe the blood off my face—I still have the scar below my eye, a dimple of puckered skin—and marched me out of the castle. I was afraid. I had never been caned in my life, only spanked once when my cousins, Crow and Drustan, and I climbed out on the crumbling section of the ramparts at the eastern end of the curtain wall, where the castle had fallen into ruin, and Drustan nearly fell to his death. That was all Crow's fault, she being the eldest, and whatever her father said to her then was worse, from the look on her face afterwards, than any spanking.

In silence, my father and I hiked and clambered among the rocks along the swift River Roshing until we were both exhausted, and I, at least, had lost the shaky, panicky urge to scream and burst into tears like a baby.

I loved the river, despite the fact that the great-grandfather I hated and feared had been named after it. All my life, the river had sung its song beneath my windows, a thunder in the spring, a lullaby like wind in pines in the low water of summer, the bell-like chime of a current of open water leaping amid the ice-covered boulders in the winter. It comforted me as no words could have done.

Sitting precariously on a rocky ledge with the water churning beneath us, we talked awkwardly, not looking at one another. My father found loose crumbs of rock and threw them, one after another, into the water, where the ripples vanished amid the froth of the current. It was perhaps the first real talk of our lives. He told me about my mother, young and scared, returning from hunting to find her grandfather's killers standing over his body.

"She slew one of them and wounded the other," he said matter-of-factly. "They were Yehillon. They were looking for the secret of Kanifglin Pass, the secret that her family had guarded, generation upon generation. They would have tortured and killed her and Robin, had your mother not been so swift with her bow."

And he told me why he thought my Maker-strength grew so strong and wild, and why I, more than most young Makers my age, needed to learn to control my temper and my fear.

"Witch-blood?" I repeated when he was done.

My father threw another stone into the river.

"You're not a freak," he said. "Well, in a way, you are. Have you never wondered why there are so few great Makers these days, men and women like those who set the enchantments on the Greyrock Pass and the coast? Why there's no one else like Maurey'lana?"

"The Warden is half human," I said, "like me."

"So are other people, especially children of your generation," he said, "but only you and Maurey risk killing bystanders when you lose your temper. You show every sign of being stronger than any other Maker in the land except Maurey himself, Nethin. Or maybe even stronger than he. Who knows?"

I said nothing, hugging my arms tighter about my knees. I knew that, like Maurey'lana, I had the power to be a great Maker, a magician that humans would call a warlock. I had left my tutors behind in skill and strength and understanding long ago. My father was a powerful Maker, but I was stronger.

"There have been so many debates about why the prince is so strong, one of the old heroes come again. But I've solved it, I think. There are no Makers like him in the earliest histories, the earliest tales. Only later, when the stories talk of humans and Nightwalkers living together in Eswiland—your mother's ancestors and mine."

"By humans, you mean the original Eswyn humans. Not the ones who came from the continent with Bloody Hallow."

"Yes. And then after Hallow came and drove us into the west, the Makers dwindled again. But we had forgotten the old ways of power. We no longer remembered that Makers were meant to work together, in groups, to achieve the great spells. We had become, I suppose you could say, lazy, because of the great Makers. Do you see it?"

"See what? You mean…witch-blood? The great Makers were all descended from human witches?"

"It's not human ancestry that makes an unnaturally, dangerously strong Maker. It's witch parentage. And so many of the original humans of Eswiland were witches, and there were so many marriages between humans and Nightwalkers in those days, which we have both forgotten…But after we sealed ourselves into Talverdin, humans and Nightwalkers hardly ever met, and the witches—the true Eswilanders, I suppose you could call them—were mostly slaughtered by Hallow's folk or driven into the Fens or the mountains."

"But Maurey'lana isn't a witch."

"His mother's mother was a Fenlander woman married to a Dunmorran lord. She was niece of the Steaplow of Clan Steaplow. And"—he chuckled—"Clan Steaplow folk are by tradition archenemies of Clan Moss'avver—which amuses me no end, though the Moss'avver has nobly forgiven Maurey for turning out to be Steaplow. Who knows if the prince's grandmother was a witch or not? She would probably have hidden it if she were, marrying out of the Fens."

"I'm like this because Mama is a witch?"

"Powerful, dangerous—and going to become more so as you grow into your power. This is not something to discuss. It's better that people don't know how it comes about, so they don't try, against all sense, to achieve it for its own sake. So many of the old Makers of your talent died terribly, Nethin. Or ended up forswearing all contact with society, becoming hermits, because they were so dangerous, because they were always so close to losing control. Children who are going to suffer that risk should be born of love, born *despite* the risk, not *because* of it, not born to be weapons. Ask Maurey what really happened to the Yehillon's Prince Alberick. I'd guess he was another one with some witch-blood, for their so-called Great Gifts to go the way they did in him. That's why you're going to Greyrock next summer. Maurey'lana's the only one who can teach you to control what's in you, if anyone can."

After that conversation by the river I stopped wondering if my mother, who had killed the Yehillon who had murdered her grandfather, was a murderer herself, and I stopped wondering if I was going mad.

I spent the winter sitting at a desk in a corner of my father's study, recopying the manuscript I had nearly destroyed. I also tried to write a history of the war with Bloody Hallow in verse, imagining the deeds of the humans of the Westwood, the witch-prince allies of the Nightwalkers from whom my mother was descended. I went for a lot of long rides and practiced sword drills by myself until mind and body were both exhausted. Mostly what I practiced all that winter was becoming as cold and quiet inside myself as people said—untruthfully—Romner'kiro, my father, was.

My father had always been afraid to let on that he felt anything for fear of being hurt, and the habit was hard to break. But I had always known that. That was one of the secret things I had confessed to my father that day by the river.

It was not my father I disciplined myself to emulate. It was the queen's nephew, Maurey'lana, the Warden of Greyrock, feared and respected in equal measure by humans and Nightwalkers alike. I practiced as hard and as harshly as I practiced my solitary sword drills to make myself cool and calm and still inside.

I had to.

Normal Makers had to put up with unexpected outbursts of power when they were young and still growing into their magic. These days, Maker-skilled youths usually went away to study with a master. Around the time I was born, the old way had been revived. Skilled Makers—warlocks—established schools and took on apprentices. Young Makers were once again learning to work together, to weave their magic in choruses, as had been done in the old days that were almost forgotten. Near-forgotten spells were also revived, spells that needed the power of the Makers working together.

I was different. For the first time, I accepted that, at least so far as my Maker-skills went. Like the Warden of Greyrock. I couldn't afford tantrums and humors and loss of control. In the rare great Makers like Maurey'lana and me, who were known of mostly in old stories, not from real life, such outbursts could be deadly. It was a dangerous power in a youth on the edge of adulthood, full of sudden temper and moodiness.

"And all the usual nonsense that goes with being your age," Romner'kiro had said that time by the river, as if it wasn't so bad after all, an ordinary thing I had to live through and try to outgrow, just like everybody else had.

That, more than anything, had comforted me like an embrace. But it was no comfort to me as I lay helpless in the coffin.

✴ CHAPTER THREE ✴
NETHIN: ALONE

Late spring, end of Fuallin-month

Useless though it was to have panicked and screamed like a silly child on finding myself nailed into a coffin when I should have stayed calm and immediately set to work on freeing myself, panic welled up again. I should not have been *able* to panic and scream like a silly child without all the rage of Genehar's demons breaking loose around me, like the slammed door shattering into needles of oak, but worse, far worse. I had lost my self-control utterly.

And nothing had happened.

Almost more afraid than when I had realized where I was, I began shaping a spell. I set the symbols on the lid of the box over my face, cutting them with my thumbnail. My hand trembled, and I tried to brace it, cupping my elbow in my other hand. The planks scratched easily; they were only pine. I chanted the words softly, letting my breath and the rhythm of the syllables carry the power of my will to the lines.

Nothing happened.

I could feel with the first words that nothing was *going* to happen. There was nothing there, inside of me.

My Maker-strength, my magic, was gone.

Maybe even worse was the emptiness of my mind. I had been too confused and afraid to realize it, but now it sank in. I was alone, as if in a room full of people I had suddenly gone deaf. The feeling of other minds around me was the thing I had never admitted to anyone, even my mother, even my witch-blooded human cousins, until that day by the river with my father when suddenly it all spilled out. I had denied it even to myself all my life, while relying on it for everything I thought I knew about the people around me.

Now, though the coffin was jarring and rattling, the wagon that bore it in motion, presumably with a driver, I could feel no other minds around me. All my life I had been able to sense the hearts of others, their emotions, their hidden souls. I had denied it because that power meant I was a witch like my mother, and therefore a human.

I did not want to be human. But with the sense of other minds taken from me along with my Maker-strength, I was alone, as I had never thought I could be. Alone, and powerless, and…and why didn't someone come? My father was a noted Maker, and tracking spells were among his specialities. He was a lord with knights at his command, a warrior who had fought the Yehillon. My mother was a witch like the Fenlander humans, even though she was from the mountains. Why didn't they come? Why weren't they here already, cutting these enemies down? And were they Yehillon, these enemies? Was that Nightwalker-hating human sect reviving again, and had I been taken in some plot as the Baroness of Oakhold had once been taken?

Had Hayonwey Castle been attacked? Were my parents besieged, betrayed…dead?

Pale, dark-eyed faces. My captors were my own people, Nightwalkers.

I beat on the sides and lid of the coffin, pounded again with my feet. The end of the coffin never creaked, the work of a skilled joiner. I screamed—the hoarse, voiceless wail was all I seemed to have left. My hands ached, throbbed and then went numb and damp. And still I pounded, wailed, though I could not shape the words, *Papa, Mama, why don't you come? Why doesn't someone come? Why doesn't someone come to me…?*

The wagon ceased to jolt. Nails squealed, being drawn out. If I could fling myself up, strike swiftly enough...Light blinded me, people cursed and shouted, someone struck me in the face as I flailed feebly—too slow, too weak. They dragged me to sit upright, but it was only to force more oily poison down my throat.

Papa, Mama...There was nothing, no sense of them at all. Mama...Then *Crow!* Crow, like a spark flying in the darkness. There and gone, as briefly as that spark.

After that, the nightmares returned.

✳ CHAPTER FOUR ✳
WOLFRAM: IN OAKHOLD

Late spring, beginning of Therminas-month

I learned only later of the parts others played in this history, but it seems best to me to set down in its proper place what I afterwards learned and guessed, to make my story complete. Wolfram and Alabeth, Crow and Hermengilde'kiro, even the Moss'avver, my uncle Korby, witnessed what I could not, so I will tell their parts of the story as I come to them.

✳ ✳ ✳

I never believed I could be abandoned and forgotten, not in the midst of the worst of the nightmares. I did not know, then, of the attack on my parents, of the message-ravens flying to the royal seat at Sennamor and to the castles of Greyrock and Weeping Valley that guarded the Greyrock Pass out of Talverdin, of the queen's knights searching wagons and barges and even checking every traveler who seemed unnaturally quiet for spells of disguise. I didn't know of how, three times, the procession bringing the body of a grieving widow's only grandson north to her ancestral village for burial was stopped and searched, and how once, just once, a knight said, "We should open that coffin." But the widow wept, and the stench of decay, despite the spells of preservation clearly painted on the lid, was strong, and so they did not.

I did not know of my Aunt Robin's wild ride to Greyrock and onward, with an escort of Nightwalkers from Greyrock, through the pass and down to Hayonwey, passing on the road when my funeral *cortege was on the river. I did not know how my Uncle Korby, seeking me even in the midst of a vital mission against the greatest Yehillon threat Talverdin had faced since Prince Alberick discovered the Kanifglin Pass, turned to the drugged teas that increase a witch's ability to sink into visions, but which can kill.*

I did not know of the young man whom Genehar and Sypat, Powers of fate and chance, had flung into the pattern, long before I was ever born.

"My lady?" Wolfram hesitated in the doorway of the library. The baroness was pacing up and down before the fire, which was blazing high, despite the heat of the summer's day. That was not a good sign. Neither was the feverish gloss in her eyes when she turned his way.

"Wolf. Come in."

"Are you well?"

She waved a hand dismissively. "Well enough." A quick smile said she knew what he meant, which meant she was...well enough. In her right mind anyhow—not lost in some nightmare, one of the bad spells where her thoughts went wandering. It wasn't his fault, but it hurt him nonetheless to see her in those states. "Wolfram, you have to go. Now."

"My lady?" His heart lurched, as though the floor crumbled under his feet and he fell, with nothing beneath him, no hope. "Leave here, my lady? Why?" Then sense returned. Not leave for good, she wouldn't mean that. "You're sending me to the Warden in Hallaland?"

"No. To Talverdin. To the town of Dralla." Her eyes were growing dark and remote. "No. Not to Dralla. To the Coronation Shrine, north of Dralla, in the mountains."

"To—my lady, that's..." He didn't say *mad*. Some might say she was, but it was only an old head injury stirring up the

Fenlander witchery in her blood that set her adrift in dreams of time. "You can't send me into Talverdin. Even the Warden couldn't. Prince or no, they'd never let him do that."

"Don't let them catch you," the baroness said. "Wolfram, I know what I'm asking. I know. I do. I see...But you must. I've seen...you must go. No one else has even a hope. Maurey's too far away; he couldn't come in time. There's no one but you. There's always been no one but you."

"They'll kill me if they take me." It wasn't refusal. It wasn't even an argument. He just wanted to be very certain.

"They may. But Mannie and Crow are at Sennamor Castle. They'd speak for you, if you were taken. They'd...at least the queen would send to Maurey, to demand to know about you. She wouldn't kill you out of hand."

"She wouldn't? Not even me?"

A rueful smile tugged at her lips, and he found himself smiling back. He'd go. He'd go anywhere his lady sent him. It wasn't anything her husband the prince needed to fear; it wasn't even the courtly games bored young noblemen played, convincing themselves they had fallen hopelessly in love with some unattainable woman twice their age and proving it by fawning devotion. It was simply...that he would.

"Not even you, not out of hand, with no trial," she said. A frown chased the smile, just as swift. "I think. I trust. Wolf, you're all the hope there is. I saw you, long ago. I've known you, always. Did you know? Did Korby tell you?"

"No."

"Before you were born, I saw you. You will be there. I think." She shrugged, wound slender fingers into the coiled braids of her hair, faded copper, as if her head pained her. She was prone to headaches and dizzy spells that left a dark and quiet room her only refuge. Not his fault either, but he carried the guilt of it. "So many ways you could come to that point, so many chances. Friend and enemy."

"I'm not your enemy," he said gently.

"Don't be silly." The baroness was sharp and focused again. "You'll need to travel light. I'll send a letter with you to the Lieutenant Warden at Greyrock; Jehan will see you have all you need by way of re-supply there. You can get through the Greyrock Pass undetected."

"Human blood…," Wolf said uncertainly.

"Bah. What the spells detect is Nightwalker blood. An affinity for the halfworld."

"Those aren't the same thing."

"Aren't they? Stay in the halfworld and you'll be fine, if you're careful and remember that the Weeping Valley garrison patrols in the halfworld, and likewise the halfway watchtower. But I don't have to tell you that, do I? No. If you were dimwitted, Korby wouldn't have brought you home no matter what I said."

"But all the hope for what?" Wolfram asked. "My lady, you haven't told me…"

"Oh." She faced him again. "No, I haven't. They have Nethin. Fuallia's son."

"Who?"

"Korby's Nightwalker nephew," she clarified. "I never dreamed of him. Never, or I could have warned Fu. But the courier came today. From Greyrock. He's gone."

"Who's gone?"

"*Nethin*. Vanished. Abducted over two weeks ago. His parents…poisoned, it seems. Nobody at Hayonwey thought to tell me at once; nobody thought it was urgent I know right away. A message-raven was sent from Hayonwey to Greyrock, of course, but Lord Jehan only sent word on to me by regular courier. He didn't think I could do anything, I suppose." A wry shrug, a bird-quick gesture of empty hands. "We can't blame Jehan. But I wish Romner's seneschal had thought to send a message-raven directly here from Hayonwey. I wish Mannie or Aljess or someone who would think of such things had been in Greyrock. And Korby has to have known nearly as soon as it happened; he's bound to have dreamed of it, or Robin will have, and what she knows, Korby knows. Korby's with Maurey, and I have the other half of a speaking-stone Maurey took with him; those idiots could have told me almost as soon as it happened. I suppose they didn't want to worry me. *Idiots*. It may be too late."

The speaking-stones were made by Prince Maurey, a great magic: cloven thunder-eggs, as they called them in the desert, each of which carried speech to its twin, no matter how many miles separated them.

His lady's distress was painful to watch, but Wolfram wasn't her son; he couldn't go and put arms around her to still her restless pacing.

"Nethin was to come to Greyrock later this year to study with Maurey," the baroness went on, plucking a book bound in soft leather from her worktable as she passed. "He's like Maurey, you see. Like you. Strong enough."

Wolfram frowned. "Strong enough for what?"

Talking with the baroness took patience sometimes, but she had earned it. It wasn't wooly-mindedness; it wasn't foolishness or lack of thought, no more than an old soldier's limp. Scars didn't have to show on the skin. Her mind leapt and skipped the connections between thoughts, as she saw patterns others realized more slowly. His eyes widened even as she began to answer, realizing what the book she now held was...her own study of one of the great secrets. He had watched her writing in it, during long afternoons of interrogation by the Warden and the Moss'avver, when he was newly brought to Oakhold, a chimera of prisoner and guest and, yes, rescued stray dog. Her own questions had been few but startling, striking to the heart of secrets he had thought he alone in all the living world had discovered.

"Strong enough for the shadow road."

"Who has Nethin?" he demanded, all urgent attention now, if he had not been before.

"I don't know."

"Are you sure he's in Talverdin? He's not being taken to Rona or Hallaland somewhere?"

"The Coronation Shrine," she said. "It's burning…"

He caught her as she staggered, a hand under her elbow.

"You have to start now, Wolf. Today. You have to be there in time. They can't be traveling very quickly. A wagon…a barge… a wagon…lavender palls…Look for a funeral on the road."

"A funeral!"

The baroness shook her head. "No, you won't be in time. Just go straight there."

"Where, my lady?"

"I said, didn't I? The Coronation Shrine. Before it burns. A wagon is so slow, but if they go by river up the South Branch Senna, they'll gain time on that stretch…you must be there before them. They need him to open the gate."

"Phaydos help him," he said, thinking of the boy he had never met. Powers knew whose hands he was in, but the use they meant to make of him…"They must be mad to try it. Odds are they'll kill the boy and fail anyhow. It's not a spell I'd want to risk."

"You may have to, if you don't come to him in time. But fail, succeed, whether he dies or not doesn't matter. Save him if you can. If you can't…it doesn't matter." He stared in shock. "Better he dies than they succeed. You're his hope. You're all our hope. I've seen it raining fire over Greyrock, Wolfram. I've seen the sea roll over Talverdin and smash against the mountains. I've seen Oakhold slide into a chasm in the earth and the stones of Cragroyal burning, and Rensey drowned, yes, and Rona and distant Berbarany too. I've seen the end of the world, Wolf, and it starts with the shadow road." She held out the book to him. "It's here. What I've seen, what I know, what Lord Romner's discovered and guessed and deduced. What you brought us too. Learn it. Pray you don't need it, despite what I've seen."

That flash of smile again, and a dimple, and sorrow as well. "Though it's all I knew of you, when I set Korby to hunting you. A man on the shadow road."

"I—couldn't wish you hadn't," he said, which was awkward but honestly meant, and even saying so much was stripping himself naked. "No matter what happens, my lady."

"Go on then," she said, as if sending one of her own sons on some minor errand.

He bowed, Berbarani fashion, the book in hand. He would have liked to have embraced her as a son might, especially if he wasn't returning, which seemed all too likely.

When he glanced back from the doorway, she was standing with her arms wrapped close around her, looking cold before the great fire. Her eyes weren't watching him though.

Lord Ranulf met him on the stairs, a youth a few years younger than himself, all arms and legs. Ranulf, like his three younger brothers, looked entirely human. But like his elder sister and unlike the three younger boys, he could walk the halfworld and was a warlock, though of less than average strength. Still, that meant there would be a warlock in the barons' council of Eswy-Dunmorra one day; being the eldest male child, he was his mother's heir. But because he was fair-haired, gray-eyed and discrete, no one questioned his humanness, despite his half-Nightwalker father.

And like his mother, like all his family, Ranulf swept Wolfram up as if he had always been part of the household. As if Wolf were a long lost elder brother. It frightened Wolfram, sometimes. At least the admiring little ones had no idea who he really was, but Lady Hermengilde—Mannie—the baroness's eldest child, and Lord Ranulf had no such excuse for their acceptance, their trust, their...yes, affection. The open hostility of the Moss'avver's heir, Gwenllian, whom everybody called Crow, was easier to understand, though even she mistrusted him only where Hermengilde was concerned, because being a witch, she saw things he would rather have kept hidden.

"Wolf, there you are." Ranulf stopped him with a hand on his arm. "Why the rush? Want to go down to the river for a swim? It's sweltering. The brats and their tutor have already gone, but Mother had me hunting through Father's study for a map of Talverdin. I told her he was bound to keep all that kind of thing at Greyrock, not here, but she insisted. I don't know what she wants it for…"

"Did you find one?"

"Actually, yes. Along with a number of dust mice."

"The map's for me. Give it here. And go to your mother."

"But what about—is she all right?" Ranulf thrust the rolled map at him and made to push past.

"The baroness isn't ill. Just…just go to her. She's alone." That sounded foolish. Ranulf might put it down to his imperfect command of the Eswyn language.

Ranulf paused and frowned at him from a step above. "What do you mean? And where are you going looking so grim anyway?"

"Talverdin."

"Talverdin! Wolf, they'll cut your fool head off and feed what's left to the message-ravens!"

"Thank you, Lord Ranulf."

"There's nothing happened to my sister, is there? I'd better come too. Or go instead. *You* can't…"

"So far as I know, Mannie is…Lady Hermengilde is fine. I don't expect I'll be seeing her. And you can't do anything. It has to be me."

"This is some Geneh-damned vision of Mother's, isn't it? She's got no business sending you off to get killed. She's got no business having dreams. She's not a Fenlander. Why can't she leave worrying about that sort of thing to the witches? She shouldn't have to—"

"Shouting doesn't change anything."

Ranulf was only a boy despite his height, and his anger was at the illness, anger that in all his life his mother hadn't been whole, hadn't always been there, ordinary and entire, when the little boy he had been had needed her.

Wolfram shook his head. "Just go to your mother, Ranulf. Do you think it's easy for her, seeing things she fears she can't change? I'll be fine. I know what I'm doing. I've known a long time, really. Your great-aunt, the queen, will have no idea I've ever crossed her border, and I'm harder to catch than your father and the Moss'avver put together. Really." Perhaps an exaggeration. After all, the Moss'avver had caught him.

"You're not leaving right now?"

"Within the hour."

"You are mad. Take Russet then. Your own mare's in no state for a hard journey."

"And whose idea was it to breed her?"

"I told you, a Berbarani-Kordaler cross will make you the envy even of Lord Romner." The boy sobered, remembering that horses were likely to be the last thing on that horse-breeding Nightwalker lord's mind these days. "Wolfram?"

"Yes?"

"Whatever you're up to, make sure you come back safe. For Mother's sake. And Mannie's."

"Lady Hermengilde—?" He felt his face grow hot, damn the boy.

"Idiot," said Ranulf. "Go on then, if you're in such a rush. I'll go to my mother."

Wolfram didn't know what to say, so he merely nodded. Ranulf clapped him on the shoulder before continuing up the stairs, two at a time. "Mother!" he called. "You can't waste a day like this stewing indoors. Let's ride down to the river and watch the brats swimming."

✳ CHAPTER FIVE ✳
KORBY: HALLASBOURG HARBOR

Late spring, early Therminas-month

The network of spies and informants that had been built up over the past decade or more by Maurey'lana for his brother, the human king, and for our own queen had discovered the threads and footprints of a Yehillon plot. A word here, a whisper there, a strange caravan crossing the deserts of Berbarany with minerals that had little common use, a Dravidaran master gun-founder murdered far from home in Rona, particular people they watched gathering in Hallasbourg...all these things began to paint a picture. In time, it led the Warden, Maurey'lana, and my uncle Korby, the chief of the Fenlander Moss'avver clan, to certain ships being prepared over the water in Hallasbourg.

The mission was not something they could drop, to return to Eswiland because one boy had vanished. It was not something they could abandon, even if their close friends had been poisoned. If they walked away from what they had chosen to do, hundreds, even thousands, in Talverdin might die. But I don't suppose it was easy for them. Maurey'lana was the greatest of warlocks, Korby one of the most powerful witches of the Fens. Both must have felt that they had a chance of saving Fuallia, if they could have been at her side.

T he three of them, the Talverdine prince who was also the Dunmorran Warden of Greyrock and his guard-captain Aljess and the clan chief of the Moss'avvers of the Fens, stood on a steep hillside overlooking Hallasbourg

Harbor and the walled city that clung to its eastern edge, nothing around them but thin, wind-whipped grass and scrubby rosemary. Korby, the Moss'avver, knew it might be considered an act of war, this attack on ships in a foreign port, if it could be proved, which was why the last of the prisoners—and there weren't many, because once the hired crews had fled, most of the actual enemy had preferred to die with their vessels—were being bundled onto a Gehtish ship.

The recent betrothal of Maurey's nephew, Crown Prince Lovell of Eswy-Dunmorra, to a princess of Gehtaland might have been a love match, but it had its political and military advantages, too, for Eswy-Dunmorra and its Talverdine ally. The *Golden Salmon* and her two sister ships would be out to sea within an hour with a strong wind behind them, and there was nothing riding at anchor here that could catch them, not with Gehtish wind-witches aboard.

A grim night's work, but a successful one; the crown to a year of secret inquiries, of agents risking their lives—and losing them too—in places as widely separated as the eastern deserts and their own port of Rensey.

"Eugeneas is dead, Abner's dead, Lola went over the side and is probably dead…" Captain Aljess held up a finger for each of the Yehillon High Circle, the secret leadership and aristocracy of the cult sworn to wipe Nightwalkers from the face of the world. "Twenty-six prisoners: a dozen of them capable of entering the halfworld, the rest ordinary humans. A lot took Lola's way out, if they couldn't get off before the ships started burning. Some may have made it to shore, but not many. They were anchored too far out. I think the harbormaster must have known something about their cargo and didn't want them in very close."

As she spoke, a gout of white flame burst upwards on one of the burning ships, showing masts and rigging stark and black. Sparks climbed a pillar of smoke.

"All right?" the Moss'avver asked the two Nightwalkers. They didn't have a name for what was burning. Each ship was armed with at least one eastern cannon, and they had fired hollow shot filled with some alchemical compound that burst and burned like philosopher's fire when the projectile struck. Or when the ship burned around it, of course.

"We're downwind," the Warden said with a shrug.

"Good thing too," said Aljess.

To the Moss'avver, both Nightwalkers looked a little unhealthy, a little gray and sick. Not a Talverdine knight there was immune to the taint of the poison in the smoke, and entering the halfworld only increased the pain and the poison of it. The Powers' own justice that those of the Yehillon who had what they called the Lesser Gift, the ability to enter the halfworld, were just as badly affected. It helped single them out. Even worse, once the stuff started burning, it seemed to suck the strength out of Makers' spells, twisting and tearing them, so that the fogs that had cloaked their attack on the anchored Yehillon-hired ships had dissolved away into the moonlight, and sleeping watchmen had awoken. The Warden had expected that, from his agents' reports. That was why he had persuaded the queen of Talverdin and the king and queen of Eswy-Dunmorra that they had to take this dangerous and provocative step and mount an outright attack on the Yehillon in Hallaland, before they could sail.

The alchemical shot was intended to destroy warlocks' magic. It was intended to cut through the spells that defended Dralla, the only port of hidden and magic-guarded Talverdin, where rocks moved to catch and grind human ships, and sudden fogs, whirlpools and violent tempests rose in moments to defend the coast.

"Time to leave," the Moss'avver said. "M'lord, captain. Come on. Before the Hallalanders get themselves organized and find they have a prize worth a fleet in their hands."

An Eswyn soldier dressed as a common sailor ran up then, with a quick bow for each in turn. "Your Highness, my lord Moss'avver, captain. Your Highness, Captain Berric says he's got a prisoner on the *Salmon* you'd better speak to. Now, sir. One of the High Circle. They fished her out of the harbor, unconscious, but she's come round. Nasty piece of work, shouting and cursing us all…but she's saying three ships already sailed, sir, disguised as Eswyn merchantmen. At least two weeks past, maybe more, she's not clear. But sailing under our own colors, Highness."

"Damn," the prince said. Some of the reports had said the Yehillon had nine ships; more had said six. They had identified six definite and two possible. Not the right two, when their agents searched them.

"Damn is right," Korby agreed. "M'lord, let's get out of here before we start arguing what to do. There's soldiers in the city streets."

Captain Aljess began to say something, but her voice came faint and distant. She was still there before him, but hazy, red-edged, fading as if smoke rolled between them. Korby felt, strong and present as if the boy stood before him, his wife's abducted nephew. He spun and stared into the smoke…fog… deep and shifting waters. "Nethin…?"

The others stared too, at nothing. He could feel Maurey's hand on his shoulder—feel his concern, his hope. Nethin had been there a moment, calling, reaching…But now there was nothing, which was all there had ever been when he sought the boy, as he had every day since the morning in Fuallin-month when his wife Robin dragged him into a waking dream of fury and grief—her sister poisoned and possibly dying, the boy's horse limping home, the boy…vanished, beyond any warlock's searching or witch's dreaming ability to find. Wisps of smoke and shadows of night.

"You saw him?" Maurey demanded, the escaped ships forgotten for the moment. "Dead or alive? Now, past, future?" The crucial questions.

Korby ran a hand over his face, muttering in the Fen tongue. "Gone," he said thickly. "He's gone. Again. I can't..." His whole soul reached after the boy and grasped nothing. He switched languages. "Nethin was alive. I felt him. Alive. It wasn't a vision of the past. Sure of it, m'lord. *Now,* now or some time to come, that's when I saw him. So he's still alive. Wherever he is. Whoever has him. However they're hiding him." He felt ill, reaching into that nothingness, and stood for a moment with his head bowed, the prince's arm over his shoulders. "Lost," he said at last. "He's lost. But he's alive. And even that's a thread of hope for Fuallia to cling to, if Robin can get through to her." He took a deep breath. "Right. I'll hunt for him again tonight. I'll do what I have to, take what I have to, to go deep enough into dreams. It's never worked before. But at least now...hope."

"Hope's good," said Aljess quietly. "Better than thinking him dead. But right now..."

"Yes. Ships. Three ships already sailed for Dralla? I did hear you. And, m'lord, you need to get back aboard the *Salmon*. We've got enough problems to sort out without the Hallalanders capturing themselves a Nightwalker prince to burn."

"We can't overtake the three Yehillon ships," Aljess resumed, as they all began to pick a way down towards where the boat waited to carry them to the Gehtish vessel acting as the prince's flagship. The scent of crushed rosemary followed them, counterpoint to the reek of smoke and alchemy. "Not now the wind's swung round to take us north."

"I have the speaking-stones," Maurey pointed out. "I can warn Cragroyal and Sennamor. My brother will turn the fleet out from Rensey to hunt them—a fast courier can get from Cragroyal to Rensey in three days with the best post-horses.

My aunt can warn the governor of Dralla in a day by message-raven. Al, I want that prisoner brought to me, once we're aboard. Sounds like we can't count Mistress Lola among the dead after all. Korby, you stay with me. I'll want to know if she's lying."

"You think she's just taunting us with those escaped ships, lying for a last petty revenge, Maurey?" Aljess asked.

"Probably not. No, I want to question her to find out what she knows about the kidnapping of Nethin."

"He's not here," Korby said. "He isn't. I'd have known—I'm sure I'd have known. I'd never have let you torch a single ship if I thought there was even a chance he was aboard."

"That doesn't mean the Yehillon don't have him somewhere," Maurey said grimly. "*We* know it's possible for Yehillon with the Lesser Gifts to get into Talverdin; the current High Circle may have rediscovered that fact. They've lost one warlock; they might plan on breaking another to their will."

✤ Chapter Six ✤

Nethin: The Stolen Spell

*About a fortnight later, early summer,
middle of Therminas-month*

T he nightmare continued when my abductors got me to where they were going. I knew we were there, wherever it was, because I woke on a narrow bed with a cobwebby attic roof above me. The corpse stink was mostly gone—that must have been some spell—though a trace of it lingered a little in either my clothes or my imagination. I pulled myself from the bed, falling, tangled in the blanket, and struggled to the window, which let in a thick yellowish light through a horn pane. It was too small for even such a scrawny person as me to squeeze out by, and besides, squeezing out an attic window was likely to lead to a very short and fatal moment of freedom, no more. It was hinged to let in air though, and I undid the catch and pushed it open to peer out, blinking in a bright noon.

I was in the mountains. There was no view but the rising mountainside, steep stone and pine trees and in the far distance, a glimpse of more peaks pushing into the sky. A raven flew, steady and swift, over a glint between those peaks that might be the course of a brook. Talverdin was surrounded by mountains. I could be anywhere.

Footsteps sounded, and I cursed my foolishness in not having tried the door first of all, little hope though there was of it being unlocked or unguarded. I tried to retreat to the bed, to pretend I was still asleep, but I fell, or half fainted, from turning too quickly. They found me crouched like a frog on the floor.

There were three of them. One was a short, dumpy old woman—so short, for a Nightwalker, that most would suspect some human ancestry in her family. Even cut off from my ability to feel her emotions, I recognized her type: the sort who goes through life with a lying smile fixed on her face, never so poisonous or manipulative as when she appears to be conciliatory, though she didn't waste that smile on me. One was a middle-aged man wearing the blue stole of an apothecary, a maker of medicines, perfumes and alchemical ingredients. Or poisons, of course; though, like the red-stoled physicians' guild, that of the apothecaries took an oath to do no harm. For what that was worth.

And one was my great-grandfather, my father's father's father, Roshing'den. I had only seen him a few times in my life, but he and my father looked so alike…although my father would never have such lines of bitterness and anger twisting his face. I am glad that my bones take after the portraits of my father's mother's family, the hereditary lords of Hayonwey. I do not ever want to look in a mirror when I am old and see Roshing's face.

Whenever Roshing had visited us in the past, the visit always ended with my father throwing the old man out and telling him never to come back. His constant sneering insults directed at my mother and me, his constant belittling of everything human, every interest and friend of my father's…I don't know why my father ever allowed him back at all, unless it was guilt, as the old man, who had once been the elected lord or councillor for the Upper Roshing Valley (I have said he was named after the river, and I think he felt the name gave him possession), had raised him after the deaths of his own parents. Even guilt has its limits though. Last time, a year ago, Roshing'den had been caught by my mother going through my father's private papers. He had then called my mother a stinking illiterate animal to her face when she summoned my father.

I do not think he would ever have been allowed to visit again. I had certainly expected never to have to face his contempt again.

I lurched up and swayed under that sneering gaze. Merely standing on my own two feet was a challenge. I felt as drained of life as I had been after the black fever. My very bones felt too heavy, though there was little-enough flesh on them after what I thought must be days, weeks, poisoned with sleeping drafts and drugs against magic, locked in a coffin, with nothing but barley broth to keep me alive.

"Are you sure about him, Sarval'den?" asked the apothecary. "He's only a human. What if you took one of the human cousins by mistake?"

"The only human at Hayonwey Castle right now is his mother," Great-grandfather said, his tone making clear his opinion of the apothecary's intelligence, or lack thereof. "That's Nethin. You've half killed him, Eslin'den. Don't blame me if he's no use to us after all."

"I said those drugs shouldn't be used for more than a few days at most. It was you who said we had to—"

"My agent in Hayonwey saw the letter his father wrote to the blasted Warden. Nethin's the one we need, and he's too dangerous to manage without the drugs." Great-grandfather made a dismissive gesture. "Can he start now?"

"He needs to get a little strength back before he's good for anything," the apothecary said.

"He needs to study the spell," the woman—Sarval'den— said. Her voice, like her face, was sweet and false. I didn't need my lost witch-sense of people's minds to see her as some sort of venomous insect. "And if he's a very good boy and does what he's told, perhaps he can go home afterwards."

I didn't need to be a witch to hear the lie in that either, and yet I wanted to believe it.

Where was my father? Why hadn't somebody found me already?

The threesome left without ever having spoken a word directly to me.

I curled up on the bed. Much as I wanted to escape into sleep, I could not. I knew enough about medicines to understand why. Without the sedative that had kept me corpse-like for so long, my body was racked with fidgets, nerves twitching, mind dithering in fruitless circles. Dodge them when they opened the door. Break a leg off the bedstead and hit them with it. Do what they wanted and then escape before they could kill me. Do what they wanted and they really would let me go. My great-grandfather would not really let them kill his only descendent; he put too much value on his family and his bloodline for that.

But he thought I was a mongrel, a pollution. He had tried to get my parents' marriage—blessed by my father's cousin, the head of House Rukiar—declared unlawful; to get my sisters and me declared bastards; to force my father to marry again. He would be happy to see me dead. I had nothing to lose by defiance, by a mad dash out the door. Nothing to lose by attacking him. If I could hide until the other drug, the one that still suppressed my Maker-strength, wore off as well, I would be stronger than any of them.

For quite a long time, I could not tell the difference between what went on in my hallucinatory waking state and the nightmares. They faded in and out of one another. Certainly my captors brought me food: bland, soothing things like porridge and milksops and beef tea. There were cups of poison, which they called medicine and which I knew were keeping me from touching my Maker-strength. When I refused and batted the cups away, they held me and forced them down, and, as on the road, a Maker was there to bespell my churning belly, so that I did not vomit them up again.

The strangest, the most nightmarish part—stranger than the shades of the ancestors I kept thinking I saw from the corner of my eye, creeping close from behind to smother me—was the studying. That was what I was there to do: study. They woke me nearly every time I tried to crawl into the bed and sleep, forcing me to sit up, the papers on my lap again. Always at least one of them was there with me, often two. I think there must have been some other drug than the one that suppressed magic, some stimulant for those days, because I do not remember that I ever slept properly, and my mind was on fire. I muttered and babbled to myself, flapped my hands at the faceless shades that huddled in the corners, waiting for me to fall asleep so they could devour me, and sometimes I wept, knowing I had gone mad and it would break my mother's heart. But in that state the core of my thoughts felt sharp-edged and alert and focused; I did what they wanted. I studied.

The spell was the longest I had ever encountered—a vast, interwoven, multilayered construct. It had been compiled from two different sources; even in my delirious state my Maker's mind still grasped that. Parts were written in the traditional language of spells—Maker's tongue, we called it, though I had heard my father and his friends, the Warden and the Baroness of Oakhold, call it Early Talverdine. Parts were in something that, when I sounded it out aloud, seemed to be like the Maker's tongue, but as if written by a Ronishman. In these sections the syntax, the order of the words, was appalling and often made little sense. I had to guess what the writer had really meant to say.

My captors were horrified when I drunkenly demanded pen and ink to correct the spell.

"Do you know what happens when a spell goes wrong?" I demanded. I was truly flying at that point, lofty and lordly, a master among ignorant children who could not possibly do me harm. I was still bruised black about the mouth from my great-grandfather's hand, though I could not remember what I had said or done earlier that day to warrant it. "The forces will recoil on the Maker, and on those around him. Are you planning to trust me to go off on my own—with my powers restored—

to work this? Because if you're standing anywhere near, you'd better be praying to the Powers there's no mistake in it."

The pair of conspirators with me—they spoke of themselves as Homelanders—looked at one another nervously. They were a weather-beaten yet still handsome woman-at-arms wearing the badge of House Langen and a round-faced young man a few years older than I was. He was, like me, half human. Sarval'den called him derisively "our Ronish halfbreed," and from something the man said once about "my spell," I understood that he had brought them some part of these papers.

"This is all wrong," I told the young man owlishly. "And you're a fool if you think otherwise. Are you a fool? Did you copy this yourself? Are these errors your fault? If I tell my great-grandfather Roshing'den…Were you trying to undermine it, whatever it's meant to do? Are you a traitor to Homelanders?"

"No! I steal it from the Yehillon; I risk much. Is true spell." The youth must have been raised among humans in Rona; he spoke very bad Talverdine. "You is only stupid little child. I bring whole spell, complete. Other one wrong. Mine true, work of very great prince of Yehillon."

So despite his having brought them what he thought was a complete spell, they had used his material only to patch what was missing in the other, better version. That made sense.

I knew the other. I had never seen it, never studied it before, and the handwriting was strange, but almost every sentence, every phrase, echoed with familiarity. I knew it as you know a piece of music or a poem to be the work of a favorite, familiar artist, their voice, the rhythms of their spirit, in every note and phrase.

The spell had been composed by my father. And copied badly, hurriedly, perhaps by a spy of Great-grandfather's or by Great-grandfather himself. Had he missed some pages or been unable to get the whole thing, or had it been left unfinished deliberately? Left with gaps to prevent anyone doing just what these Homelanders were doing? That was what old Maker-Masters had done to protect their most dangerous secrets, in the days before the guild when Makers always lived as disciples under a Master, working their magic in concert, not alone as we had come to do in later times: left gaps, inserted errors that only the truly wise, or at least truly knowledgeable, would recognize.

I prayed to the Powers, and especially Eyiss the Great Power, whose special care was craftsmen and Makers and poets, that I was capable of recognizing every such trap. I did not really want to die, though if this spell were some great evil, some spell of last resort...What if it exploded the Greyrock Pass in earthquake and rockslide? What if it caused the waters of Dralla Harbor—the only port of our treacherous coastline, bound by spell-storm—to boil? What if I killed the human king and queen in Eswy-Dunmorra, my father's friends, by working this spell? What if I destroyed Sennamor Castle and killed our own queen? There was nothing on it that *said*.

"The very great prince of the Yehillon was a fool, and this is wrong!" I shrieked, crumpling the page before me into a ball and hurling it at the man. I couldn't stand him. He had pale skin like a human who had not been out in the sun enough, and his eyes were human brown, but his hair was black. He looked more a Nightwalker than I did. For all Sarval's and Roshing's insults, he was treated as one, and I was not. "I need to make notes. I need to make notes and correct this, or we're all going to die, and I hope you burn in Genehar's fires forever the way the humans say the wicked do."

"Go find him a pencil, Orlando'den," said the woman-at-arms. "Quickly, before he does himself harm."

She shoved the Ronish Nightwalker out the door and picked up the crumpled paper, smoothing it.

"Don't make them hurt you again," she said, kneeling down by the bed, grabbing my wrist—like a puppet's, it seemed all bone and cords, alien to me. "Nethin'kiro, listen.

Listen to me. You're very ill and you're not thinking clearly. Look at me. Look me in the eye. Are you still in there? Can you still control yourself?"

I looked at her. She wasn't making sense. She stared into my eyes. Few people would. I looked like a shade of the dead at the best of times, with white-pigmented Nightwalker skin and my mother's white-blond hair, pale eyes like a washed-out sky.

"What?" I asked sullenly.

She sighed as if something she found in my gaze relieved her. "Nethin'kiro, you're not alone. Don't do anything stupid. You're far too ill to risk the mountains, so just play along with them for now, all right? Do you understand me?"

I blinked.

"Good lad. Roshing and Sarval were so secretive about their great plan, I didn't know what they intended until they dragged you out of that coffin and I realized you were what they—I've sent—" She dropped my wrist and stood up. Orlando had come back already. "He won't try that again," she said grimly and cuffed the side of my head, not too hard. "Will you?"

I shook my head dumbly and reached to take the stub of pencil, the lead stick wrapped in a twist of rag to keep the fingers clean. Orlando snatched it back from my grasp.

"No-no. Not till the bad boy say sorry."

"Maynar help me, you're as much a baby as he is." The woman-at-arms plucked the pencil from Orlando and dropped it on my lap with the papers. "We don't have time for games, halfbreed." It took a moment for me to realize that particular insult was directed at Orlando, not me. "Powers know you can't claim to be a Maker, let alone one of this brat's strength, none of us can, or we wouldn't be taking all this risk with him. Let the boy write notes if he has to."

After that I was lost in the spell and the maze my drugged mind had become, where only the spell seemed real. For all I knew, I had dreamed the soldier's words out of my desire for an ally. She showed no other sign of being a friend. It was she who marched me down the narrow stairs by my collar, when, under my great-grandfather's interrogation, I admitted I could now hold the whole spell in my mind.

"But I can't work it here," I protested, as the woman-at-arms, whose name I gathered was Arromna, pushed me stumbling into what proved to be the hall of a hunting lodge, the beams decorated with spiral-horned skulls. "There has to be a framework, a form to channel the power. A strong one. It has to be built of stone…" I could use sand and ashes for part of it, though I would need an enclosure of stone. But stone for the whole thing would be better, and would make my captors have to work harder to collect what I needed. That would take time, maybe time enough for my father to find me…

"You'll have what you need," Roshing said.

"Is he ready?" asked Sarval, turning from speaking to Orlando the Ronishman.

"He says so," Arromna reported. "But wouldn't it be better to wait a day or two, Roshing'kiro? He's so weak. There's so much risk in it anyway. Do we really want to add more than we need?"

"When I want your opinion, I'll ask for it," Roshing grunted. "Sarval'den is the best Maker among us. It's her decision."

"But it isn't she who'll be working the spell, Roshing'kiro," Arromna protested, giving my great-grandfather the honorific of a lord, which had not been his since he left the queen's council. He had always had a human obsession with titles, resenting that my father's children's lordship was hereditary and his own had been only due to his office, ending when he lost an election.

"If he can stand and do the spell, he'll be fine," Sarval said. "All he needs to do is get the pattern right. A parrot could do it, if it had his Maker-strength."

People who believed that all you had to do was rattle off a spell by rote—the right words, the right gestures, the right symbols inscribed and the right symbolic objects forming the correct patterns—were the reason our Maker-craft was in such sorry shape these days, my father said. Without understanding, without focused will, magic was a knife in the hands of a child. Usually a dull knife, but when it was not...He always snorted and left the rest unsaid. There was a theory that said a spell should only be used once and created new each time, but that idea was not very widespread. Those who held to it left small gaps in their written spells, forcing Makers using them to improvise, but only in some small way. My friend Lord Ranulf of Oakhold claimed this was cheating, not truly making a new spell each time, but I don't think my father felt spells had to be new, although he certainly believed a Maker should be capable of crafting new workings on the fly. But maybe I was wrong about those gaps in my father's spell that they had filled in with Orlando's; maybe it wasn't for secrecy after all, or to keep the ignorant from unleashing great magics. Maybe I was supposed to improvise, to make the spell new and my own. Maybe it was all of these reasons. Maybe I should...

Arromna shook me. I had begun muttering to myself again.

"You can see the state he's in," the woman-at-arms protested. "Give him another couple of days to recover."

"No," said Sarval, "we go today." But she made it a question with a look at my great-grandfather.

"Everything can be ready in an hour," Roshing said.

"Are you sure he's strong enough?"

"The longer we delay, the greater the chance my traitor grandson will have the Warden and that vicious Baron Moss'avver helping him hunt for the brat, and none of us want to go up against *them*."

"No, sir. You're right. Does that mean we make Nethin ready now then?" Arromna asked. "I can take him to the apothecary."

I didn't like the sound of that.

"Don't be a fool, Arromna'den. That's far too dangerous."

"But if we leave it till we're there, Roshing'kiro, we risk it not taking effect in time. We don't want to be hanging around there come daylight. There might not be any villages close, but there are shepherds. If we're seen…Surely it's better to have him prepared beforehand. I can keep him quiet. He trusts me, and I've told him that if he's good and does what you want, he'll be sent home after, so I'm sure he'll behave even if Eslin'den makes him ready now."

"Such decisions aren't yours to make, Arromna," snapped Sarval. "You had no business getting soft with him. Roshing'kiro and I decide his fate. It's us he has to please."

Arromna shrugged and gave a little bow. "Just trying to help," she said. "I thought that—"

"Don't question my judgement," Roshing snarled. "Nobody is to give him anything yet. I want him out of my sight until we're ready to leave. Make him go over his text one last time. Make sure he knows the price of failure."

With a spell this powerful, the price of failure was all too likely to be my death, if not theirs as well. That was a way out, of course…

No. My parents would be searching for me. I believed in that truth before I believed in the Powers themselves.

Arromna was sent off to do something about the horses, and I was left to the tender care of a man-at-arms and Orlando, who amused themselves by interrupting my dutiful attempts to read over the spell—which floated and seethed whole in my mind by that point—with insulting my mother. I won't repeat what all they said. "Human harlot" from the man-at-arms and "Murderer—I hear she like killing mans" from Orlando were the least of them.

"My mother fought the Yehillon!" I screamed, and weak as I was, I threw the papers aside and went for Orlando. He yelped and made the mistake of defending himself as if I were a little boy to be fended off with a few slaps.

A mistake he wouldn't make twice. I might be short for a Nightwalker, but my tutors in the arts of battle had been among the best. Not to mention a lifetime of having to hold my own among my Moss'avver cousins.

A blow from my foot knocked Orlando's breath out of him and doubled him up. I got him on the jaw as he started to straighten up. He crumpled to the ground, rolled over and tried to crawl away, shouting in Ronish, "Get him off of me, you stupid warlock. Help me, for the Powers' sakes!"

I struck from the side, at his shoulder, and knocked him over sprawling on his back. Then in pure animal madness I flung myself on him and got my hands around his throat. Blood stained his skin, but it was mine, from all the cracked and crusted scabs on my hands. His brown eyes went wide and terrified. A coward. He didn't even try to fight.

"Don't!" he begged. "I'm not really one of them! Let me go and I'll help you!"

I didn't listen. I didn't believe him. With that kind of fear in his eyes, he'd have given voice to any lie to make me back off. If I had had my powers, I could have, would have, split every bone in his body, shattered him like the door of my father's study. As it was, I merely dug in my thumbs and listened to his breath go raspy in his throat.

✤ CHAPTER SEVEN ✤
NETHIN: THE STONE CIRCLE

The man-at-arms hauled me off. The Ronishman lay gasping, his mouth working. Then he scrambled up and punched me in the face as I hung in the grip of Sarval's retainer.

"Enough," the man said, swinging me out of Orlando's reach. "Halfbreed coward." He meant Orlando, not me. The Ronish youth might be their ally, but he was never going to be one of them in the ways that probably mattered most to him. We had that in common in our mixed blood. You couldn't belong. "You should have fought when you had the chance," the man-at-arms added.

Orlando sneered and spat at his clear contempt and turned away, rubbing his throat.

"You damage the blue-eyed freak any further," the soldier told him, "and you'll be answerable to Roshing'den."

Not one person remarked on my bleeding hands or swelling lips once our little expedition got under way, although Arromna's eyes went wide a moment. She had no chance to get close to me though. Sarval sent her ahead in the halfworld to scout the route.

We traveled for about four hours on horseback, judging by the stars. The mountains lay behind us and rolling hills to either side. My hands bound to the saddlebow, I rode a pony with a kidney-jarring trot, led by Roshing himself. They were taking no chances with any son of my horse-racing father. Only about half of their horses were of the white breed that can walk the halfworld on its own. If I had my hands free and could get to one of those once we stopped and they all dismounted… a breakneck ride down the hillside…maybe.

It finally, slowly, dawned on me that in my drugged state I could not work a spell, any spell, certainly not this massive interlaced epic of magic that they expected of me. They were going to have to restore my powers somehow. That was what Arromna had meant by having the apothecary prepare me. And with my Maker-strength back, I would perhaps be offered a better chance than a desperate, knee-wobbling attempt to steal a horse, when I could barely walk five paces without sitting down to catch my breath.

The trails twisted and twined along streambeds and over sheep-cropped upswellings of green, and when we passed between the first pair of the carved wooden posts, renewed with every monarch, I knew where we were. The hunting lodge must have been on the edge of the mountains, where they dropped towards the coast. This was the processional road to the Coronation Shrine, high on a headland north of Dralla, where every king or queen since Hallow's conquest had been crowned. Before that, my father claimed the coronations were held at a similar ancient shrine near the heart of the island, now a ruin in the Westwood.

My father also claimed the shrine was far, far older than we Nightwalkers, that the central stone circles of it and the others like it around the island had been holy gathering places for the humans of Eswiland since time immemorial. We Nightwalkers had only added to the original structures, removing stones, adding stones, adding the widely spaced outer rings. We had changed the shape and the purpose, putting up the odd, randomly placed trilithons, the three-stone gateways that had since been pulled down at all the other shrines. He had never said why he thought our ancestors had done this. Only now did

I begin to wonder what more he knew that he had not told me, and what it might have to do with the stolen spell.

We dismounted and walked on afoot, though the horses were kept close and no one slackened their girths; they expected to be riding again soon. The scent of the sea, perhaps a quarter-mile distant and below a high and tumbling cliff, was strong in the night air, and its pewter glow limned the horizon. I stumbled, caught at the last minute by Arromna'den, who had appeared once more out of the darkness. The brown and golden night-color of the wooden pillars gave way to the stones' cold blue-green, swirled with waves of darkness. A faint pinkish tint showed some flower among the knee-high grasses. It was easy to believe the place was ancient, and holy, though I had been up here before for nothing more awe-inspiring than a history lesson. It was so quiet, despite the soft mutter of the waves far below, so...listening. The stones could hear me breathing.

Oh. *Oh.* I could see...the pattern described in the spell which I had thought I would have to lay out in river rocks or sand and ashes within a containing circle. It was already here, laid out permanently in stone, on a vaster scale than I would have dared try. And where I had meant to put mere gaps in my lines of stone and sand, there were the big trilithon gates, the purpose of which had always puzzled anyone I asked. The Coronation Shrine was a series of concentric circles of widely spaced boulders. Each ring had a single gateway of roughly worked stone, a lintel placed on two uprights. The gateways weren't aligned. You had to travel quite a long way around, between the rings of boulders, to get from one to the next, though there was no reason you would have wanted to, as there was plenty of space to cut across the circles in a straight line to the gap in the inner ring, where the stones made a fence. Inside the inner wall of tightly spaced stones was a single central boulder carved with ancient symbols of Maynar. This was where our monarchs first wore their crowns, swore to protect the people and were acclaimed by the heads of the Houses and the guilds.

For generations the historians' guild had puzzled over the symbolism of the stone circles. They had concluded that part of the structure was a human thing, its meaning forgotten.

They were wrong. I didn't know what it meant, but they were wrong. Humans might have built it, thousands of years before, but this stone circle was no longer a human temple. We had remade it into something completely different.

I felt myself falling, dissolving into the stones. The headland rose and fell like the distant breath of the sea, the waves sighing and soughing among the rocks at the foot of the cliff. If I could fling myself off, I could fly down…I shook my head and clenched my bound hands so that my ragged fingernails dug into my palms. I was poisoned, drugged, not in my right mind. I couldn't fly. All I could do was play along. Arromna had warned me…

A hazy time followed of people milling around, Sarval and Roshing arguing with one another over where they should stand.

"We don't know how long it will last," Roshing insisted. "We need to be right by the boy, ready."

"And if it's more violent than you think or if it goes wrong, we'll be ripped to pieces by the forces unleashed, or incinerated."

That sounded like a good idea to me, so long as I wasn't included.

It seemed Sarval had decided to keep her distance. First, though, she drew a knife, took my hand and, before I realized what she was about, pricked the ball of my thumb, smearing the upwelling bead of blood onto a clean handkerchief. Then she cut a good chunk of my hair, even as I flinched. My hair was already raggedly cropped as short as a human knight's—something done when I was first captured, I supposed. There was a lot they could have done with that much hair.

Sarval wrapped the hair in the blood-smeared handkerchief—I was bleeding far too much for such a little nick—and retreated. Roshing and Orlando stuck close as I wandered, unsteady on my feet. I wondered uneasily about Orlando. He wasn't one of them, he said. I preferred Arromna as an ally, but perhaps Orlando took his role-play further. Too far. My lip was split and my nose still dripped. I snuffled blood when I tried to breathe through it.

"Find where you need to be and stay there, mongrel," Roshing said. "These stones are supposed to be the form to hold the spell, in case you haven't figured that out."

"I tell you that," Orlando said proudly. "That in the Yehillon spell I find. You not know that till I say."

I ignored them both, my eyes on the ground. I had thought I should stand at the center, where Roshing had brought me, but that wasn't right. I wandered, tracing a winding route around the circles, passing through each gate in turn.

It was a sort of a maze, except that you couldn't get lost in it. It was just a pattern to follow.

For a moment the world lurched under me. Oh, no, you could get very, very lost. The stars danced and I saw them beneath my feet, as if reflected in water.

Too many drugs.

I finally returned to stand outside the gateway of the outer circle, on the sunken lane that was the processional route to the shrine.

Roshing and Orlando stuck close as shadows. The others bunched between them and Sarval, farther down the lane. They were nervous; even a night-blind human could have told that, just from their voices.

The armsfolk held the horses' bridles. There were mules laden with packs among them. A picnic, I thought hazily. They looked ready for an expedition into the mountains. The apothecary loomed before me, Arromna at his side.

"Are you ready, Sarval'den?" Eslin'den asked over his shoulder, and in answer the old Maker began to sing. My thumb throbbed with the rhythm of her spell.

It was a curse, a forbidden Making, and the punishment for such a crime was death. They were likely to be executed for imprisoning and abusing me so anyway; they had nothing to lose. I had much. I felt the curse reaching into my veins, seeking my heart, my lungs.

"If you are disobedient, if you try to escape or trick us or threaten us in any way, Sarval'den will freeze the blood in your veins. Your heart will burst and you will die," the apothecary said. "Do you understand, halfbreed?"

I nodded. For a moment I could barely breathe, the curse seizing me. Sarval'den was clumsy.

"I am going to give you a draught. You will drink it. It's an antidote to the drug that suppresses your Maker-strength. Do you understand?"

I nodded again. Then I shook my head.

"What?" Roshing snapped.

"I need my hands free. I can't do this tied up."

Arromna, without waiting for permission, knelt down and sliced the cords binding my wrists. In the process she dropped her knife. Roshing made an irritated *tcha* sound, and while Arromna retrieved the blade, her hand groped over my ankle. Something rigid slid down into my boot. I hoped it was sheathed.

She stood and slipped her own knife, which was still in her hand, into its scabbard at her belt.

Eslin'den brought out a little flask and held it to my lips. I gulped greedily, despite the foul taste of bile and honey.

The breath left my body. I couldn't inhale. My ears rang, and my vision went to a sort of blotched red and black with a strange white flaring around the edges. There was a horrible, distant keening noise, which I faintly knew was myself.

Someone shouted my name, over and over. Mama...no, it was the woman Arromna, who was holding me as I lay thrashing on my side, trying to keep my head from striking the base of one of the big gatepost stones. I gasped and coughed and found my mouth full of grass and spittle, my eyes full of tears. Roshing struck Arromna a backhanded blow. "Stop your yelling! If there are any shepherds sleeping out within a mile of here, you've woken them for sure."

She ignored the blow. "Nethin'kiro! Nethin, can you hear me?" Roshing had always been far too free with his hands, as I remembered, ironically human in his contempt for those he considered lower in rank than himself, but he was old and frail now.

"There's nothing to worry about; it's not an unexpected side effect," the apothecary babbled. "It should pass in a moment."

"You could have warned us," Roshing growled, and Eslin, already safely out of the way, took a few more steps back. He was terrified he'd killed me. I felt his fear; felt Arromna's fear for me and a great anxiety about something, a sense that she was tense as a drawn bow with anticipation; felt Roshing's disgust at the sight of me lying there by his boot; Sarval's annoyance at this delay as she sang, over and over, the phrases of her curse, sinking it home, blood and bone; and the fear and excitement of the other Homelanders. Whatever I was supposed to be doing for them, it frightened them. Orlando...there was some great deception he hid...

I sat up, astonished by how slow and heavy my body was. Was that wasted hand gripping Arromna's really mine? In heaving myself up I managed to feel inside the top of my boot and touch the narrow hilt of a slender knife. I squeezed Arromna's hand as Roshing seized me by my collar and hauled me upright.

"I'm all right," I told the woman-at-arms, meeting her eye. She gave me the slightest nod.

I stretched, and in a way, I stretched inside too, feeling the return of my strength, the feel of power flowing through my heart and the landscape of the minds about me. But I was weary, so weary, and the curse gripped me. Sarval was intending to let the curse strike once I had completed the spell. There was no pity in her or in Roshing, though some of the others felt it; in the old Maker there was just an eagerness, in my great-grandfather a grim determination and the physical disgust he had always felt for my appearance.

"Begin," said Roshing. "No more delays."

"Shouldn't he rest, first?" Arromna was trying to hold things up. She was waiting, yes…for someone or something? An ally or just an opportunity? I couldn't tell.

My heart stuttered, and I staggered, gasping. Sarval's doing.

"Get on with it," she called.

I pushed Arromna's hand from my shoulder. "Stay back," I ordered, as imperiously as any senior Maker with a crowd of young guild apprentices cramping some demonstration. Roshing and Orlando fell back a step.

"You," said Roshing, "Arromna, go join the others guarding the perimeter. You've gone soft on him, and I don't want you interfering if he starts to whine. The Ronish halfbreed too. Your part is done."

Sarval broke off her curse to repeat the order to her guardswoman, reminding Roshing whose commands Arromna was supposed to obey, but the pause was too short for me to take advantage. The Maker's chant resumed as Arromna walked away into the darkness, sliding into the halfworld as she went, vanishing from my senses. My witch's ability to feel other minds could not reach into the halfworld, though in the halfworld myself I could still feel those in the solid world, just as one could hear and see them while remaining unheard and unseen. The apothecary beat a hasty retreat as well, very afraid of whatever was about to happen. Orlando went a little ways and vanished, like Arromna.

A sharp pain lanced through my heart. I could feel Sarval's satisfaction as I gasped and doubled over. I was not going to be able to delay this. I couldn't tell if Arromna had some plan, or if she was just hoping for a chance to snatch me onto a horse and run—witches read emotions, not thoughts. But I was beginning to sort out the shape of Sarval's curse, the way you might run your fingers over a knot in the darkness, if you were a night-blind human who couldn't see it, and come to understand the shape of it.

Another lance of pain, worse. I grabbed a dragging breath and started, my voice cracking on a false note, and then started again, half singing, half dropping into a chant.

My words, my voice, formed a channel for the power within me. The rings of stones, or rather, the circuits between the rings, provided the mold into which the power could run, like molten bronze into clay. I could, I realized—as in some remote way I watched myself—have drawn a circling and switchbacking pattern in the dust, trampled one in the grass, so long as I had some symbolic fence in stone, even mere pebbles, to mark its outer boundary. The stones weren't the important thing; the pattern of the gates was. But it came easier here, in this place, as though the stones themselves held a memory of what was meant to happen.

The Coronation Shrine was a map, a map set in stone, so it could not be lost or miscopied. But it had been forgotten. The air around me began to liquify, to burn. I fell into liquid light, cold and silvery, a damp dank fog flowing into me. Sparks danced around my feet.

This all may have taken much longer to happen than it does to describe. Certainly I had the dim, distant impression of stars turning over me, of people zipping around like bats, though I don't know if they were real people or shades of the past, or things I only imagined. I passed into the halfworld without intending it but felt a rightness in being there, another part of the spell that had not been written down. Roshing plunged after me, reaching to seize me, and dropped his hand when the sparks flared up between us. Orlando was right behind him, a hungry, tracking mind, as intent on this as my great-grandfather, if not more so.

The sparks drew together, spun, burned, turned into a shroud of blue-white lightning, engulfing me, flaring around me like a cloak, like the great wings of the mythical star-eagles. I should not have been able to see the blue of it, not in the colorless halfworld, but I could. I could feel Roshing and Orlando, terrified, all their eager anticipation vanished in animal panic as they were pulled, drowning, into the icy flames in my wake. The lightning coiled and spat and forked and was a road before my feet, and my voice held it together, kept back the shadows—the deadly cold, the darkness, that lay under and over and around, flowing, reaching, striving to collapse in on me.

I added a line to the verse, another, began to weave small gestures into just one of the layers of the spell, nothing I had read in my three days of delirious study, nothing I had written in the margins. There...and there...and...that. The curse unraveled, its tendrils snapping free of me, running back up the lightning road. The bloodstained handkerchief Sarval held clenched in both hands burst into an oily orange flame that clung to her, running up her arms as she yelled and flailed about, setting her own tunic on fire. I seemed to be somewhere above, watching that, as unemotional as though it had nothing to do with me, something long ago and far away. She flung herself to the ground, rolling, but the flames clung and embraced her. Her hair burned.

One of the men-at-arms dropped a cloak over her, incorporating it into a spell to still flames, and another joined him, crouching over Sarval, the clasped hands of the two Makers forming a bond between their power and voices as she stopped thrashing and lay mewling, motionless. They might despise my father and all his works, but it was from his theories that they had learned to combine their Maker-strength that way, to work spells more powerfully than an ordinary Maker could alone.

Sarval wasn't dead, but she was no threat now. My attention was drawn by the sudden moon-silver flash of a horse, a white horse galloping over the eastern end of the ridge. I saw the cold, hungry, iron-blue glow of naked steel and mail hauberk, the blue and ruby night-highlights of hair. Arromna. She wove in and out of the halfworld, dodging fellow House Langen guards and Homelanders, but it was clear that, though an able rider, she was not a knight used to fighting on horseback. She gained herself a little space, sheathed her sword and whirled a sling around her head, spun the horse about, let the shot fly.

It was a mountain ranger's weapon. How strange, I thought. A man drawing a bow went down like a felled tree.

"Traitors to your House," she shouted. "Traitors to the queen. Child killers! Fools! Lorcanney'kiro knows all about Sarval and Roshing. Queen's knights are on their way to arrest them. Think to whom you owe your true oaths. Throw down your weapons. Take Sarval and Roshing!"

In my remote delusion of safety, I was a bit insulted by "child." And she was confusing her fellow guards by demanding they disarm themselves while at the same time doing their duty to their lord, Lorcanney, the head of House Langen, by arresting Sarval. She must be a spy for the head of the House, I thought, finding that interesting, the way the weave of the blanket can be fascinating when you have a fever—interesting but of no great emotional importance. So Lorcanney had suspected Sarval was up to something. Was this a private House Langen affair, or did the queen know? Was the Royal Office of Inquiry involved? Was rescue just over the hill, a company of royal knights galloping to save me?

Apparently not. Arromna was still alone as she kicked the horse forward into the white flames that danced over the stones, shouting my name.

But then a second horse appeared, dark in the night, velvet brown, froth flying from its bit, its chest lathered. It charged for the entrance gate to the shrine, where the white lightning burned. I could see myself, a small pale figure, a shade, walking slower than a funeral procession, but I was as faint as a shade, growing fainter. I could see stone through my own body, and grass, see the pale pearly white of fog that was all those outside the reach of my spell could see of the white fire I had raised. I could see my great-grandfather reaching for me, engulfed in the lightning, and Orlando seizing his arm as Roshing finally grabbed a fistful of my tunic.

A white horse and a bay galloped through the three of us, through a road of light and shadows they could not see. Both riders shifted to the halfworld, circling like racers on a track, still finding nothing. The white horse hung in my vision a long moment, as if the flow of time had paused for breath. Arromna'den turned, so slowly, catching sight of the rider behind out of the corner of her eye, and she drew her sword again. Not an expected ally. What then, was the rider of the heavy bay destrier?

A stranger. Human. A human, here in Talverdin. It wasn't possible.

The man ignored Arromna and her sword. He began to sing, and his deeper voice wove through mine. Half of what he sang was meaningless, the distorted nonsense of an ancient lullaby, but his intention, his will, was as firm and fixed as granite. What he wanted it to mean overrode the nonsense, which was the same

Ronish misunderstanding of the Maker's tongue as the sections of the spell Orlando had stolen from the Yehillon and brought to the Homelanders. The stranger's spell merged with mine, pulling him after me, and the big warhorse came thundering, dancing through the white lightning, snorting at me, shying aside, her eyes rolling. We both fell silent. The spell found a stable place and hung, incomplete—a pause for breath, no more.

The man leaned to grab me and I dodged away, catching a glimpse of a biscuit-colored human face marked with some scribble of blue on the cheek, black eyes, a conical helmet loosely wrapped in a headscarf that smouldered with streaks of green and purple—still seeing color though I was in the halfworld? A splash of green and black on his dusty pale surcoat. Was I in the halfworld or someplace else entirely? Fallen into madness and hallucination perhaps, because for a Berbarani warrior to appear was surely dreaming nonsense. He was too pale to be native Berbarani, but their merchant princes hired many mercenaries.

"Lord Nethin!" he shouted in accented Eswyn. "Catch my hand!" And then the big horse wheeled around for another pass. He yelled, "You!" in Ronish and drew his sword, a curved, single-edged blade.

"Run!" Orlando shrieked, and he let go of Roshing to grab my arm instead, fumbling to draw his own weapon. Truth burned in his mind with his words; truth and fear. "The Prince of the Yehillon! Run!"

✠ Chapter Eight ✠

Nethin: Through the Gate

Orlando tried to drag me one way. Roshing yanked me the other, shouting abuse at Orlando. The white lightning turned ice-blue and wrapped around me. I had faltered in the spell, and it was not yet whole. Cold bit my fingers and crept up my legs. Cold flooded my veins. I could feel myself starting to dissolve, to become nothing but particles of cold, if that were possible. The stranger and I realized the danger at the same moment, and together we resumed the spell, singing, chanting, weaving around one another. Orlando and Roshing stood as if frozen, still gripping me. Even they had the sense to recognize the danger.

In another place and time, the beauty of it would have entranced me. I'm no musician like my human friend Lovell, who would be a singer if he were not the crown prince of Eswy-Dunmorra, the only surviving child of King Dugald of Dunmorra and Queen Eleanor of Eswy, but I understand the power and grace of two things so perfectly joined in one act—voices, dancers, lute and recorder, horse and rider. It didn't matter that the Berbarani mercenary was Yehillon; it didn't matter that he was my enemy, not for that moment. Together, we made something that neither of us could have built so well, so strong and true, alone.

And then the spell came towards its conclusion. His voice dropped out, and I finished on my own, like a soloist drawing a great choir work to an end, chanting rather than singing, my voice slower, softer, the keystone of an arch dropping into place.

Silence. No, there was a faint sound, as of distant water or leaves, hard to hear at all unless one concentrated on it. The current of the lightning, white and bluish white, flowed past us, as though we stood as islands in a river of it, but it was faint and ghostly. We seemed to be standing on dusty, dry stone, stone that had never known water. Around us was shadow.

We were wrapped in thick black night, more solid, heavier, than any night could be, even to human eyes. It pressed with the weight of mountains and seas against the barrier of the lightning. It was cold as cannot be imagined. It had never known life, or warmth, even the warmth of ice, and never would. It was death, a void: pure nothingness.

The human warlock turned from side to side, frowning, momentarily distracted from us. His horse laid her ears flat and tried to back away.

"This isn't the Homeland," Roshing'den said. "Powers damn you, brat, you useless human, what have you done?" He swatted my head with the back of his free hand. "What is this place?"

"The shadow road," breathed Orlando. "The true shadow road at last." He switched languages and addressed Roshing. "Is not place. Is place *between*. Long journey to Homeland yet. I know. I study Yehillon writings of great prince. Roshing'den, kill this Yehillon. I save boy."

Orlando was afraid. A dog would have smelled it on his skin; I could smell his mind.

Roshing wore no sword and was no Maker. He was a very old man. How Orlando expected him to fight a Berbarani mercenary who was also a warlock, I don't know. He certainly didn't offer his own weapon as Roshing, failing to protest being given orders by a halfbreed, stepped forward, long knife in hand. Perhaps Roshing had as poor a notion of Orlando's fighting skills as I had.

The Berbarani muttered, "Yerku save me from fools," and sheathed his scimitar. "Out of the way, old man," he yelled and kicked his horse forward. He meant to grab me, sweep me up like a sack of bran and gallop past; I sensed his predatory intention. I didn't wait. I twisted free of Orlando, leaving a piece of my shirt half torn away by his hand.

"Nethin!" the man shouted. "Don't—" But I was already preparing a defence. The Homelanders had worked something like it against me when they captured me, on that early morning gallop in the dew-sparkling beechwoods, when Bold went crashing over, her legs snarled in invisible snares and they plucked me, stunned and battered, from the ground.

I wondered what had happened to my white mare, how long it had taken her to find her limping way home, to alert the castle...or had my mother known the moment I hit the ground?

I ripped the rest of the rag from my sleeve, tore that into two strips and twisted them into a sort of cat's cradle. It was a variation on a technique to draw something out of reach towards you, the sort of thing that's fun to play with when you're a student but rarely has any use in everyday life. The horse was almost upon me when I spoke the words and dragged the big bay Kordaler's haunches one way, shoved her forequarters the other. She squealed and skidded on the cold and dusty stone, which was only an illusion shaped by the great spell to give this place substance in our minds. Another twist and she fell entirely. Her rider managed to roll clear. I wasn't done yet. I dropped to my knees and spat in the dust, using the dark stain to trace a few hasty syllables, linking them with bindings. The shadows grew fragile, brittle. The white lightning seized the stranger, wrapped around him. Even as he shouted in horror, he was gone, pulled away into the storm.

I staggered to the horse and got her reins as she heaved herself up. She was trembling and sweating, her hide scraped and scratched. I found no more serious injuries, though, and by the time I had done feeling over her legs she was nuzzling my hair affectionately.

Orlando and my great-grandfather watched me warily but made no move towards me.

"Good," I said and found my voice hoarse, my throat still raw from the great spell. I had no idea how long I had been singing and chanting, but it felt a lifetime. "I can do that to you, just as easily."

Orlando was afraid. Roshing'den was merely angry, as if defeated in some game by an opponent he had underestimated.

"I'm going back," I said and, never taking my eyes off them, began adjusting the stirrup leathers. The Yehillon had been a good deal taller than I.

"You cannot," protested Orlando.

"Don't be a fool, boy," said my great-grandfather. "We need you."

"You wanted me to work the spell and get you here. Here you are. I'm leaving."

"This is not the place you were meant to take us," Roshing'den said. "You were meant to open the gateway to our lost Homeland, so we could rejoin our ancient kindred and seek their help in ridding Eswiland of the human invaders."

"What? That's nonsense. What ancient kindred?"

"Our people. Our own kind. Your father knows, the queen knows, but they're all under the Warden's spell: his puppets, his lapdogs. They keep it secret. We came from another land, boy, a distant land Korian'lana hasn't yet found with all his fleets and all his exploration. And before he does, I mean to make certain the right people are the ones to open up contact with our long-lost kin. Not the human-lovers of the court."

Prince Korian the Navigator had discovered the human empire West Overseas and opened up a trade with them in exotic spices and the teas called black and green cha—a trade that was making Talverdin and Eswy-Dunmorra wealthy, as the only shippers of such luxuries to our eastern neighbors. There was even talk of Talverdin being allowed a small, stony island

off the West Overseas coast to found a trading colony. But if
Korian'lana had not in all his voyages discovered another land
of Nightwalkers, it was difficult to believe there could be one to
be found.

"You're dreaming. There's no such country."

"Where did we come from then, eh? Are you really so dim
you have no idea of the secrets your father and the Warden's
human woman are hiding? They uncovered the truth, and
they've hidden it ever since. We're not from this pitiful little
island. We came here—"

"From some other land, yes; that's not a secret, you can find
that out reading ancient histories with your eyes open," I snapped.
"I know Eswiland was a human land before it was Nightwalker,
which you seem to be overlooking." My anger wasn't against
Roshing; it was a shield to hide behind from the thoughts of
what I had just done. "*My* human ancestors didn't follow Hallow
the Conqueror. Maybe you and Hallow's folk should both go
back where you came from and leave Eswiland to the Fenlanders
and the mountain-folk it belonged to in the beginning."

"Peace, peace," said Orlando, holding up his hands. "We
must not fight here. Lord Roshing, Roshing'kiro, this is not
gateway. We come through gate onto road, yes."

"The shadow road," I said, repeating the term he had used
when we first found ourselves in this place.

"Yes, yes. Shadow road."

"That's what the Yehillon call the halfworld," I pointed out.
"Some of them with what they call the Lesser Gift can go into
the halfworld like us."

"Yes! Yes, Yehillon call halfworld 'shadow road' but is wrong
name. *This* is shadow road. They not to understand. I read this
in papers of Prince of the Yehillon."

He felt very anxious to be believed by both me and
Roshing. He was also telling the truth, though fearful he
wouldn't be believed.

"That man just now was the man you stole the spell from?" Roshing demanded. "The Prince of the Yehillon?"

"Him? No, no. This man Aldis, this prince very dangerous man. Circle think he dead, want him dead. No, papers written by other prince, great scholar prince. Alberick. This Aldis father. He work on great spell before he die."

"Why?" Roshing demanded.

"Because he want Yehillon to go to Homeland and kill Nightwalkers there, I guess. Of course. Destroy all Nightwalkers everywhere."

I did not like the feeling Orlando gave me then, a sort of greedy excitement. He was edging towards me as he spoke. I somehow got a toe in the high stirrup and dragged myself up the mountain of horse. Roshing and Orlando looked very small from this height. I could just ride over them...

"Look, Lord Nethin, we can't go back," Orlando told me, speaking Ronish. "We've come so far. We need to go on. Make us a gate out of here, into the Homeland."

"I cannot," I said.

Roshing understood enough Ronish, though he wouldn't admit it, to catch my negative.

"Can't do what?" he demanded. "What are you two talking about?"

"You didn't understand the spell, did you?" I asked. "This isn't a gate. I made a gate and we came through it, but that's only the start. Orlando has said it, but he doesn't understand what it means. This is a road. No, more like"—I fumbled for the right words—"a river. And it's a path through a maze. It's not like opening a door and going through. There are places we can leave it, but most of them are places we shouldn't. Bad places. Gates into death or into dead places. I can't open a gate just anywhere, once I'm here. We have to—to follow the road the right distance. To take the correct turns. Otherwise we'll end up lost. At best." Some of the parts of the spell they had copied had not been actual elements of the magic, but comments on what it would create, cryptically written so that they only now made sense. Guesses, maybe, but after what had happened to the Berbarani I was not about to doubt any sort of warning.

"Stuff and nonsense," said Roshing, but his voice lacked its usual venom.

"Then go ahead and try," I said. "Walk off into the shadows and the lightning, the nothingness that's out there in the dark. Do you think you've ever given me any reason to care what becomes of you?"

"So how do we get to the Homeland?"

I sighed. "We don't. I told you, I'm going back. You can come, or you can stay. But I made the road and neither of you is a Maker. Once I leave…I don't think it's going to be here anymore, not for you two, unless either of you is capable of maintaining the spell yourself."

I turned the mare's head. We had not come far onto the road. The gate back—the proper gate back—would be near.

"No," said Orlando behind me, still speaking Ronish, and the fear that had washed through him ever since I regained my ability to sense it was gone. He burned with an animal-like single focus of a sudden: a navigator who had found his lodestar. "We go on. We're going to the Homeland."

"What the Powers do you think you're doing?" Roshing demanded, but I didn't look behind to see if he was talking to me or Orlando.

"You can try to find your Homeland if you like. I'm going home."

"No," said Orlando. "I'll kill you first."

I did look back then. In his hand he held a nasty little crossbow, its stock barely longer than the length of his hand. I had never seen anything like it. It probably didn't have a great range, but it wouldn't need to. I was close enough for it to punch right through me.

"The dart," he said, "is coated in a mixture of resin and *chiurra* dust. You won't know what that is. It's a mineral pigment found only in a remote part of the mountains of southern Berbarany. Very rare. Fresco painters in Old Rona used it for a particular shade of yellow. It has certain alchemical uses too. For instance, it's one of the main ingredients you need to make philosophers' fire."

I felt my skin go cold and clammy. "You're lying."

"No. Shall we test it?"

"You wouldn't dare carry such a thing. It would kill you."

Philosopher's fire burns white and cold to human touch. Harmless. It kills Nightwalkers in agony worse, more prolonged, than any normal flame, and its effects can be felt before the fire even touches you, or so I had been told. The Yehillon had other weapons that combined alchemy and magic to kill Nightwalkers in similarly agonizing ways.

"But I do carry it. I'm very careful. It's only on the points. Now, come back here."

"No. The spell is mine, rooted in me. If you kill me, this road will dissolve around you. The lightnings will take you." I didn't know that, but I suspected.

"I'd rather die than fail to reach the Homeland," Orlando said, which was the sort of threat a boy in a temper would make, but I could tell he meant it. In this one thing, his mind was coldly resolute. He would die. The question was, was I willing to die to deny him what he wanted?

I was not.

"What?" demanded Roshing, who had only followed a little of this Ronish conversation. "Don't be a fool, halfbreed. Shoot the boy and we'll be trapped here."

Orlando swung the crossbow around at him. "It's only a little *chiurra* dust," he said, still speaking to me. "It won't be fatal if it's just a scratch. Maybe you need to see what it can do though." My great-grandfather's mouth folded into a thin line, and he took a step back. I didn't think it was just because he suddenly had a small crossbow bolt nearly touching his chest. His hand went to his heart, and he stepped again. Orlando followed. "If I just prick his hand," he said, "a little demonstration. But imagine what it will do to you, sinking into your flesh, carried throughout your body by your blood...Just stand still, Roshing'kiro. We show the boy why he should not run, yes? Then he be good and he take us to Homeland."

"How dare you?"

"Stand still. We not want accident."

I was nearly sick. Orlando was enjoying this, the gleeful pleasure of the foul sort of mind that liked hurting animals. My great-grandfather—and I never saw anything admirable in him until then—stood fast, glowering and defiant, still not quite understanding, but refusing to retreat any further. The tip of the bolt touched the back of his hand.

His lips went gray, his eyes wide, teeth clenched on a scream. He crumpled up, gasping with pain.

Orlando jumped back with a jolt of fear. He hadn't expected quite such a dramatic reaction?

"Sorry, sorry," he said. "Have to show the boy. Serious."

Roshing'den climbed up again, knife in his right hand. The back of his left hand was blistering, livid purple-red. "You filthy, misbegotten human..."

Orlando gestured at him with the bow, smiling, and he fell silent. "Now," the Ronishman continued to me, "imagine what that will do, if I shoot you with it."

"I'd die."

"Yes. You'd die screaming, in agony, burning in the marrow of your bones. But I'd rather we all died here than not find the Homeland," Orlando said. Even Roshing heard the passion in his words. "Are you going to turn around and take us to the Homeland, or do you need more proof that I mean what I say? I'll start with your grandfather. It's up to you."

I couldn't watch him kill my great-grandfather in cold blood, much as I loathed the man. I couldn't become that sort of person. And I was afraid, too, of dying, of feeling the bite of that dart in my back.

"Why does it mean so much to you?" I asked bitterly, turning the mare's head once again.

"A whole world, and all the people there are Nightwalkers," Orlando said. "Imagine what could happen, if they decided to come through the shadow road to our world. If they could send an army..." And again, passion burned in his mind. Eagerness. Devotion. Hatred.

He must truly loathe his humanity, I thought wearily, that hating them so could drive him to such lengths. Did he dream of Nightwalkers conquering all Eswiland, even all the continent? I could imagine that was behind Roshing'den's hopes for rediscovering the land of our ancestors. For all Orlando knew, though, the people of this Homeland in which I did not really believe would all be like my great-grandfather, and Orlando and I would find ourselves outcast, driven back to Talverdin, or worse yet, killed as mongrels, impure freaks.

More strongly than anger at Orlando, my great-grandfather felt disappointed in me. Satisfied, yes, to have me turned to his will again. But disappointed. No great-grandson of his should have given in to a bluff like that.

Orlando had not been bluffing. I would not tell Roshing'den how I knew. Like most people, he did not believe humans had any magic of their own. Rumors of Fen witches were for children's tales.

"How do we know where we're going?" my great-grandfather demanded, walking at Orlando's side as if the incident had never happened. He meant to see Orlando dead though. With all that hate and anger from both of them, my head throbbed.

"Think of the pattern of the stone circles," I said, too exhausted to give him anything but the truth and wanting to distract them both from their emotions. "Think of the rings. There are gates between them, right, at different places? Well, that's the pattern. The map of the maze. I have to…to keep that pattern in my mind, to travel the proper way around the circle, to leave where the gate is for the next circle, not at any other point. Those stone trilithon gates are markers. Milestones, or descriptions of landmarks in an itinerary. They were built to record the pattern. Something that couldn't be lost or changed or miscopied easily. There are other branches in the road, other forks in the river, but if we take one not marked by a gate in the stone circles, we'll be lost. Or dead."

Orlando listened with keen attention but then complained, "I can see nothing. No circle. No gate. Just white light, and blackness."

But Roshing had a point. How could I know? There were no trilithon gates here, no convenient way-markers telling us where to follow a new branch. We could walk this road till we faded into shades.

Shades on the shadow road. Someone had said something about that in my hearing once. Had it been the Baroness of Oakhold, Prince Maurey's human wife? Overheard, half understood…grown-ups talked of so many things that sounded mysterious and turned out to be dull; one tended, growing older, to forget them all. But the shadow road…I had to remember this broad path of stone was not real. The true shadow road was all around me, flowing through me.

"I can feel it. Can't you?"

"No."

"There's nothing to feel," my great-grandfather said.

There was no point debating it. I started to sing, or rather, to chant. It was not the notes that mattered now but the breath and the rhythm, the words. I called up the shadow of the Coronation Shrine around me—a ghost, a shade, a memory—and I felt it settle over me, so I moved half in a dream.

It was vast. The circles stretched miles and years across. They twisted the night between the stars; they rode the currents of the suns.

It wasn't any land Prince Korian could ever reach with his sailing ships that we went to. Did Roshing and Orlando understand that? I barely did. It was what the spell implied, but it was, at the moment, almost beyond imagining.

And the back of my mind prickled. Yes, Roshing talked as though he believed the Homeland was merely some as-yet-undiscovered continent, another West Overseas. But Orlando had said "world." Orlando knew more than he had told the Homelanders about his spell. But I was too weary and battered by their raging emotions and the need to hold to my spell to chase that thought.

Once I had my bearings, I let the chant fade. I could call the image back to memory at need. The spell still rode in my mind.

I could see the way.

And so we went on.

CHAPTER NINE

NETHIN: ROAD OF WORLDS

Time out of time

Orlando lagged behind. It was only my imagination, but I felt that *chiurra*-poisoned dart, like a compass needle, always swinging to a point between my shoulder blades.

There. I felt it, like a breeze on one cheek, a rushing in another direction. A fork in the way, a branching of the road. Two possibilities to choose between.

I held the image of the stone circle in my mind. We walked the outer ring between the stones and the gate was…not here. Not yet. I didn't tell them. I hesitated, moved towards the gap. A turning in the road, yes, and also a way out. If I just exerted my will, bound up in this spell that wrapped the shadow road and me together, I could leave the road, abandon my enemies here, to perish as the road collapsed around them. Once I was out, I could rest and then, so long as I remembered the pattern, perform the spell again, pass back onto the shadow road, and retrace my steps. I weakened the walls of lightning a little, beginning to form an opening.

Red landscape, rock and sky. Waft of stinking, choking air. The horse flung up her head and shied back.

"What was that?" demanded Roshing.

I shook my head. "A dead place," I said. "A poisoned place. We can't go through."

"Through what?" demanded Orlando, looking around as if he expected to see a door, hinges and latch and all, that we could open.

"Never mind," I said and went on.

When we came to the place where the trilithon gate stood in the second stone ring, the gate between the first enclosed track and the next, the path before me forked again. *Turn, turn, turn,* sang the dull voice in my mind that had become most of my conscious thought by then. But there was a way out as well as a branching of the road. A place beyond, if I stepped *through* rather than turning. I could see it, feel it, though whether that was because I was the Maker of the spell and the road was flowing through me so that I touched all it touched, or because I was a witch, I didn't know. I hesitated, drawn by the vision of warm earth and towering green trees where jewel-like birds flashed from branch to branch.

Not birds. Winged lizards with long tails streaming. The whiff of air as I weakened the walls of the road was fresh and moist. The bay mare stretched out her neck and snuffed greedily, her ears pricking forward for the first time.

"We here," Orlando proclaimed and made to push past me. He must have been able to glimpse the world as well, or the potential opening at least. "Open gate, Nethin."

I was warier now. The scent in the air was green and living but subtly wrong too. It smelled like no forest I had ever known.

"This isn't where the map leads. This is just the first fork, the first place we turn onto a new branch of the road. We're supposed to go past here, not leave the road. Think of it as a milestone, a landmark, like I said."

"But..."

"Don't be a fool, boy. Don't think you can deceive us. I can see it, like a reflection on water. Our Homeland's there. Open the damned gate." Roshing seized my arm and dragged me half off the horse, hit me yet again across the face when I struggled to break his grip and haul myself upright once more. "Don't think you can get away with lying, you ugly little monster. That's our

homeland through there, and you and your traitor father have
no right to keep it secret."

"Fine," I snarled and dragged myself straight in the saddle
again as he released me, getting my foot back into the stirrup,
wiping an arm over tearing eyes. "Go through and be damned."
For the insults he never ceased giving my mother, for my sisters
whose miserable deaths had so pleased him. I spoke the words to
change the balance of the place, to open this gateway fully, and
I reined the horse back as she tried to bull her way through them
to the shifting crack that opened in the flow of the lightning.

"It must be quite far south," Roshing'den said. "Look
at those birds." As Orlando started forward he seized him.
"No, halfbreed. You aren't even supposed to be here. You and
the boy follow. And if you do anything to disgrace me when
we come to inhabited regions, I'll see you suffer for it."

Roshing strode forward. I could see him, standing amid the
trunks of trees that rose like pillars to hold up the sky, trees as
big around as a house, their rough bark overgrown with strange
lichens and flowering plants. A sparkling two-legged lizard
the size of a cat, its throat pulsing ruby red, wings feathered,
glittering blue, breast glittering with pearly scales, swooped to
cling to the bark of the tree above him. It perched like a squirrel,
clinging with claws on its feet and at the angle of its wing. Its eyes
were a deep amber, and it made soft churring noises, its tongue
darting in and out, tasting the air. We all stared, entranced.
It showed no fear at all, only curiosity, studying Roshing as the
old man studied it. The lizard came a step or two closer down
the bark, to the height of my great-grandfather's head, not quite
brave enough to sniff him. While the lizard thought about it, it
helped itself to a mouthful of white flowers and chewed them
up, staring at him the while.

"So tame." Orlando started into the forest as well.

"What sort of land is this?" my great-grandfather breathed.
"Such wonders." He stretched a hand out and plucked another

spray of the white flowers from one of the thick-leaved plants rooted in the bark. The lizard stretched down a cautious neck, almost as if it thought he might feed it.

Roshing ignored the creature. He rolled the stem of the spray between his hands, sniffed the blossoms. "Smells a little like one of those oil beans Korian's fleet brought back," he said. "The one the apothecaries make perfume from. I wonder if this is some island south of West Overseas? And which way do we go to find civilization, boy? Trust you to dump us in the wilderness."

Then his eyes widened. The flower dropped from his hands. His fingers clutched like claws, and his face went fixed and frozen. He made a strange harsh noise in his throat, once and again, unable to take a breath, staggered a few stiff steps back towards us and fell motionless, his rigid arms still outstretched, lips gone blue. The lizard made an alarmed noise and launched itself into the air, soaring up and out of sight.

Roshing'den was dead. I doubled over, fighting for breath myself. I'd felt him die, felt the sudden tingling in his hands, spreading up his arms, felt the numbness, the moment of horror when his chest could not rise, when the air could not come.

Orlando backed away. "An apoplexy?" he asked. "The excitement was too much for him?"

"Poison," some part of me said, calm and matter-of-fact. Orlando was panicking, a rising swell of animal gibbering in the back of his mind. He almost fell, there in the shadowy threshold on the lip of the jungle. If he did fall, if he did get any sap on his skin from the lacy green fern things that covered the forest floor..."It paralyzed him. The whole world's poison to us, Orlando. I'm closing the gate." He retreated, and I reshaped the shadow road around us. "We turn here," I said gently, as if it were he who had just watched the grandfather of his father die. "As I said, we don't leave the road here, we turn." I sang the words that told the lightning to fork, to follow the flow, the pattern of force, made by this world's presence, and we started forward again on the next circuit of our road. I didn't look back. There would be nothing to see. "Third waymarker, counting the one we came in by. Four more to go. Or we could turn back."

Why by all the Powers hadn't I closed the shadow road on him, while he stood on the threshold of the poisonous forest? Why hadn't I kicked the crossbow from his hand, at least, as he staggered back to me shocked and stunned? My father, my cousin Crow, they would have acted; they wouldn't have sat paralyzed and sickened until it was too late to take advantage.

Too late. Orlando had his wits about him again. He eyed me speculatively.

"You say 'world,' Lord Nethin. Not land. Do you mean that? Do you understand what that means?"

"World," I said, stubbornly refusing to join him in speaking Ronish. "A world Korian'lana could never find in all his sailing. Not our world, not our sun, not our stars at night. Another world. That's what you think you want to find. And without Roshing, do you think they'll welcome us? You and me, two mongrels, like he said?"

"We go on," he said. "Another world, yes. I've known the truth; I've dreamed about this for years. You might be in trouble, but at least I look half Nightwalker." He found that highly amusing.

We went on.

Time passed, but there was no time. Like my weeks drugged in the coffin, it was a nightmare that cycled back on itself. We grew no hungrier, no thirstier, than we had been when we set out. The scabs on my battered hands changed but slowly. Chins prickled but never needed to be shaved. We slept when exhausted, which might have been every hour, or rarely in a week. Then we trudged on, the horse as dispirited as we. She had already been exhausted, hard-ridden, when her rider appeared at the Coronation Shrine.

Orlando occasionally tried to take the horse from me, but I was so ill and weak I could not walk. I ended up huddled on the stones, waiting for the sudden stab of the crossbow bolt and wishing it would come soon, so each time he was forced to relent and let me have the horse again. Sometimes we both rode her, but he was oddly squeamish about that, hated to have my body so close to his, hated to touch me, as if he felt I carried some disease. His physical loathing at contact between us was like what Roshing had felt simply looking at me. My pale hair, probably.

Only Orlando's threats, the little crossbow he clutched like a child's toy, even dozing, kept me going. The circles seemed to stretch larger and larger, or somehow my own weakening strength affected the road, made it resist us more. Sometimes I felt I was fighting my way through a solid mass, struggling through snow, swimming in sand.

We both slept lightly. Orlando opened his eyes at the slightest movement, and took Arromna's knife from me the first time he woke to find it at his throat. Though I tried, I never succeeded in stealing the crossbow from his sleeping hand. Only once did I get open the heavy pack he carried. A small wooden case looked about the right size to contain the crossbow bolts. Another much larger case, wrapped in oilcloth, was inscribed all over with flowing Berbarani script where I peeled back its wrappings. It was locked, so I left it alone, but the poisoned bolts would be as deadly to him as to me, if I could get one and use it to stab him. I was trying to fish out the smaller box when Orlando stirred and pressed the crossbow against my back. Even through shirt and tunic, I felt the burning. I mewled with pain and rolled away, and the fight went no further. Neither of us had the strength for it. The shadow road was slowly poisoning us.

Orlando ceased to speak Talverdine at all. I found my Ronish growing slow and stumbling, as if my mind began to stiffen, to grow thick with sludge. It was harder and harder to rise out of the gray weariness after our periods of what I supposed was sleep, though the lightning and the wind-rushing darkness flowed through my dreaming mind, and I felt myself becoming more and more a part of it.

In the wind noise, the sound of pines and water and a storm that never ended, I heard voices. In the oily, flowing darkness, I saw dreams.

My mother lies motionless, her long braid of silvery hair trailing over the coverlet. Her skin is the sickly color of buttermilk, gray where it should be golden rose, dry and sagging. She looks old. She has never been old. Her lips are cracked and bloodless, the orbits of her eyes dark. Only the rapid, shallow rise and fall of her breast says she is alive.

Two bluehounds lie at the foot of the bed. Another three keep watch by the door. Wherever my mother goes, there are dogs.

Another woman lies on the bed, atop the coverlet, clothed in hose and doublet and a practical leather jerkin, fashion for a human man. Exhaustion lines her face; her hair, short and curling brown, is snarled and knotted. She smells of horses, and her rough brown hand is interlaced with my mother's. Aunt Robin, my mother's elder sister. How has she come into Talverdin? They must have sent her with an escort from Greyrock; humans cannot cross the Pass alone. The spells wake to protect us, and some are deadly, though Robin's husband, the Moss'avver, destroyed one defence, freeing the trapped shades of the invading dead, and for doing so got himself barred from ever coming to Talverdin again.

I can feel the strength of my aunt, like her mountains, flowing into my mother, holding her to life. I can feel it, like cold glacial melt, trying to soothe the bitter poison, fighting to wash it away.

But the tides of poisoned blood are strong. I do not feel any great hope in my aunt, only her bull-grim stubbornness, her refusal to let go.

She opens her eyes, blue as the sky, like my own, and frowns at me. "There you are," she says. "Korby did say you'd know what you were one day. Help me!"

I need help myself, but I can't find the words to say so. I don't know what to do. I am a shade, lost, and this is only a dream.

I am a witch, and I know better. Not only a dream. But I don't know anything. I can't help. I reach out a shade's hand, feel the shock of warmth as Robin, the Lady of Kanifglin, the witch of the mountains, seizes it in her own free one. Am I really here? Am I real?

I can smell the sweating horse I ride; I can see her black-tipped ears. I hear Orlando's feet scuff behind me. He mutters to himself as if rehearsing, the words empty of meaning to me. Another garbled spell.

I don't know what to do, how to help, but I want to hold my mother, to bury myself in her enfolding arms and cry, and so I do, but I am the parent and she the child, small and fragile and cradled against my chest, wrapped safe in my warmth, safe against all the world, as I pour my heart into hers. She feels like ice. What do you tell a child? Be strong, be brave, be safe, be well. My tears, my warmth, the strength of my blood, to burn the poison away. Not ice, I want to tell Robin, not water, not for this. Fire. But I have lost all my words. I feel my mother melting, or I am. I hold her tighter…

…catch myself falling. I lie on the dusty stone of the shadow road. Orlando paces, muttering again, Ronish abuse of me. Then I am back in the saddle, and he is leading the horse, still muttering…

...and my father mutters, shouts, strikes at a gray-haired man trying to force him down in his bed.

"You'll kill yourself, riding out again," the man says. I know him. He is the castle physician, a friend. "If your lady does recover, do you want her to find she's lost both husband and child?"

"You are a fool," my father says and falls over onto the floor in his struggles. The physician and my father's seneschal get him back into the bed.

My father is riding, riding, the webwork of a tracking spell wound about his hand. The trail leads west, down the Roshing River. A mess of cloth caught on stone. A body. No. Straw bundle, a cloak—mine. A braided knot of bone-pale hair, man-shaped, five-armed star-shaped. Also mine. He screams. I've never seen my father weep. He is so ill he can barely keep his seat. When he dismounts, leaving his stallion standing, head hanging, sides heaving, he slips and falls in the river. The poison eats him, but he must see the simulacrum, he must unpick the spells in it, the spells that led his own astray, that lost him his son, because in their design he may find some clue as to who has done this, who has poisoned his wife and left her at Genehar's very gate, and poisoned him and stolen his son. But he falls, and the knights who have been riding hard to keep up get him back on the near-foundered horse, and they return to the castle. In bed he tosses and moans, sweating poison, striking out at any who come near, calling for Fuallia, calling for me. They tell him the librarian is fled.

"Roshing," he says. "She was Roshing's creature. Warn the queen." But he does not say of what Queen Ancrena should be warned.

He strikes at the physician, who is trying to force him down in bed.

"You'll kill yourself, riding out again," the man says. "If your lady does recover, and there is yet some hope she may, do you want her to find she's lost you?"

Dreams circle. They come too late, they come too early. Is my mother living, dead, saved? The past is too late to change.

The dreams were stronger than any waking thoughts.

I saw my parents again and again, always the same dream, or so it seemed, with slight variations, but I was never able to hold on to the moment when my aunt saw me and spoke, as though the effort to make myself really and coherently there disturbed the dreaming, as smoke parts and swirls and vanishes when you try to seize it in a fist.

In another recurring moment I saw my uncle the Moss'avver and the Prince-Warden of Greyrock, leaning on his shoulder, both men staring away from me.

A ship burns, at anchor in some foreign harbor. Aljess'den, captain of the prince's guard, comes to them and speaks, gesturing at the lurid reflections on the dark water. I cannot hear what she says. Another man, human, joins them, speaking. Whatever news he carries alarms them all. Then the Moss'avver turns suddenly, eyes meeting mine. His face is streaked with ash and blood, his scarred left eye runs trails of tears through the ash, but relief lights his expression and he calls, "Nethin!" and Maurey'lana turns too, but they fade and dwindle as though I were a bird soaring away, lost in the smoke of the burning ship.

Dreams rarely tell *now* from *then* from *may yet be*, Crow and Drustan say. Sometimes I think I still lie in the coffin, drugged and struggling to fly, to let dreams carry my cries to those who can hear them. Perhaps I dreamed these dreams then too; perhaps years from now Korby will look away from a burning ship and see the shade of the nephew they long ago mourned and buried. Perhaps my mother is long dead, and I am nothing but a shade, doomed to patrol the shadow road as the shades of dead humans once patrolled the Greyrock Pass, till Korby freed them.

I see two young women, sleeping back to back, sleek Nightwalker-black hair and tousled brown braids tangled on the pillows. The room is small and the bed plain—a barracks, I think. Gear of war is stacked by the door, as if the dawn will bring them some journey. Mannie, Lady Hermengilde Elspeth of Greyrock, the Warden's eldest child and only daughter, is one of the women. A freak caught between races, like me, but better accepted, because Mannie, to both humans and Nightwalkers, is beautiful: tall, graceful, with hair like black silk, pale honey-tinted skin, her mother's green eyes. She is recently graduated from Asta College and is scholar as well as knight, serving in her cousin Crown Princess Imurra's guard now but expected to take up a position as a Master at her college within a few years. The other girl is my cousin Lady Gwenllian, Crow, the Moss'avver heir and Mannie's shadow as her father is the Warden's. She is a witch as strong as her father.

Crow wakes. In this dream, she always wakes. She blinks sleepily. "Coz," she says, as she always does, and then she wakes up fully. "Nethin? Where—?"

I know she will shimmer away like an image in oil, spreading on water. I have been here before. "Shadow road," I cry. "Homelanders. Help me. Tell Maurey'lana…" At the time it seems sensible. But I am gone, as always. In my dream my voice is thin as a distant bird's, and I am certain she has not heard.

My mother lies motionless, her long braid of silvery hair trailing…

In the end, there will be nothing left of me. A husk of ashes blown away into the endless night.

✢ CHAPTER TEN ✢

WOLFRAM: A PRINCE OF THE YEHILLON

The same, with memories of years past

Time is strange on the shadow road. While Orlando and I trudged onwards, towards we knew not what, Wolfram, behind us—miles behind, days behind, but perhaps mere moments for him—fought his way out of the lightnings.

Wolfram clutched a looping knot tied from a single hair of Russet's; he gripped it as if it were a lifeline, his nails slicing into his own palm. For a long time he lay still, breathing slow and shallow, as though he hovered on the edge of ceasing altogether. The stone began to fade beneath him, the shadows rolling in. Tendrils of white light moved like hairline cracks through the shadows. He pushed himself up. For a moment he thought about simply lying down again. Breathing seemed too much work. But he clutched the knotted horse hair and climbed all the way to his feet. After a moment he began to sing, recreating the spell. When it was stable, he pulled tight the patterned knots in the horse hair and tied it around his little finger, to keep safe the hair and the tracking spell bound into it. Then he held his left hand out before him, studying the pattern tattooed in blue on his palm.

Seven circles about a central boss, each connected to the next by a single short line. The symbol of the Yehillon.

His lady had seen him here, in this place, seen him before he was ever born, she said. It had not been so he could lie down and die.

With the symbol clear in his mind and the shadow road secure about him again, he set out on foot, following his quarry down the shadow road, assured he was going the right way by the warmth of the hair about his finger, a rope holding him fast to the bay mare. It seemed as though he walked forever. One foot, then the other, the spell cycling through his mind, a hum to which he set the rhythm of his steps. One. Two. One. Alone. Lone wolf. A lone wolf was a mad wolf. Wolves needed their packs about them. He had none. Dead, all dead. Everyone. He was dead; he just didn't know it yet. He hadn't stopped moving, that was all. Because if he stopped, they won.

When the boy was very small, he was named Aldis, and he was nothing but a cowed and beaten puppy. The men and women who raised him kept him that way. His life was lessons and beatings, and he believed he deserved it, because he was wicked; he was evil—a necessary evil, a sacred and holy evil perhaps, but evil nonetheless. The Powers could not forgive him. Those who represented the Powers in his life, Mistress Lola and Master Eugeneas and Master Abner, could not forgive him either. It was their duty to the Powers to beat every evil impulse out of him, so that he would be good and obedient, and do what he had been born to do. He understood this, and cringed and cried and tried to please, because every child, every puppy, wants to please those in power over it. He tried, but they beat him anyway. He could not change the color of his eyes; they could not beat the color out of him, though sometimes it seemed they wanted to try.

Then, when he was five or six—he was not certain just how old he was, in those days—he discovered he had an uncle. It had never occurred to him that he had an uncle, or that he had family at all, the way normal people did. His uncle appeared suddenly, at the barred window in the room on the second floor of the house, a pale face pressed to the glass.

Aldis did not scream. Good boys did not make noise. But he left off the silent, hopeless weeping of weariness and pain—he had been beaten again for asking a question he should not have asked, though "Why did the Powers make warlocks at all?" seemed a reasonable enough question to him, because they could have not made them; they didn't have to make evil. He stared, his stomach falling away, at this thing like a drowned shade trying to force its way in. Perhaps it was Fescor himself come to carry him off to Geneh's damnation. He huddled back against the wall, but the thing gestured, beckoning him, and the habit of obedience was so set in the boy that he unfolded his skinny self from the grimy cot and went, shaking, to unlatch the window and swing it inwards.

A hand came through the bars, ancient nursery bars meant to keep children from falling out. It groped for him and caught him, and the man's face—not drowned after all, just wet with rain, though it was not raining—pressed even harder against the bars, as though will alone could dissolve them.

"I've found you, thank the Powers, I've found you." The hand squeezed his so hard it hurt, and rain streaked the man's round face.

How ignorant he had been to think it was rain. But the boy had not known that grown-up people could cry.

"I'm your uncle," the man said. "I've been searching for you since before you were born. Come—what do they call you?"

The boy answered haltingly, the first word he had spoken to the stranger, the uncle. The man shook his head. "Your mother wouldn't have named you that. You need a new name, my boy, a true name. A strong name. I had a friend when I was your age, an old groom, who was more a father to me than... Anyway, he was an honest, strong, true heart, and I'd have been a better man, if I'd lived more with him in my mind. He was Wolfram. Would you like to be named Wolfram?"

Uneasily, he nodded, though at the time he did not really understand. It was all too strange.

"So, Wolfram, I'm your Uncle Gerhardt, your blessed mama's uncle. Let's get out of here."

Getting out was not so easy, but the man—the uncle—had a sack of tools slung at his hip, and he prised at the iron frame of the grille until it came loose and dropped it into a bush. Then he came over the sill in a rush, and though the boy flinched from the sudden movement, his body knowing that such movement led to shakings and being thumped against the wall, he was only engulfed in warm arms, pressed to a warm chest. Somehow that was what stuck with him most, the strongest memory of that moment: the warmth of his uncle's embrace, the scent of him, which was mostly coffee, because his uncle had been working as a merchant's clerk in a warehouse. Ever after, coffee to him smelled of love and safety.

He went down the ladder clinging to the man's back, which seemed so broad and strong, though time taught him his uncle was not a big man.

That was Wolfram's first small victory over the Yehillon.

Now he drowned in this storm, deaf and blind to anything but the mad flare and flash, the sheets of lightning that wrapped around him, the roar of the tempest that never ceased. A fitting place for him to die maybe, blown to ash amid the storm of the shadow road, which, on all the evidence, was how his father Alberick had died, in this place or some place similar, some rift torn into the foundations of the world. But Wolfram wasn't his father, that abductor of women, and he didn't deserve such a death, though in the darkness of his mind he sometimes thought he did. Everyone he had ever loved before he came to Oakhold's service (and he could count them on one hand and still have fingers left over) had died because of him.

They were gone. All gone. It was easier to stop, to let the threads of the spell slip from him, and lose himself. But he had been born bloody-minded stubborn, and so he did not. If he gave up while he still had breath in him, they won. Surviving was a small victory.

All he ever won were small victories.

After the flight down the ladder came the golden years, his golden years, when he traveled with his uncle, listening to the stories of that brave, beautiful, laughing girl who had been his mother, abducted and betrayed by the Yehillon. In those years he truly became Wolfram, not Aldis, though he and his uncle both took name after name as they traveled, shedding them again like costumes, like masks. There were lessons: woodscraft and the fighting arts, books and languages and alchemy. Mostly fighting, with one weapons master after another, Gerhardt bartering his labor, however menial, for the teaching of the boy. There was the constant running, the hiding, year after year as Wolfram grew, until they drifted to sanctuary of a sort among the reclusive Brothers of Holy Otho, who dedicated their lives to contemplation and prayer on the edge of the eastern desert. Gerhardt's heart was older than his years, worn down by some past sin and guilt. He said he had much sin to pray for—nothing to do with Wolfram; the sin was not Wolfram's. The sin was that Gerhardt had listened so long to the poison of the Yehillon in his youth, and had done a terrible thing for them, not using his own Powers-given heart and head to judge right and wrong.

Gerhardt found a peace among the brothers that escaped him everywhere else, which was why they lingered so long.

Too long.

The hand of Phaydos lay over the monastery, but it was not over Wolfram and his uncle. They were found when Wolfram was thirteen. And all Wolfram's skill and speed and strength with sword and dagger had not been enough, not against grown men. His uncle died there in the desert, crying with his last breath, "Remember, Wolf..." And Wolfram was taken back to the Yehillon High Circle that had bred him, his uncle said, as other men bred hounds.

He fought them, and they beat him until he learned again not to. He blasphemed them and their idea of the Powers; he was rude in six languages, and sarcastic and insulting, and they beat him and proved their words were stronger. That was because he listened, and they did not. He gave their words power by believing them. But then one night, the last time they had beaten him—it had been Master Abner's heavy hand and the dog-whip he deserved, being a creature as base and filthy as a dog in Master Abner's view of both—he had crawled into his bed and waited to die. He had wept, yes, and whimpered, and cried for the mother they had let die of childbed fever the week he was born. He had cried for his uncle and begged Fescor to take him into death, where he could be with Gerhardt again, and be loved and free. The blankets glued themselves to his bleeding hide.

He nearly did die. Mistress Lola had words with Master Abner, shouting and screeching in the next room. It all meant nothing to him at the time, because his dreams had drifted far away, back to that day when he was a little boy of five. Again he saw his uncle come through the window, but he looked young, younger than Wolfram had ever known him, and no tears streaked his face; only sorrow stilled it. He was silvery like mist, a shade. One should invoke the protection of Fescor and the Great Power Geneh for oneself and pray for the rest and peace of the unquiet dead when shades walked, but he did not. His uncle did not look restless or unquiet; he looked like a man in his own home, calm and confident and at peace, though sorrowing, and he reached out a hand to Wolfram. In it lay something that glowed softly, faintly gold and ivory. An egg. It was only an alabaster darning egg, such as a gentlewoman might use when doing her mending, if she was not the sort to dismiss such work entirely to the servants. It had been his mother's, his uncle's treasure, the proof Wolfram had that his mother Katerina truly had existed, not as a wonder-tale of his uncle's but a living woman who owned a simple alabaster darning egg, lost the night she was lost, and come into his uncle's hands, his only memento of her.

Wolfram had had it in the purse at his belt the night they were attacked.

He reached out a hand from where he lay curled on the cot and felt a faint warmth in the air, like the brush of breath on the cheek. Then Gerhardt was gone. Wolfram sat up, hissing with pain, weeping with it, as the blankets tore from his skin, but he did not notice his tears. He crawled—he could not walk—across the room, found the floorboard by the hearth which he had prised loose. He lifted the board to grope beneath. The stone egg was still there, along with a few other things he had managed to squirrel away—a handful of coins and a garnet-headed pin belonging to Mistress Lola, which was worth a lot more than the coins, if he could sell it without being turned in as a thief. If ever he escaped again.

When, not *if ever*. His fingers found the egg, cool and smooth. He had nearly forgotten it. A miracle his captors had not bothered to take it from him, when they searched his unconscious body and found his last weapons and the Ronish silver one-mark coins sewn into the lining of his doublet. He had hidden it when the journey back to this villa in northern Rona ended, lest they change their minds and take it from him as a punishment, seeing how he valued it.

He held it cupped in both hands, like a live thing, like a bubble of promise, of memory. That was his uncle's message, fever-dream or vision sent by the Powers, or true returning soul allowed to bring his message of hope. It didn't matter. He understood what his uncle had meant to say as he lay dying amid the desert stones.

Remember, he was Wolf. Wolfram, not Aldis. He had never been Aldis.

He was not strong enough to do more than lie in wait within himself. But in that fever, or vision, or gift of grace, he learned to understand patience. The wolf crawled on its belly, but it kept its eyes open; it no longer fought his captors, but it remembered they *were* captors. They were wrong in what they did, and he was not wicked.

An egg could be a timid, earth-hued partridge; an egg could be an eagle, bold against the sun. An egg was something that waited, until the time was right. The stone egg reminded him that the wolf within him would dance like a performing monkey if they asked it, but inside it would be true to itself and to his uncle's shade. Every trick his enemies taught him would be a weapon some day.

Eggs hatched.

When Wolfram recovered from the whipping that had so nearly killed him, he was changed.

"You have to break a beast to master it," Master Abner said complacently, and Mistress Lola sniffed. Master Eugeneas said, "What were you planning to do if he had died? How many generations before the Powers sent us another prince with such a strong Great Gift?"

"If we didn't have Aldis, we'd be content with my nephew Roland," said Mistress Lola. "And I still say it's my sister's boy we should make our prince, even if he doesn't have this brat's gifts. My Roland has more of the Great Gifts than any but Alberick and Aldis have had in a century, and he has a pure and dedicated heart, which is more than you can say for the brat."

"Great Gifts of such strength in two succeeding generations are a sign from the Powers," said Master Abner. "As is the fact that Aldis didn't die. The beating merely proved him. The Powers won't allow us to fail this time. And if we do, Roland will preserve the bloodline for another generation. He's not enough on his own, not now the warlocks have the Warden, and who knows what others like him."

Their bickering debate ended at that, and it seemed Master Abner had been right, even Master Eugeneas admitted it, because Wolfram—Aldis, or even Prince Aldis they called him, granting him the title his blood proclaimed was his—never had to be beaten again.

He devoured every lesson they gave him, mouthed their thoughts back at them, excelled and never questioned, so that they gave him more and more to learn. They set his cousin Roland, Mistress Lola's nephew, to study with him, and though rivalry dragged Roland on in an endless race to overtake him, Aldis did not need that spur. Knowledge was a weapon, Uncle Gerhardt had said, and understanding put the edge on that blade. He devoured whatever books were set before him, truth or lies, because even in the lies there was something to be learnt.

Good behavior earned rewards. He was treated like a young gentleman, most of the time. He had a chess set and a fire and fine clothes. He had a horse in the stables and rode out every day with an escort of Master Abner's liveried men, and played tennis in the afternoons with Roland or with Master Eugeneas when he was home and not off on secret business, as he usually was.

He had his alchemical experiments, harmless amusements. His father had made great discoveries, invented alchemical poisons against the Nightwalker that no one else had ever discovered. They hoped he might have his father's genius for the science, along with the other talents he had inherited. He certainly made discoveries, though he didn't necessarily pass on what they were to his captors, who now styled themselves his court, his High Circle.

Best of all, he had his father's books, sent away with his mother before the great battle that had wiped out so much of the old High Circle. They even trusted him to study his father's library, and though they never left him unwatched, they rarely understood what he was reading. Much of it was in languages they did not themselves know. Like the alchemy, they assumed the knowledge of the library could point only towards their ends. They did not understand that an arrow could be shot in any direction, once you knew how to draw the bow.

"Learn the things you might need," they said. The truth was they were all poor scholars, no match for the High Circle of his father's day, who had mostly perished in Dunmorra or died mysteriously in the years since. "The Powers have given you grace and their blessing. You are to be the one who will learn the way to destroy the Nightwalkers for good and all, and cleanse the world. The Powers will guide you to what you need to know."

Wolfram had always intended to destroy something when he was finished his studies. Preferably the Yehillon.

Stone circles. Scraps of ancient verse, sense garbled. The tattoo on his palm, which they had done when he was too young to remember and which branded him as theirs. His father's notes, a bold square hand he knew as well as his own, and hated. Notes, more notes, and the tentative shaping of a spell…Roland took too much interest in that and pestered him with questions as to what he thought it meant. When he found the stolen copies of Dunmorran research, the work of the Baroness they cursed as being somehow guilty, along with her halfbreed lover, of his father's death—writing that seemed half scholar's treatise and half the dreams of a madwoman or a poet—the wolf within the egg knew he now had what he needed, and those, at least, he managed to keep from Roland's eyes. He hoped. The secret Alberick had begun to understand came clear in Wolfram's mind, the secret that might destroy the Yehillon in doubt and confusion, if he could escape and find his proofs, and throw them at the feet of the High Circle.

There were voices in the roar of the wind of the shadow road, the crash of the lightning, the endless thunder of the sea stripped of rhythm and made mere noise. His name, cried on the wind. Shades hunting him. Men he had killed, maybe. Yehillon hunting him. Enemies of the merchant prince he had served in Berbarany, the man whose life he had saved, never understanding the cause of the ancient feud between the two tribes. It was stupidity to fight over forgotten causes. He'd won honor by it, and a wife if he had wanted one, and adoption into the tribe—home and family and a nation, if he had accepted. He hadn't. He couldn't. He had his own ancient tribal feud to settle, he told his lord, and someday he would have to leave to do so. And yet he had killed then, not worrying about the right and wrong of the greater argument, only that he kept his word to the man whose salt he ate. Did that make him an honorable mercenary, or a murderer, as his uncle, in his moments of blackest despair, had called himself?

Then came the day he had finally been able to get his hands on the last ingredient he needed for a burning fluid that combined alchemy and the secret arts. Master Eugeneas had procured some for an experiment, and Wolfram had palmed a lump of mineral the size of an almond, managing to stow it in his shoe when neither Eugeneas nor Roland was looking.

The iron bracelet had been welded onto his wrist when they captured him from his uncle. He had grown, and it cut into the flesh now. Master Eugeneas said, about once a month, that it needed to be replaced before it crippled his hand, but no one did anything about it. A crippled hand would not affect his usefulness to them. His name—the name they had given him, Powers alone knew what his mother had called him, or if they had laid him even once in her arms before she died—was part of the formula inscribed on the bracelet. The iron band kept him from being able to touch the halfworld or work the magic—not that they called it by such a name—that he studied for so long every day. They wouldn't call it a spell; warlocks made spells, but the Yehillon practiced the philosophers' secret arts, regarded with horror by most true philosophers, those honest scholarly seekers after knowledge.

It was a spell as foul as any worked by wonder-tale warlock.

He made the books and papers that he wanted into a parcel in the middle of a blanket. Master Eugeneas praised his diligence, that he carried his studies to his room. Then, using the stone hearth of the fireplace as a workbench and the chamber pot as a crucible, he set to work with some common liquids and uncommon powders and the lump of mineral, all stolen from the alchemical workroom in the cellars, a wet scarf tied over his nose and mouth against the poisons.

The clear liquid he ended up with looked harmless enough. He painted it onto the bracelet with the untrimmed end of a quill and hissed when a trickle of the stuff ran down onto his skin. He knelt there, left hand clenched in right, while the metal spat and smoked, and turned his head to bite the heavy cloth of his jerkin to stop himself moaning aloud. He was shaking as, protecting his fingers with a stocking, he prised the twisted wreck of the iron band off. The furrow of the bracelet was raw and angry, looking in places like uncooked meat, and blisters broke the skin like a boiling pot where the stuff had dripped on him. He wrapped it in the wet scarf.

The philosopher's secret arts and the Gifts he had learnt had little to do with medicine. Experience said he should keep it clean and hope for the best. If it scarred, at least it would match his back.

He felt so much lighter without the bracelet. Crossing to the bed, he put his throbbing left hand on the bedclothes. Under his breath, he began to sing, syllables whose intent he knew, though not their literal meanings. It was such a relief to feel the power rush through his blood again, the will wielding the words unconstrained. Like flying. When he turned away, flames were spreading from a scorched handprint, and the straw tick was beginning to crackle. There was no other source of light in the room.

"Aldis is dead," he said aloud, touching the alabaster egg, which he carried like a holy talisman in a leather purse around his neck.

Wolfram grinned to himself, slinging the heavy bundle of books over his shoulder, staggering a little. He felt so very light without that bracelet.

He took the shadow road and walked out straight through the door, as no other Yehillon, no matter how Gifted, could do. Wooden planks were as much a barrier in the halfworld—he used the Nightwalker term, defiantly—as anywhere else, but for him, they could be no more substantial than mist.

He could do almost anything necessary to survive. Uncle Gerhardt had seen to that. Gerhardt had fitted him for that life: mercenary, scholar; he was both and neither. Gerhardt had wanted him to survive.

To survive long enough to grow and learn, and understand what no one, not even Prince Alberick, his mad and murderous and so-brilliant father, had understood. Then, if the Yehillon were very unlucky, their prince might come back.

But revenge didn't matter so much any longer. He had made deeper promises, better promises, of life and honor and service, to his lady, to Oakhold.

True, he had once promised service to his Berbarani prince, and that was over. A mercenary's oaths of fealty had their time and could be put aside when that time had passed, if one's lord released one. He had been sailor and armed guard, huntsman and city soldier, before he ended up a mercenary knight in Berbarany. All these things served his needs for a time, and that time ended. Yet he had served his lord faithfully until he knew the hunters were closing in on him again. There had been assassins, twice before; the Yehillon had given up trying to recapture him, it seemed, and had decided to destroy what they could not control. He could not bring that danger down on the household of a man he liked and respected. He resigned honorably from the service of his Berbarani prince and prepared to vanish once more. At the time he had thought that perhaps he would go as a sailor again, go north as far as he could and vanish into the cold depths of Rossmark. The Berbarani tattoo on his cheek made vanishing harder, but it hadn't been something he could refuse, a sign of his honor among the warriors. He had saved his prince's life, and that must be acknowledged.

So when the time came and he felt the hot breath of a hunter on his heels, he took his leave. Family matters to deal with, he said. Blood feud. His Berbarani lord kissed his cheeks and forehead in the fashion of Berbarany and called him "son," weeping, because in Berbarany men wore their emotions like banners on such occasions. A pretty niece of the chieftain, who might have been his wife if he had not refused to be adopted by the old man, wept also, and so, with perhaps better cause, did a certain imp-faced camel girl. He had left her, at least, with fond memories on both sides, and—his lord had been generous at parting, gifting him with his horse and weapons as well as gold—what wealth he would not carry on the run. She could purchase beasts of her own and maybe follow her own dreams, turn caravaneer.

But not all oaths of fealty could be so easily dissolved, even by mutual consent.

The hunter he had felt lurking in rumors of strangers in the trade camps and questions asked in the bazaars of the city, in a watching shadow on the dunes or among the palm orchards at night, which vanished before he could draw near, had fallen upon him as he journeyed by the little-used rockway, the smugglers' winding route through the dry, knife-wind, stone country. He had been camped for the night, hidden from the track itself by a ridge of stone, alert but thinking himself protected, his spells better than a dog for giving warning of danger, and the horse, desert-bred and keenly alert to the scent of predator and stranger on the wind, an added sentinel. Then for the first time since the monastery and the death of Gerhardt, he found himself bested, but the shadowy hunter was not the one he had feared after all.

He had been confused, mistrustful, afraid, yes, but still found himself wanting to trust the man, after the first shock of defeat. His captor was the Warden's infamous Fenlander, the Moss'avver, not Roland with a gang of Yehillon assassins. The Moss'avver was a flashing kingfisher, no silent-floating sandhawk. He should never have gotten within a mile of Wolfram, let alone been able to walk up on him as he slept, through spells that would have alerted him if so much as a gerbil crossed his camp's perimeter.

He had to trust the Fenlander. Easy to say when every blade had been struck aside and you had a dagger to your throat and a man laughing in your ear about how "Little Gerhardt taught you better than he ever managed himself, didn't he?" But… the Moss'avver knew things about Gerhardt, about Katerina, Wolfram's mother, that no one alive in this world but Wolf knew. Things even he hadn't known that nevertheless rang with truth.

So he went with the Fenlander to Eswy-Dunmorra, to Oakhold and the household of the Baroness and the Prince of Talverdin, the Warden of Greyrock, whom the Yehillon had done their damnedest to teach him to loathe and dread. The Moss'avver walked him into the lady's presence and…he felt himself a lost dog found at last.

"I knew your mother," Baroness Oakhold had said. "I knew your mother. She saved my life." The baroness pulled him, stiff and astonished, into her arms like he was a little child and not half a head taller than she. Since that once, and the giving of his oaths, she had never touched him except for an offered hand, as any great lady might give a hand to her vassal to kiss or take in escorting her, and he had never presumed to treat her as her sons did, with unlordly affection, dragging her into impromptu dances like the little ones, or, like Ranulf, flinging an arm over her shoulders as if she were a lad his own age, sweeping her along in some enthusiasm.

But that once, it had been as if his mother, long lost Katerina, held him in her arms.

He had sworn service to Baroness Oakhold on his knees, hands between hers, but it was not the mere words that bound him.

True oaths were founded not only on word and honor, but on something deeper in the heart. He couldn't take leave and walk away, even if the baroness released him. He would fight going if Geneh herself stood beckoning.

So.

That brought him here. One foot after the other. If the Yehillon were hatred and fear, he served what resisted that. Simple.

That meant going on. It was too soon to die.

✧ CHAPTER ELEVEN ✧

ALABETH: SAND RIDGE

Early autumn, under another star

If I had known what awaited me in the Homeland, would I have dared Orlando's chiurra-poisoned crossbow quarrel and fought him to turn back?

No. Because amid all the suffering and the horror was Alabeth.

Dawn, on an early autumn morning. Alabeth Narran Kiron lay on her belly in the crunching lichen, chin on her folded arms. The wind—it was always windy up here on Sand Ridge—whined around the fallen stones of the old mage's circle. The cold of the earth seeped up through her coat as she watched the distant herd of sardeer. They weren't the brown-and-white-spotted ones that belonged to the Wanderers. No herders followed them; these were wild. The Wanderers should have been back six months ago, like the deer. But neither they nor their spotted deer and their halfworld-walking tawny dogs had returned from the north this summer. What that boded... she knew Aunt Mara worried about it and read her ancient texts for signs. There had been lurid sunsets around midwinter.

When she went home and told the village council of this wild herd, there would be a hunt. Alabeth would insist she be allowed to join, young as she was. She was a good shot with the bow, a good stalker, and she and Aunt Mara needed a share of the meat and hides—a decent share, not a charity allotment of cheeks and shanks and tails. Her mouth watered. It had been a long time since she had tasted roast meat, other than fish and fowl. Meat was good, but still…she liked to watch the deer. She liked the way they seemed a part of the wind, of the green-brown roll of the hills and the mountains white against the sky.

Not part of the stones though. The stones had been here before the sardeer, when sardeer were something that lived in the distant south.

When ice was something that lived in the distant south.

A rock quail wandered around the nearest stone and froze. Alabeth forgot the sardeer, but she couldn't shoot lying down. She reached for the bow lying beside her, and sat up, but of course the bird noticed and scuttled off, out of sight over the ridge. She sighed and got to her feet, leaning back against a stone still upright. Willow brush and dwarf birch grew in its lee, bent and sloped by the wind even there. If she stood still enough, long enough, the bird would wander back, and now she had her bow in hand and an arrow ready. Supper. She didn't plan to go home without something. Aunt Mara was ill, and, despite what she claimed, it was no passing ague. Aunt Mara, bundled into bed, the bedstead pushed as near to the brick stove as Alabeth dared, needed something better for her supper than eggs and kale. Alabeth had not dug the botati tubers yet, though she could grub up a few if the Powers didn't bless her hunting. They had not yet received their allotment of the communal rye crop; it would be meagre enough. No milk or cheese; their only milch sheep had borne nothing but male lambs for the last four years and then died in the winter, and such was the villagers' respect for Mara, Mara Leor Hedenor, the last Hedenor, the last to carry the caste name of the ancient emperors, that though the village flock was large, no one had offered them another, not even the promise of a ewe lamb to rear. Mara had nothing to trade but her skills, and those skills—always regarded with suspicion— had become even more suspect last spring, when the quakes had started again.

The earthquakes foretold a hard year, everyone had said. A bad summer, an ice summer, and that had come true. Not so many miles upriver, ice still choked the Great Aganan, once, so the tales said, the great golden river of the Old Empire, and Little Aganan out of the mountains had not thawed at all. Late and then early frosts had blighted the gardens, and the rye was mostly hollow husks, seedless.

Because of the tremors and last winter's quake, they watched the sky for the signs from the old tales: for a shrouded sun, for green dusks. And some—too many—said, "The Powers are warning us. It's as they used to say in Rivermouth: the Calamity was brought upon us by the pride and wickedness of the Kiron, and here's Aunt Mara rearing that orphaned Kiron brat from Overhill and teaching our children Kiron ways."

In the long cold winters, Aunt Mara had taught three generations of children in Watersmeet to read and write and do more than add on their fingers. Taught them to think, she claimed, to reason and understand, to carry their past with them and not forget what the world had been. But nobody cared, nobody wanted to read and remember—only to tell and retell distorted tales that grew more fanciful with every winter's telling—and the parents stopped sending their children, or outright forbade them. Their hands were more use at home, spinning, weaving, turning the heavy quernstones to grind the grain, which even before this year had not grown so well as it had when the parents of this generation of children were young. Their minds were more use...doing nothing. Not asking questions. Questions led to wonder, wonder to exploration, exploration to the death of the world.

If...*when* Aunt Mara died, there would be no one but Alabeth to read her books. There would be no one to teach another generation the ancient, complex way of writing, with its syllable characters heavy with poetry in the High Court tongue, no one to read the histories and the tales and the knowledge of the empire's scholars and mages. Only Alabeth herself, to carry what was left of a whole world's knowledge. Of young people her age, only a handful could even read the simplified single-sound characters that had always been used for business and everyday matters.

Nobody in all the world but Alabeth, because in Watersmeet they were all the world.

For generation upon generation, there had been three settlements: Watersmeet where the Little Aganan met the Great; Rivermouth down by the turf-buried ruins of the Old Capital, where they had quarried the ruins for fine dressed stone for their houses; and coal-mining Overhill upriver, nestled in a fold of valley. Overhill, where the Kiron caste had still kept a library, the Last Library, and guarded the past and hoped for the future. They had taught, as Aunt Mara did, and perhaps they had worked their forbidden spells in secret, though they claimed all magic had been foresworn and they were only historians. Then folk from Rivermouth sailed upriver in the fall of a bad year, when storms smashed the shore and drowned the fishing boats and rain rotted the botati tubers and the rye in the fields.

The Last Library burned, and most of the Kiron caste with it, trying to save their books. And the survivors, who had put out the fire with the spells they claimed they had foresworn generations ago, died anyway, because there were too many angry people from Rivermouth and too many of Overhill who stood by, or even picked up stones and axes themselves, against their friends and neighbors and kin. And perhaps too few of the Kiron knew more than the most basic of spells and so had no weapons more than bows and farm tools and stones to defend themselves anyway.

Alabeth's parents had died there. She didn't really remember, having been a baby at the time. Probably it was better not to remember that night.

Then one summer day five years ago, all Rivermouth was destroyed, when the sea rose up and smashed the town, the last town, the largest population left to the world. Even in Watersmeet the river rose and swelled in a great flood, but they lost only cattle pastured in the water meadow and one man who had been tending his eel traps. But when a party paddled down to Rivermouth…it wasn't there. Wreckage. Bodies and other flotsam washed far inland, men and women, children and beasts. All dead.

Whispers in Overhill blamed the Kiron caste, which meant Aunt Mara and Alabeth, though no one in Watersmeet had believed that. Not then.

And now Overhill was gone, this year. In the depths of winter the stones had shrugged, and in the mine, men and women, half the adults of Overhill, had died. Then some plague had come upon the settlement, and most of the rest of the population had followed them. Sheep and cattle had perished too. The few survivors had come to Watersmeet with the spring, abandoning their settlement and their mines, which meant no more coal for the fires, and they had begun at once to mutter that a plague would come to Watersmeet, or worse, for their tolerance of Kiron-caste folk among them. Kiron knowledge, Kiron practices had blighted the world. Its continuing destruction proved they were still at it.

Watersmeet and the Wanderers were all that were left in the world, and the Wanderers must be lost, because there had never before been a spring when they did not return.

That left Alabeth as, maybe, probably, the last of the Kiron, the Kiron caste who had broken the world. She and Aunt Mara, who was Kiron even though her caste name was Hedenor. The last mages.

The rock quail showed no sign of returning. Well, Alabeth had meant to do her hunting farther west anyway, where a forest of spruce and dark-needled varnor sheltered grouse. She had come to Sand Ridge for another purpose.

With her heel Alabeth scraped a patch free of gray lichen, uncovering black sand beneath. All the top of Sand Ridge, within what had once been a fence of upright stones, was deep with sand. Aunt Mara had brought her up here once and showed her how you could grub up fistfuls of it, black, white, pink, green, blue, carted here from beaches long lost to the changing world. Here the mages of the Kiron caste had once poured out the sand to draw the many paths of their shadow roads, and had walked them in the sacred emperor's service, exploring, bringing back the exotic luxuries of a hundred lands, or simply shortening the road from one province to another, for the Old Empire had truly been vast, containing all the world. And then they would sweep the design away and pour out a new road, the gathered Kiron singers weaving power out of words and the patterns they traced.

Here, in this place, began the shadow road.

Here they had broken the world.

It was all the Kiron mages' fault, the Calamity, fifteen hundred years since. Those tales they didn't forget, and told again and again around the stoves. The great volcano. Dark skies and poisoned rains and years without summer, and all the province of Veralin buried under stone and ash, an entire province, men and women and children, beasts and birds, fields and forests—dead. Winds had carried poison across half the world, so that other provinces of the Old Empire, especially here around the Old Capital, Royal Province west of Veralin, had seen death come upon them, though more slowly, in a season or two, as poisoned animals died of grazing poisoned fields. Then the generations of wars, as empire broke into petty kingdoms and republics, little states fell into feuding cities and warlords.

Plagues had come, and famines, in drought and storm, summers of cold and waterlogged fields, seasons of mold and blight, summers of frost, till nearly all the people of the world died. Sun returned, but never as it had been, and cold crept up from the south, down from the mountains. "They sailed east, and they sailed west. They sailed north and south, and they sought new lands, but the seas are empty. There is only one land in all the world, and it is the Empire," one old song said, and another story told that, "They gathered all the folk who had survived, a family here, a village there, and as the ice grew they summoned them all to the Royal City, to make a new kingdom and start again and leave the other provinces lost to the ice." "They" were the survivors of the Hedenor caste and the Kiron, though that did not stop the villagers from distrusting the descendants of their heroes. Overhill, if the stories held truth, had not been the first massacre of the Kiron.

Probably all the summoning and founding of new settlements did not happen so swiftly as that, or so easily. The chronicle Aunt Mara kept began in the one-thousand-and-seventeenth year after the Calamity. The earlier volumes had been lost to wars and other disasters, so the details were vague. Watersmeet had been here, and Overhill and Rivermouth, when Mara's chronicle was begun. But even then it spoke of few other settlements. Now, no one, even the Wanderers, ever found any other villages, except maybe deserted homesteads, fallen walls. Watersmeet really was all that was left of the world that had been, when an Emperor ruled in Old Capital and the Kiron caste were his bodyguards, his mages, the princes of his court.

Fifteen hundred years ago, Alabeth would have been one of those scholar-warriors guarding the sacred Hedenor emperor, riding a shadow-walking moonhorse, powerful, respected, a great knight and a mage and a prince of the empire. Maybe she'd have been wise, wise enough to say, "No, leave the shadow roads alone. They bring death to the world."

But probably not. Nobody had known. Probably nobody could have known, because if they had, surely they would not have done what they did. What had it been like, to see the world dying and know what you had done?

Alabeth shivered, here on Sand Ridge, where it had all begun. It was an ill-omened place.

Where better for the last Kiron to pray?

Alabeth felt in the deep square pocket of her long coat for the bundle she had gathered in the garden: a few herbs, nothing more, things pungent and bittersweet, fitting for death offerings. With broken twigs she laid out a pattern atop the prepared wood and spoke a few words in the High Court tongue, the language of magecraft as well as of history. Flames licked up, and she laid the herbs on, watched them blacken and shrivel.

"Please," she begged the shades of her ancestors, "help me. Give Aunt Mara strength. Help us find a way..." A way to do what? She couldn't do anything to change the world. She couldn't stop the ice, stop the cold. She couldn't even keep one old woman well fed or stop a sick sheep dying. "Please," she said, "help me. I'm alone. I'm..." She hadn't realized how she hurt till she came here, to this forbidden place where once people of her caste, people like her, had gathered in their schools and choirs, in their scores and hundreds, men and women and youths. Tears ran down her face, and the wind stung. "Please. I'm alone. I'm the last one who knows, the last one who'll remember..."

But perhaps it was better forgotten. Rivermouth died and Overhill, and Watersmeet would follow. Without the Wanderers, they were too few. Babies were already born sickly. Even if no plague came upon them or their herds, no blight to their fields, no flood or drought or summer of snow, they would dwindle and die from inbreeding, and the world would be empty of all

but animal life. And it would be as if all the history and poetry
of ten thousand years had never been.

Sparks danced over the lichen at Alabeth's feet. She sprang
up and took a hasty step back.

Lightning arched from one fallen stone to the next, searing
lichen, starting small fires in the dry mosses, until the ring that
had once fenced off the ritual floor from the outside world was
marked in smouldering clouds. The air grew dark, as if night
had taken the sun, and a web of white light crackled over the
circle. It was like the work of a thousand mad spiders spinning
in lightning, and it shifted and flowed and changed. Alabeth
felt as though she were peering into something vast from some
unimaginable distance, felt as though she were falling forward,
plunging into bottomless water. Thick cold shadows clung and
set the ache of deep winter in her joints.

Then the shadows shattered, and the white fire was not
a web but a vortex of lightning, reaching into the world. Shapes
within it grew thick and solid and loomed over her. She yelled,
reaching for the knife in her belt.

No lightning. No shadows. She blinked in sudden daylight
and stumbled to her knees, pulled off-balance by shock, or by
the tilting of the world.

A horse shambled away from her, its rider huddled small
in the saddle, but the man who followed turned her way. He
was young and quite short and had not shaved in several days.
His beard stubble was pale with dust, and his skin had an
unhealthy livid and mottled hue, like a bird plucked naked.
He was lightly dressed, not even a summer coat, just an odd
long shirt, belted, that reached to his knees. He carried a heavy-
looking bundle over his shoulder, held a strange little device
in his hand and wore a narrow-bladed sword.

He stared at Alabeth as though she were a shade herself and
then turned towards his companion. The horse, which was huge,
a deep red-brown with hairy black feet, broke into a labored

trot that still managed to hint of grace and power. The beast was gaunt, her coat dull and ribs showing. Her rider, a thin old woman, cast one hollow-eyed look over her shoulder and then urged the horse on, out of the ring of half-buried stones and down the long grassy slope. The man shouted and raised the thing he held in his hand, which Alabeth now realized was an odd miniature crossbow, already spanned. She didn't need to understand the words to know that the old woman on the horse fled the angry man. She fumbled and dropped her arrow, her hands shaking. The thought of having to kill a man...she left it and ran through spells in her mind. Tangle the man's feet, call up a fog...too slow. Strike him momentarily blind... no. She dropped her bow and caught up a twist of grass, lost from her fire-making. She shaped it, muttering over it, twisting and tearing.

While the man still took aim at the zigzagging horse, the cord of his bow snapped with an audible twang. He shouted in what almost seemed horror as the weapon bucked in his hand and a bit of broken cord whipped his face. Then he flung the weapon away, taking off running. He began to shout in a rhythmic, hoarse way, sounding as though his throat were parched. A spell? He knelt down for a minute, doing something with pebbles and twigs. The rider reeled and flung out a hand, and the ground erupted between them, sand exploding upwards like a fountain, shards of rock slicing every which way. The pursuing man screamed, abandoned his spell unformed and fled, down over Sand Ridge, stumbling and falling and rolling and picking himself up. A sharp chip of stone had grazed Alabeth's cheek, but she hardly felt it. Such strength in that fleeing rider. Alabeth hadn't even heard the spell or seen her make any pattern.

Well, the man wasn't likely to come back in any great hurry. He couldn't have escaped without a dozen cuts, and she'd definitely seen a stain of red on his neck and on his hand. The white-haired rider was in trouble though. She slumped again and fell, sliding down the horse's side, only enough wits or strength left to kick her foot free of the stirrup. Alabeth ran to her.

"Are you...?"

Not an old woman. Not a woman at all: the narrow shoulders and near-white hair together had deceived her. A slightly built youth, a boy a few years older than she, and his snarled, roughly cut hair the color of undyed linen, of silver with the warmth of sunlight. His face was nearly skeletal, sickly gray around his eyes and mouth, bruised as if he had been beaten, sunken and shadowed. The wrists hanging out of his filthy, threadbare sleeves—coatless like the other—were scrawny as a hare's foot, all tendons and bone, his hands torn and bleeding. She didn't bother asking questions. He was unconscious anyway. She got an arm under the boy's shoulders, her elbow supporting his neck, and dragged him half onto her lap, off the cold ground anyway. She had meant to pick him up, but he was no light weight after all.

"I think he's dead," she said aloud, which wasn't sensible, as she could feel the swell of his ribcage against hers, even through her coat. "Don't be silly," she told herself, because she was in serious need of good advice from someone just then. "He's only fainted. But he may die if I don't get him someplace safe and warm. So..." She looked up at the horse, which, viewed from this angle, was a monster of a beast. "I need a ladder."

At least the animal seemed quiet. Completely ignoring Alabeth, it had fallen to grazing, tearing up almost frantic mouthfuls of the sweet-scented grass that grew in tussocks amid the lichen.

Somehow, Alabeth got herself to her feet, lugging the young man. Her knees trembled with the effort. She tried to push him up the side of the horse. It flicked its tail and sidestepped away, and they both fell, though she managed to keep the boy from hitting his head. He stirred and muttered, and then his eyes snapped open and he started to struggle.

"It's all right; you're safe. Don't be afraid. I'm trying to help." He didn't seem to understand, but his eyes fixed on hers, blue as a rain-washed sky, blue as unicorn eyes in poetry, a color she'd never thought a person's eyes could be. "I want to get you up on your horse, but you weigh more than I do, which is ridiculous in a scarecrow like you." Her voice was shaking. Stupid. She wasn't going to cry again. She couldn't carry him home. She could leave him, cover him with her coat, try to find saplings she could hack through with her knife to make a litter on which to drag him. She could…

"Horse," he said.

"Yes, the horse."

He said something more, incomprehensible. But his struggles now were to get his feet under him, so she helped, and this time, when he clutched the reins and the front part of the saddle, the horse merely flicked a resigned ear and didn't sidle away. The boy tried to get a foot in the stirrup, but he was too weak. Alabeth caught his leg and boosted him and then shoved at his hip. Somehow he floundered into the saddle again, swaying.

"Don't fall and break your silly head." She kept hold of one leg. He looked down at her, said something. When she shook her head, protesting, "I don't understand you. Where are you from?" he held a trembling hand down to her, fumbling his foot out of the stirrup.

"What? No. I'm not coming up there. That would just mean two of us breaking our heads." But for a moment she was tempted. No. She'd fall and pull him off with her. He was obviously a horseman, quite capable of keeping his balance so long as he stayed conscious. She was not. Only Rivermouth had kept horses, though the Wanderers rode—had ridden—sardeer, and no way was he from dead-and-ruined Rivermouth. Nor was he a Wanderer.

But that was impossible…

Alabeth left that thought for later and firmly returned his boot to the stirrup. "Come on. We go that way." She pointed downriver, east. "I'm taking you to Aunt Mara. Where did you come from? The north? The west? Are there more of you? Why was that man trying to kill you?"

But the other questions ran in her mind, no matter how much she would rather have left them for later. She knew he hadn't ridden up to the top of Sand Ridge without her seeing him. Not on a horse of such evident breeding. Horses in Rivermouth had been chosen to be small and sturdy, to work hard and eat little, not to tower grandly over the landscape, to move like solemn dancers, as this one did. The last tame moon-horses, horses that could walk the halfworld, had belonged to the Kirons of Overhill and had been slaughtered, vindictively, for their meat, after the final massacre.

Alabeth took a breath. "You came by the mages' road, didn't you? The shadow road? How? Are there enough Kiron left somewhere, some hidden valley, to work the spell? It takes dozens of mages at least, doesn't it? A full choir? Why haven't they come to help us before now?" The fate of her parents should be answer to that. "Is there an island that was never found, back when we still built the great ships, someplace safe from the ash and ice? Have you come to help?"

No answer. She shivered, looking up at him. Was he even a real person? Tales said the Powers were served by spirits of air and fire, who took fleshly form as men and women of eerie and heartbreaking beauty. Silver hair, silver-lashed unicorn eyes… No, he stank of sweat and sickness, as much a person of flesh and blood as she.

"Aunt Mara," the boy repeated. "Nethin Kiro Rukiar." He touched his chin, obviously indicating himself. He must have understood that it was a name, but...

"No, no! *I'm* not Aunt Mara. I said I'm taking you to..." Hopeless. She shook her head, tapped her chest. "Alabeth Narran Kiron." She pointed away, down and over the moorlands. "Aunt Mara."

He actually grinned, or tried to, and said something, understanding his mistake. Probably now he believed she was taking him to a village called Aunt Mara.

The boy—Nethin—slumped forward again, catching himself, clinging to the saddle. She took the reins from his unresisting hand, passed them over the horse's head.

"I'll lead," she said. "You just hold on."

He nodded as if he understood.

She led him back to pick up her bow. The horse, thank all the Powers and the Lady of Beasts in particular, followed obediently, almost treading on her heels.

So much for hunting, and now she had two invalids on her hands.

There was the little crossbow the man had flung too, when she snapped its cord. It would be valuable for its metal alone; the smith's family had begun to claim that any scavenged metals from the ruins of Rivermouth were theirs by right, to call salvaged iron and bronze and copper the gift of the Powers. They'd even told Aunt Mara she was a liar when she had said metals came from stone. If people forgot that, forgot how to smelt ore, they'd have to go back to using flint and bone like the Wanderers when scavenging and reforging failed them, as someday it must.

When Alabeth picked up the bow, Nethin stirred and then, as she hunted for the bolt and found it, shouted, "No! Nay!"

Alabeth froze. That was almost comprehensible. He shook his head violently, tried to reach and grab her, swayed.

She jumped to steady him, and he took firm hold of her coat, trying to get the reins back, repeating himself. She caught, "No." Then, she thought, "Poison!" But…well, it might have been poison in the High Court language.

"It's all right. I won't touch it." She left the bolt and dropped the crossbow as well, just in case. She assembled words in her mind and tried, "Is the arrow poisoned?" in the court tongue.

A smile lit his face. "Thou speakest the Maker's tongue! Touch not the arrow. The poison is deadly. Thou art Alabeth, yea?"

"Alabeth. Thou art Nethin?"

He nodded. And having established that, he seemed too exhausted to go on. His eyes closed.

"Dost thou be strong only a little more. We go to my"— she could not think of any word for aunt, which Mara was not, anyway—"my old lady." That sounded foolish. "My dwelling-place. In Watersmeet. Not far." That was a lie, but it might encourage him. He nodded, never opening his eyes. She clucked to the horse as if it were an ox, and it started plodding onwards again.

After a little, she stopped, strung her bow and took an arrow from her quiver. She thought the man hunting this boy had run more towards the southeast, while home was east, down the Aganan and then over to its northern shore. But no point taking chances. There was no place for that would-be murderer to go, no place in all the world but Watersmeet, and he would see the smoke, eventually.

A perhaps more pressing problem was going to be getting that horse to swim the Great Aganan. It was not going to fit into her skin canoe.

They had nearly reached the place where she had left the canoe when the big horse shied at nothing and refused to move, standing splay-legged, head down, shivering.

The earth shook. Leaves rattled in the brush. Birds fell silent. Stones jumped and skipped like crumbs on a shaken tablecloth.

That was all. A jay shrieked. The horse shuddered her skin and raised her head again, looked around and blew wearily, before plodding forward once more.

Alabeth found she was trembling. Foolish. This little shiver was nothing to make her break into a sweat.

But whoever they were, the man and the boy, and wherever they had come from…It was no use pretending; they had come by the shadow road. Was there really some secret settlement of Kiron mages hidden in some distant corner of the world? Had they really sent this boy here by the shadow road? What about the man who had tried to kill him? Was he the real mage, sent to prevent the boy from waking the old evils by using the road? Had she rescued the villain?

The earth shivered again, just enough to remind her it slept lightly and that there were fires beneath.

Part Two

✠ Chapter Twelve ✠

Nethin: Burning Books

Autumn in the Homeland

I dreamed of my cousin Crow crying my name across some unimaginable distance. I called to her and, in my dream, reached out as if I could seize her hand and pull myself to her. I felt cloth and yielding flesh, and gripped, fingers locked. She had me by the shoulders, pulling me towards her. The world bucked and swayed, as if trying to tear us apart, but I clutched the harder. As if surfacing from deep beneath the earth, I dragged myself out of sleep, forcing my eyes open. I was in bed, soaked in sweat, and I had a death grip on the shirtfront of someone who was only too clearly female. And not Crow. A Nightwalker girl my own age, with wide cheekbones and long hair cut into a fringe at the front, level with her straight black brows.

The bed rose and dropped, and she shouted, dragging at me. I went from struggling to hold her to fighting, flailing around to escape her, but she wouldn't let go, and she managed to drag me to the floor, falling on top of me. I came to my senses then. The house was still. I squirmed and got to my knees, still groggy, dreams clutching at me. The girl took my arm. The earth was stable now, but its bucking had not been part of my dream; the brick stove, like those my uncle Korby described in Gehtaland, was cracked, embers spilling across its stone hearth and the earthen floor. In places the straw with which the floor was strewn for warmth crackled, already alight. Storage baskets were tipped and scattered, and pungent herbs were smouldering, adding their smoke to that of the burning straw.

"Outside," she said in the Makers' tongue, "quickly."

I nodded. *Alabeth*.

The dreams washed away. I remembered. I had been here several days now, waking and sleeping, eating ravenously, though they had little enough to offer—boiled roots that looked like fist-sized stones but tasted faintly nutty, and eggs that were the size of duck eggs but narrower, pink-shelled. Making halting conversation in the formal language of Maker-craft, stumbling with Alabeth through antique verb forms and words long forgotten in everyday speech. The old woman, Aunt Mara—Mara'lana, I thought, but that was a dream; Alabeth had never given her the title of princess, or any honorific at all—spoke it more smoothly.

"Mara?" I asked, looking back at the bed we had so ungracefully vacated. There was only the one bed. Alabeth and Mara shared it, and I slept across the foot, curled up to keep my feet from dangling.

"She is outside. Go thou to her, quickly."

She had rescued the old woman first. So would I have done. I nodded my understanding and climbed shakily to my feet. Alabeth went for the big wooden chest at the foot of the bed and began dragging it. Every other storage container in the one-room cabin was a woven basket. Of course the most valuable things they owned would be in the heavy chest. But she couldn't manage it herself. I went to help, shoving on one end as she dragged, my knees shaking with the effort. I was still weak as a newborn puppy. She scowled but didn't protest.

The hair on my arms prickled and bristled, and I nearly bolted in blind panic.

"Outside!" I shouted, and when she ignored me—wrong language—I flung myself over the chest, probably driving it down on her toes, and grabbed her, dragging us both into the halfworld. The floor, rising like a monstrous swell at sea, struck us, and the roof came down. The main beam missed us, and in the halfworld the reed thatch was of no substance and passed through us as though we were mist. We'd have been killed if Mara's cabin had been roofed with slate.

Pale flames, colorless and cold in the halfworld, leapt up through the straw, hissing and spitting. The rafters caught and ignited, dry with age. Alabeth shouted, "The books, the books!" and struggled free of me, into the flaming debris. In the halfworld such ordinary flames didn't touch her, but the chest was buried deep beneath it, and the flames were growing in strength, burning hotter, whiter, a heat I could feel now. The ground pitched and tilted. Burning timber shifted. My turn to grab and drag her, and we fought there a moment, before the hillside dropped away and we both fell into the flames.

In the distance, people were screaming and shouting, dogs barking, sheep bleating. Nearer, someone was shouting, "Alabeth! *Alabeth!*" above the engulfing crackle and roar.

"No!" I shouted as we tumbled together on the straw. "Mara, stay away! I have her safe!"

I began a spell to extinguish the flames, but I was too weak to hold the power and it faltered on my tongue. I felt dizzy, faint with the effort and the smoke, and angry at my own weakness. Alabeth was desperately singing something, but I could feel the weakness of her words against the flames, no more than a cup of water tossed hissing onto a blazing hearth. The fire roared up stronger, finding some good source of fuel, probably the straw-stuffed mattress. I reached out blind into the fire, fumbling to feel whatever it was that witches did, when they coaxed a fire to yield to their wishes. Even my mother, who was no match for her sister in witchery, could calm a fire. But I had no experience in such things. I'd spent too long denying to myself that I was a witch at all. I'd shut my ears or gone away whenever Crow and Drustan began talking about what it was like to feel the unseen forces of the world around and within them. I was a Maker, superior to all that unscholarly animal instinct.

The fire tangled me. For a moment I felt it ebbing, and then it flared up again and its heat, its hunger, was inside me. I screamed and broke away from it. Alabeth threw back the lid of the chest that was too heavy to drag, ignoring me now, and began flinging books onto the quilt dragged from the bed. Most of them weren't properly bound, mere bundles of paper or parchment tied with twine. Sparks found the open chest and it blazed up; I crouched on the quilt trying to shield the bundles with my body, with no idea how I had gotten there, as sparks darted like swallows and flames whirled around us. Spark and flame passed through me. I was in the halfworld.

Alabeth was not, though some of the books she handled, the bound ones, were old enough to have a halfworld presence. The baggy blouse and trousers that she had slept in were scorched; her bare feet and hands and face were blistered. Her eyes ran with tears, and she looked more than half mad, beating at the flaming chest with the bed's thin pillow.

"Alabeth, no!" I grabbed her into the halfworld. "Thou can'st do nothing more."

Even my father's obsessive love of books was not so desperate, I thought. She was sobbing as she slipped out again, but only to grab up the corners of the quilt and pull it with us. "Come." I took it from her, strong enough for that, at least, and, supporting one another, we clambered and stumbled out over the ruin of the wall.

Aunt Mara's was not the only house fallen and ablaze. Farther down the lane, at least three other fires lit the night.

The white-haired old lady was on her knees, a younger woman gripping her shoulders. I thought that woman had been trying to keep her from risking her life by going back to rescue Alabeth, but at the sight of us emerging safely from the halfworld Aunt Mara tried to struggle up and was forced down again.

The woman shouted, and Aunt Mara cried what I assumed was, "Run!" and Alabeth pulled us both into the halfworld again, but two men followed us there, leaping the low stone garden wall. One clouted Alabeth on the side of the head, and the other got an arm around my throat. They were shouting, but the language was too changed from the Makers' language. A scholar like my father or Maurey'lana could probably have worked it out. The only word I recognized, though, was "Kiron," which I understood was some kind of clan name—or caste, as in Dravidara. From what Mara had told me, it seemed in the past that a person's role in society was governed by their name, their birth. Kiron also meant a Maker, and in the voices of these people it sounded like humans screaming, "Warlock!" full of accusation and hatred.

While Alabeth gasped on the ground, her attacker grabbed the quilt and hurled it into the burning hut. It left the halfworld as it left his hand, and the books and bundles of pages flew, scattering. The flames seemed to leap savagely to meet them. Alabeth wailed, and Aunt Mara gave a terrible cry. Their utter despair and grief and rage hit me in a way I can't describe. The despair and grief were Mara's; she huddled limp on the ground, no longer struggling. I think she wept. Alabeth's rage and grief felt, to my mind, as though some beloved living thing had been murdered before her eyes. Her emotions overwhelmed me, as though I were dry tinder catching spark from her, and I cried out too as her rage swept through me.

I grabbed the arm that still half choked me and flung my head back, trying to break free, but the rage within me wanted destruction more than the mere loosening of his grip. The world roared: the fire, raging high as if feeding off me. The man holding me gave a cry I still hear in my nightmares and fell thrashing, pulling me down with him, but then his arm went limp and I rolled away. The man lay still, thick blood welling from nose and open mouth, eyes open and staring at nothing, horribly broken inside. I could feel it, had felt the tearing pain. The other man had gone tumbling as if kicked by a horse. He sprawled, choking and gasping, blood bubbling past his lips as he tried to get to his hands and knees to crawl away. Alabeth… I looked for her frantically, aghast, knowing in my gut I had killed her too, until I realized I could still feel her living presence. She had been saved by her captor, sheer accident, falling atop her. Now she dragged herself out from beneath his loose-jointed, flopping body, picked herself up, eyes wide and panicky, and ran over to help me to stagger to my feet, though I wrenched my hands away from her, crying, "Don't touch me!"

"Alabeth, run!" Aunt Mara shouted, using the High Court language. "Nay!" as the girl took a step towards her. "Thou must survive, thou'rt the last, the very last. Thou'rt the only one to remember. Find the Wanderers, or flee with Nethin to his people, but go. Go, if thou lovest me! Nethin, I charge thee— save Alabeth! She must live, or all that we were will perish."

The first rock hit then, striking Alabeth's back. More people were arriving, and they were throwing stones, shouting, a tide of anger and hate rising. They blamed us, blamed Mara and Alabeth, for the earthquake and the fires; I could sense that much. I simply shocked and horrified them. A diseased stranger, a monster, some supernatural creature…I could not tell what they thought, only that their reaction was that of a dog trembling and growling at some unknown thing. A stone struck me, and I found Alabeth's hand, tugged her into the halfworld. Some of the people were in the halfworld, but at least they could not throw stones there. As one took a step towards us, I held up my free hand.

"Stay back!" I warned them. "Stay, lest ye all die as those did."

That gave us space. We ran, though I felt I was falling from one foot to the other, never sure if my legs would fold up under me on the next step, and Alabeth sobbed and stumbled.

I could feel no one following, but I was afraid to trust what my witch-blood knew, that they were all back in the village, angry and fearful, the mere sight of me enough to alarm them. I did not let go of Alabeth until we were staggering up a rocky gully between steep stony hillsides, our bare feet bruised and battered and numb with cold. My breath wheezed in my throat.

"Horse," I said, at last. "Where's my horse?" And then I fell to my knees and threw up what was left of my meager supper.

Alabeth's storm of weeping had passed. She was silent, grim and angry and terrified. Taking my arm again, she rubbed my back. I was shivering, not only with cold, though the cold was enough. I wore billowy loose trousers and a shirt not my own— Alabeth's second-best, probably, because they had a few more patches than what she wore, and the shirt was too tight across the shoulders, ripped now from my struggle.

"Thou art not yet strong enough for fighting," she said. "We shall find some safe place where thou may'st hide and wait, and I shall go back for Aunt Mara."

"She feared she was about to die," I said, too weary to explain how I knew, or that it was not the fight but the manner in which I had killed, not intending to, that sickened me. "She wished thee to escape, to survive; all her heart was in that. Thou hast no right to deny her that, and she charged me to take thee to safety. But"—as Alabeth took a breath to protest—"I will not leave her to be killed by them. I do not..." Words escaped me. I could not leave an old woman, an ailing old woman who had shared what little she had to save my life, an alien stranger's, to be murdered out-of-hand by a mob.

"What else is my life worth?" I cried. Powers, but the hatred of those people, who should have been my people...I had come all this way only to meet my great-grandfather and Sarval again. "They think we have fled, so we must return quietly and secretly. But Aunt Mara cannot walk far. Have ye sold my horse?" I wouldn't blame them if they had; they had so little to spare, and a Kordaler took much feeding. "Or have ye a horse of your own for your farm?"

Of course they had not. I remembered now Alabeth's devastation a day or two before on discovering a mere two of the jairrin fowl, which laid the big pinkish eggs, had been stolen in the night, along with a basket of botati tubers she had dug that day. Orlando, I had thought and had felt Alabeth's fearful knowledge of the stranger. Neither of us had said anything then; she because she did not want to worry Aunt Mara further, and I because I was sinking again into my hazy dreams.

"I freed thy horse," said Alabeth. "It would not swim the river. And besides, the village leaders would have claimed it, and it would have revealed thee to them. I could not have kept it hidden as I did thee. Nobody in all the village has a horse in these days. I am sorry for it," she added.

"How then didst thou bring me over the river?" I asked, regretting the good mare.

"My boat."

"Then we must carry Aunt Mara away in thy boat. She is too weak to escape on foot."

"Away to where?" Alabeth asked bitterly. "To thy people? Dost thou expect me to believe that in all the long years there was some city surviving hidden after all, guarding the old secrets? Art thou truly Kiron caste and not some demon? Tell me the truth now, before thou art lost in fevers again. Thou art the one who awakened the shadow road."

I wanted to protest, but for a moment I could not think where to start.

"Why hast thou done this? Dost thou not understand the evil it brings? Have thy people forgotten the Great Calamity?"

"I do not understand," I protested. "I am no demon. But my people know nothing of any Calamity. We do not even know the word *Kiron*. We have no castes." *Kiro. Kiron.* Scholars' puzzles for my father to play with, if I ever found my way home.

She took my hand and we walked on together, not running now, but picking a way over rocks.

"Use of the shadow road weakens the fabric of the world," she said. "Do they truly not remember this, whence thou com'st? It renders all nature unstable. The Kiron caste did not know this until too late, until they had broken the world with their constant traveling on it between the provinces and to other lands of other stars, all for nothing but treasures and dainties and curiosities. And now thou openest the gates again and travelest the shadow road. This shaking of the earth is thy doing." She didn't shout, but almost whispered the accusation. "And all the books are burned." Tears streaked her face, silver in the moonlight.

The moon hung fat and near; the shadows that blotched its face making unfamiliar patterns. That, more than the strange scatter of the stars, far too few, the night sky eerily thick and featureless between, hit my very marrow with the realization of how far from home I was.

The shadow road damaged the earth? Caused that earthquake? Caused, maybe, the disaster the Nightwalkers had fled? They must have turned the old stone holy places of the witches into gates in case they ever wanted to leave again, but because they knew the risks, they did not use them, and so they were forgotten. And when a new disaster came upon them in the shape of Bloody Hallow—the invasion of humans from the continent, the massacres—they could not flee and so hid in Talverdin instead. I shook my head.

"Alabeth, I do not understand. All this land is strange to me. I come from no city of this world. The shadow road winds by many worlds. As you said, another land under another star. In my world we had forgotten all about the shadow road, until an ancient spell was made anew. Tell me—"

He was near. I felt his presence, the pressure of his hatred, a hunting eagerness. Orlando. I gestured to Alabeth to be silent, but she did not understand.

"The end of the Kiron caste," she said. "Can'st thou not understand, Nethin? The books were the last, all that survived of the past: the history, the legends, the great poetry, the science, the wisdom and the spells. The last copies, the last records, the last chronicles of the years since the Calamity. The records kept by Mara and her father and their ancestors before that, the… the princes and the mages who summoned all the survivors here centuries ago, when this was a greater town and Rivermouth greater still, the remnant of the Old Capital, the heart of the empire, when the ships still sailed. Those books were all the history left in the world, and the fools threw them to burn. They were all the memory left of the empire, of the better days. And the fools will kill Aunt Mara, as they killed the Kiron of Overhill, if they have not killed her already, and…" She fell back into her own modern speech, choking on frantic words, before I got a hand over her mouth.

It was too late. My sense of him vanished. What had Crow said? Like sound, the sense of a mind did not escape the halfworld. We had left the halfworld when I was sick, and now in the halfworld himself, Orlando stalked us. I plucked a stalk of grass and went into the halfworld after him. I had no weapon. Neither did Alabeth, half-undressed as she was for sleep.

Even without Mara to rescue, we would have had to return to the village, to get coats and boots and weapons and food, no matter where we intended to go. It seemed to be autumn in this world, and the air smelled of frost. We would perish of cold as we were, before we had time to starve.

The gully shone like the tears on Alabeth's face, silver-gray stone, silver-gray water, a sleek trickle over rocks. Stunted creeping shrubs I did not recognize overhung the steep-cut sides. The mostly dry streambed was littered with broken fragments of stone and huge boulders, rolled down from the mountain slopes in spring floods. Now I could feel Orlando again, close, very close, but he could be anywhere—behind those rocks, in those dark night-shadows, motionless, escaping my eye.

Movement and the gleam of steel disturbed the gray-lit haze of the halfworld. Orlando dropped from above, among the fragrant shrubs, and jerked Alabeth's head back by the hair, even as I hurled myself forward, a spell to bind his limbs half-formed in the knots of grass.

"Don't," he said, and I froze. The blade of his sword lay across Alabeth's exposed throat. Her eyes were wide black pools.

"Very convenient," he said in Ronish, "as it turns out. I need your help after all, warlock."

He looked almost as ill as I felt, gaunt and weary, lips cracked and eyes shining with fever. He let go of Alabeth's hair and wrapped an arm across her collarbones. His left hand was swathed in stained cloth. The hem of his tunic had been torn raggedly away to provide that bandage.

"Release her." I tried to calm my rising anger. I had no way of mastering it, and I could kill Alabeth as easily as Orlando, losing control of myself.

"Hah, I think not." He nodded up the gully. "Go on. That way. Walk in front of me, and keep your hands on your head."

✳ CHAPTER THIRTEEN ✳
NETHIN: CAPTIVES

"Who is this enemy of thine?" Alabeth whispered. "What doth he want with us?"

"He wanted to meet the rulers of thy home," I murmured in reply. Her fear pounded at me, but she was angry too.

Orlando crouched beside us, smearing awkward symbols on a strip of cloth with ashes and spit, using his clumsy, bandaged left hand. With the other, he held the point of his sword against Alabeth's ribs, a threat against me.

"I do not understand why he hideth here, why he hath not gone to the village but to steal. He hateth me because I am not…" *Of clean blood* was the only phrase I could think of, and I did not want to give my great-grandfather's words to her. "In the world from which I come, there are two kinds of people. Two breeds." Was that right? Were we only two different breeds, like bluehounds and pied sheepdogs? Nothing more? No dog cared about breed. "People in two different kinds. The humans, whose world it is. And people like thee: Nightwalkers, who came there long ago. My father is Nightwalker and my mother is human, and so Orlando hateth me, though he says he is the same, of mixed blood."

"Humans have white hair," she said with great enlightenment.

"Um…most do not. One can'st tell them more surely because they all have colored skins, not white. Like that one, but many are darker than he and do not look like the meat beneath their skin is showing through."

"I thought he was diseased."

"And they cannot enter the halfworld. That is the only true difference between us."

We sat shoulder to shoulder against the wall in the ruined shell of a little house. It was very like Aunt Mara's, a single room, but built of stone. The roof sagged and moonlight shone through gaps in the thatch. The stove was cracked. Orlando had simply built a fire on the hearth before it, leaving the smoke to rise through the decaying roof. Dirty earthenware pots showed he had been making himself at home for a few days, living off Alabeth's stolen fowl, I supposed. The two cases, the smaller one that held the poisoned crossbow bolts and the mysterious larger one, sat on a sodden, leaf-drifted ruin of a bed. Strange that whoever had lived here had left behind their cooking pots and blankets, and even the moth-chewed sheepskin coat Orlando wore against the cold.

Plague. Alabeth had talked of plagues. Perhaps it had been long enough ago that no contagion lingered here. Please Maynar, mother of us all, that it was so.

Perhaps we might not live long enough to worry about disease.

Alabeth was shivering so her teeth chattered, and I dared to put an arm around her. Orlando did not notice the movement.

He finished his writing, clearly a spell, though I could not read what it was intended to say.

"Up, girl," he ordered, and Alabeth looked at him blankly.

"He desireth you to arise," I translated. She obeyed, arms wrapped close. The sword never left off pricking her as he prodded her over towards the bed.

"No!" I shouted, lurching to my feet when I saw what he intended. He had the smaller case open, dropping his sword and fumbling out one of the *chiurra*-poisoned arrows. That was why he had forced her over to the bed: to have a hostage within reach as he switched to the more deadly weapon, fearing some sudden lunge on my part, or that we might be able to bolt out the door in the moment his back was turned. No chance of that now. Alabeth made a shrill noise like a pained dog and flinched back as the point wavered near her.

"Stay still!" Orlando snapped. He pushed her back towards me. "Sit."

She sat again, shaking now, hardly able to form a word, her eyes never leaving the arrow, sweat beading her face despite the cold. He rested the arrow on her thigh, where one move would drive it into the flesh of her hip.

"Now, Lord Nethin—" Clumsy, he dropped the ash-inscribed strip of cloth on my lap. "Tie this around the chit's neck."

"Why?" I asked, but I picked it up.

"I don't know if she's a warlock. I'd be surprised if she was. This is obviously the back of beyond, a village of someone's half-witted serfs. I haven't found the lord's house. I haven't found a town—just another village abandoned and falling down, away west in the foothills. No lords, no warriors, no warlocks. Which is fine by me. I wish that arrogant bastard Roshing had lived to see the scum his grand and glorious ancestors are though. But just in case she is a warlock, I want her wearing this."

"Why?" I asked again.

"Suppresses magic, at least for whatever weak powers an ignorant peasant like this might have." He grinned. "Kinder than the Nightwalkers' drugs, isn't it? Don't thank me. I don't have any of the apothecary's brews with me, or I'd use them."

"She is not a warlock," I lied. "She is just a...a land-worker." I could not find the correct Ronish word for a homesteader. "These people are no threat to you. Leave them alone; go inland and find the lords." That should lose him forever. I still could barely believe what Alabeth had said, that these were the last people in the world.

"What do I want with lords? I'm not Roshing, dreaming of reconquering Eswiland. You really believed me, didn't you? Thought I was a stinking halfbreed? You're all fools, you night-eyes. I'm *human*, pure human. An agent of the Powers, chosen in this age to end the pollution of the Nightwalkers for good and all."

His words rang with truth and pride and hatred.

"Yehillon," I realized.

"Hah, yes. So simple. All I had to do was stay out of the sun a month and dye my hair, and the Homelanders were all ready to believe my story of my poor disgraced mother and her nasty father, my sad half-breed childhood in Rona. I'm the prince of the Yehillon, the true prince, and I'll be remembered as the one who discovered the true source of the Nightwalker threat, the martyr who sacrificed everything to end it, while that traitor Aldis will be a damned and wandering shade, rejected by Geneh, his name spat on by all the generations to come. Ironic, isn't it, that a creature like you should do what I and even our assassins have failed at, by killing him at last."

I fumbled with the spell-inscribed rag, not refusing, not with that arrow a hair's breadth from touching Alabeth's flesh, but not quite complying yet either.

"What do you mean?" I asked.

"You killed Prince Aldis, the traitor. On the shadow road. Don't you remember? You're as feeble-minded as they say your *wallachim* peasant of a mother is, aren't you? Hurry up with that."

I let the insult to my mother pass. "But what do you mean, ending all the Nightwalker threat? You have seen how these people live. They are no threat to anyone, certainly not to us in another world. Even if they were powerful once, they cannot travel the shadow road now. From what I have seen, they have no warlock skills at all."

"So this gate is abandoned. Who knows what great cities still exist, beyond these ignorant peasants' horizons? Who knows what other gates may still be in use, what other worlds they may be conquering? I've studied the great Prince Alberick's thoughts on the nature of the true shadow road; Aldis thought he had them hidden from me, the arrogant traitor, but he wasn't half so clever as he thought. Alberick's writing says I don't have to destroy all the gates, to sever this place from the worlds. I have only to destroy one, sever it from the web of the stars, and it will be like knocking down the pillar supporting a roof. All this monstrous world will be torn free of the shadow road. They will never, ever be able to threaten us in the true world again."

"They are not threat now!" My Ronish was escaping me. "No threat," I corrected.

He wasn't listening. "And if by some mischance any other of your people have rediscovered the secret, they won't be able to run begging to their precious Homeland for help—not that there seems to be any here—when blood and fire come upon them and Talverdin lies in ruins, as it soon will. The time of the Nightwalkers is ended, brat. Your plans to corrupt the humans of West Overseas as you've corrupted Eswy-Dunmorra, this deluding of the Overseas emperor and the planting of a colony on his shores, is ended. I will cut this place off, isolate it, as one cuts out a tumor, and my people will lead the way in burning out Talverdin like blighted wood." He grinned. "It should already have begun. And I will be a saint, a Lesser Power, remembered with greater reverence even than Hallow and Miron. I will succeed where they failed, in ending the pollution of the Nightwalkers once and for all."

"You don't need us then," I said. "Let us go."

His eyes focused on me again, away from his dreams of martyrdom. He wiggled the arrow, pricking the fabric of Alabeth's trousers.

Her face was still beaded with sweat, and she was sick almost to fainting, her pain washing through me, her gaze fixed on the floor. She refused to look at me, refused to plead.

"Tie the cloth around her neck."

With shaking hands, I did so. I saw no other way. But I had been crumpling it in my hands, and the ash was very smeared.

"Alabeth, he saith the spell in this bandage will prevent thee working magecraft," I said. "But I have rubbed away a little of the writing, I hope. We must wait our chance and overcome him. He meaneth to destroy the gate of the shadow road. He is not one of your people or like me. He hath lied about his father. He is one of those who hateth all of our blood."

She nodded.

"What are you saying about the spell and the shadow road?"

Powers help me, he had caught a word or two.

"I tell her why you say she must wear it and that, like her, you say the shadow road is evil."

Orlando snorted but accepted that. "You don't need to explain anything to her." He felt satisfaction and relief when I had knotted the rag, but he did not remove the poisoned crossbow bolt from its place on her thigh.

He lifted the other hand, wrapped in its seeping bandage, and dropped it on my knee. "Now, my Lord Nethin," he said, "heal this."

"I do not know how."

"You do, you Phaydos-damned liar. A great warlock like you? Take the bandage off."

A faint mewling noise escaped Alabeth. She looked close to fainting. I untied the knot and unwrapped the bandage, flinching back. The palm of his hand was an ugly, lurid red and greenish white around an oozing, swollen gash.

"Been playing with your poisoned arrows, I see," I muttered in my own language.

"You snap bowstring," Orlando snarled in the same tongue. "You do this. You fix it."

I didn't deny it, though I hadn't done anything to his crossbow. I suspected any human surgeon would say the hand had to be amputated, before the rotting poison spread to the rest of his body, if it hadn't already. Any of our own physicians would say the same, if there was no Maker around to drive out the infection.

"And this was only a scratch," Orlando said. "So don't waste time, or it'll be your little sweetheart burned and rotting."

I cradled the back of his hand in my own, careful not to touch the wound or any of the encrusted secretions.

"Have you washed it?" I asked.

"I swam the cursed river."

That wasn't quite the same as washing it, but it had probably flushed away any trace of the *chiurra* poison.

A witch like my mother could heal a wound like this much more swiftly than any Maker's magic, but the strength to do so had to come from within herself, and I did not know the way to do it. Orlando was not expecting that anyhow. He did not know I was a witch. He probably did not believe witches really existed.

"Maker-craft doesn't work wonder-tale instant cures," I warned.

"I know that, you fool. Get on with it."

I decided not to point out to him the hypocrisy of condemning all Nightwalker Maker-craft as evil, a pollution to the world, and then demanding I use it to save his life. With another glance at Alabeth, who now sat with her eyes shut, lips clenched, I dredged from memory the spell I needed. Leaves and stems from certain plants were part of it, but Orlando was not likely to let me wander off herb-gathering, if they even grew in this strange, cold land. True Maker-craft could adapt and create spells, my father said. Time to prove him right.

I began to sing.

The wound didn't heal over right away; that would take witchery of my Aunt Robin's strength. My spell drove the toxins from the festering and dead flesh though. The livid color eased as I sang, and what was dead began to dry, like an old blister. Pus turned to filthy crust and flaked away. The heat in my cupped hands ebbed to merely body warmth, and slowly the swelling went down. The wound itself still looked raw and nasty and could get infected again if he did not keep it clean. Still, it had begun healing much more swiftly than I had expected. Usually the effects of such a spell became apparent only slowly. My unnatural strength again. Or unconscious witchery.

Orlando flexed his fingers. I kept singing. I feared that he might recognize random words in the Makers' tongue, as he had before, or as I recognized garbled traces of that language in his own spells. But now he trusted what I had done, and was doing, so…I wove words around him, to drop him, swift and sudden, into sleep.

I was not swift enough.

"Well done," he said and stabbed me in the forearm with the poisoned arrow.

Alabeth screamed. I fell into a well of red agony. Then there was darkness, and a noise like the sea. Somewhere, Crow was crying my name.

They left me lying there. Alabeth says she does not even remember leaving the shepherd's hut, whether she walked or whether he dragged her. Only that I gasped, fell, convulsed and stopped breathing. Then I was still, and Alabeth was being driven down the hillside, staggering under a great weight.

Nethin was dead. Alabeth couldn't quite believe it. Dead. One moment alive, and the next...

He had looked so strange, so much a stranger.

Alabeth could not stop shivering, though Orlando no longer held the sickening poisoned dart against her leg. She kept trying to look back over her shoulder, as if Nethin could possibly be there in the doorway, about to work some powerful spell against the foreigner. Every time she did, though, Orlando pricked her with his sword. She stumbled, and he shouted at her, putting out his wounded hand to steady the wooden chest he was forcing her to carry in a sling over her back. It made her muscles ache, not from the weight, but as though it sucked something vital from her. The smaller case of arrows he carried himself.

He had bandaged his hand with another strip of musty cloth, while she knelt shivering and whimpering uselessly over Nethin. Generations of Kiron behind her, and all she could do was cry. She had not even attempted some spell against poison or one to test if the spell binding her was broken or weakened;

she could not bring any spells at all to mind. Every calm and rational thought had fled her.

It seemed a lifetime that she stumbled, bare feet bruised and cold and bleeding, and then numb, down the gully and over sheep-cropped turf after that. The box on her back thumped until she had to clench her chattering teeth against crying aloud, as it beat its bruises into bloody galls. By pushes and prods, he steered her down through the fringes of the village, not entering the halfword but keeping to the darkest shadows. Hadn't Nethin said whatever the other kind of person was, they couldn't enter the halfworld? But this Orlando had sprung out of the halfworld to attack them. Perhaps Nethin had been wrong.

Only one house still burned; the other fires were out, and the village was silent. A dog barked and then was still. Did Aunt Mara yet live, or had they already killed her? Orlando muttered and pricked her side with his blade again. Warning her to keep silent, perhaps. What point was there in yelling? If anyone came, it would only be to drag her off to whatever fate had befallen Aunt Mara. Punishment for the earthquake and the fires.

He was aiming for the river. More empty words. When she failed to answer, he struck her with the flat of the blade, then snarled and grabbed her arm as she fell, shook her till her teeth rattled. Angry that she couldn't understand? Angry that his box had almost fallen?

Orlando jerked her around to face him, made wild motions with his bandaged hand, whispering, hissing, some word over and over. She shook her head. "Vessel," he finally might have said.

"Boat?" she tried in the High Court tongue.

"Boat," he agreed and swung her back towards the river, setting her on her way with a shove.

She kept her canoe down in the willows below where the village's few cattle were currently pastured, not that anyone would steal it but because she hated the way the village elders watched her comings and goings, hoping to catch her in some wrongdoing, hunting large game alone so as not to have to share or the like. Orlando was aiming her at the landing stage at the end of the main track. She began to push a skin canoe similar to her own down to the water, but the sword came prodding again and Orlando pointed to a small wooden rowboat already in the river, moored to the posts of the landing stage.

Not so easy to tip. She had in the back of her mind been planning to do just that.

Bleakly, she untied the knot in the sling holding the box to her back and, as he lunged forward, dropped it into the boat. He struck her across the face but didn't make her take it up again, so she untied the boat, climbing in and steadying it for him to join her, before she dragged the oars out from under the thwarts, settling them into the rowlocks with more splashing than necessary.

Nobody heard. Nobody came.

Orlando babbled, pointing not directly across the river but west, upstream, as he seated himself facing her. She braced her legs and began to row. No tiller: it was not a big enough boat to need one. Nothing she could make him take charge of to distract him from watching her. Even if Nethin had damaged the spell meant to bind her magic, there was nothing she could do, with Orlando staring at her.

His hair, why had she not realized his hair was strange? Its night-color held no hint of dusky blue or red. Amber lights were hidden in it, flickering as the wind stirred it. The tawny bull showed the very same color at night. Was that a sign he was, as Nethin had said, that other breed of person from the other world? Different night-colors? The boat's wake left a crooked, wandering trail of soft green. The boat itself seemed to be staggering, straggling over the river. She shut her eyes, feeling the current fight her muscles, which burned with exhaustion. Eyes shut, Orlando's face was replaced by Nethin's.

So still, light fading in his sky-colored eyes. An oar slipped free of her hand and somehow she caught it again, closed screaming fingers around it. She had to think about what to do. What did he want, this mad stranger, this murderer? The box. He had poisoned arrows in the small box. He had lost his crossbow. Was the larger box another, larger bow? Too heavy.

More poisoned weapons? But he went away from the village. She had no idea how the gate to the shadow road worked. In the stories Aunt Mara told her, in the histories, it was said the assembled mages of the Kiron sang, great choirs of them, and laid out patterns in sand to walk. Was he carrying sand? Special sand? It made no sense for him to have come here, tried to kill Nethin, stolen a couple of jairrin fowl, killed Nethin, and now be about to leave again. No. He was mad in his murderous evil, but not so irrational. He did something that made sense. He killed Nethin once the boy was no longer useful to him, because Nethin might prevent whatever he meant to do. He kept Alabeth because she was useful. She could row him over the river, which he could not do himself, not with his injured hand. Nethin must be a great mage among mages, to have started it healing so swiftly. He would have been able to help Aunt Mara, if only he had known how sick she was, if only she had thought to ask, if only he had not been so sick himself, if only...

Orlando was heading for Sand Ridge, of course, for the circle of stones and the gate to the shadow road. Had he found something, some lost treasure? No. The box was...there was something wrong in it, wrong like poison. She had felt it. She felt it still, in her bones, behind her—a living malevolence.

She had opened her eyes when the oar slipped. Now she realized Orlando had closed his. He looked very young himself, and exhausted. Perhaps he did not even realize how he drifted on the edge of sleep. Softly, Alabeth shaped words with lips and tongue, barely a breath to give them life. Softly, she rested her oars, shaped patterns in the air with her fingers. She had forgotten the rag tied about her neck. The power flowed into the spell, but sluggishly. It was enough. Orlando sighed and his head drooped. Still moving slowly, she fumbled with the knot at her neck. Nethin had tied it so loosely it took only a couple of fingers to pull it free. Tears prickled her eyes. Now the spell strengthened, as she completed it.

As the boat began to drift downstream, turning in the current, she unshipped the oars and, gripping them, went over the side.

The splash woke Orlando. Her spell had not been strong enough. He shouted at her, clutching the sides of the rocking boat.

The water burned on her raw skin, but the cold quickly chilled her beyond feeling anything. She swam with the current, leaving the drifting boat behind, and let the oars go once she was sure Orlando would not be able to retrieve them. They were just a drag in the water, not large enough to be any use in staying afloat. Scraps of disjointed prayer, *Please, lord of the waters, please master of mages*, ran through her head like frantic squirrels and settled into *please, please, please*.

Orlando started a spell, abandoned it, and then she heard the splashing. He was using something to paddle with. The blade of his sword? Hands, feet? Somehow Alabeth forced her legs to kick harder, but the water was so dark, so deep and quiet, that it seemed easier for a moment to stop, to sink and escape Orlando that way. But the splashing grew fainter, and somehow she had never stopped kicking. He wasn't trying to pursue her after all.

A dog barked. The current had brought her down to the village, and she had been angling across it all this while. She was into calm water, slow and gentle, and on her hands and knees in the mud, shivering. A small black shape became a dog, who nosed her all over, licking her head. Gentalir's dog. Gentalir had been her friend, once upon a time, despite her being a good four years older than him, before his mother the smith forbade him to learn from Aunt Mara any longer. Almost a little brother, until last spring. The dog remembered, and whined, licking now at her bleeding feet as she used its shoulder to push herself up. She looked back. Nothing disturbed the river. No sign of the drifting rowboat. She stepped into the halfworld, accidentally taking the dog with her—it wasn't one of the breed that could do so on its own—but Orlando was not visible there either.

Drowned, or safely ashore.

Either way, she could do nothing about him. Nothing about him, nothing about Nethin. Her mind shrank down to two thoughts: Aunt Mara; warmth. She could hardly walk. Her body shuddered so she could hardly stand. Next she would stop shivering, and that was worse, that was death. They had either killed Aunt Mara, or they had not. If they had not...she could do nothing, the state she was in. But she had until morning.

She looked at the stars over the eastern horizon. A little while. Not long, but long enough to rest in some warmth, to dredge up some last reserve of strength. The nearest building was the drystone barn behind the smith's yard wall. A blessing. And the dog was already with her; no alarm would be sounded. She let herself in. The cattle stalls and the sheep pen were empty, the animals still out to pasture, but the mows above were packed high with summer-scented hay. Her hands slipped on the pegs that made a ladder up one of the posts. She simply could not climb it. Hay fallen from the mow above made a pile in the corner, against the wall that separated the sheep pen from the center aisle of the barn. Alabeth crawled into that, burrowing deep. The dog snuffled after her, sneezed and then settled down, half on top of her. It was warm, like a small and furry stove. She fell into drifting waves of pain and tides of shivering that slowly ebbed. She needed to wake before dawn, before the shrieking of the jairrin fowl greeted the sun. She would not sleep but watch the chinks in the stone for growing light, to warn her when to leave.

It was the dog who woke her, stirring, stretching, yawning, its tail sweeping the hay. The small door set into the tall wagon door opened and closed again with only a faint creaking. Someone had come in. And as the dog trotted to him, whoever it was flung himself down, buried his face on his arms and sobbed.

Alabeth froze, not even daring to move enough to crawl into the halfworld. For a moment she forgot she was the last Kiron, that the world was against her. Her chief feeling was the embarrassment of being witness; the boy had so clearly fled the house to find someplace private for his grief.

There were words in his weeping, the mumbled, choking words that can't be kept in. Her own name. Mara's. The dog whined, nosed at him, and his arm encircled it.

Without thinking, she crawled out of the hay and clenched her teeth on a moan of pain. Her feet felt raw, and the shirt was like the box itself slapping against her back. Her thigh, where the arrow had threatened, felt burned, and her trousers stuck to it.

"Gentalir."

The boy looked up, his face smudged with dust. Then he flew to her and flung his arms around her, face pressed to her chest. "I thought the shade took you," he said, half incoherent with weeping again. "The white man. Aunt Mara's going to die."

"Hush, hush." She patted his hair, tried not to flinch from his touch. "That wasn't a shade, Genta. He was Nethin, a boy, a man from another world, from the shadow road. He—" She remembered and choked on a sob herself. "Where's Aunt Mara? Is she all right?"

"They've shut her up in the smithy till morning. Mother put chains on her. She said no Kiron could get out of her chains. And Aunt Mara's so sick. But they say she brought the earthquake by her Kiron magecraft, and she brought the shade here, a damned shade that was trapped on the shadow road, and she corrupted us by teaching us to read and write and do Kiron spells, which she didn't, so we'd want the old days back, and she brought you here from Overhill, and…and…and they're going to make me say she taught us about the Kiron, that they weren't evil, to prove that Aunt Mara *is* evil. Mother said I had to, and they're going to kill her—they're going to kill Aunt Mara! They're going to summon all the village and do it."

She rocked him, muttering, "Hush, hush," as if he were a baby she could soothe in her arms. Maybe she was trying to comfort herself. "I'll get her out, Gentalir. Don't worry. She and I will go away, far away, someplace they'll never find us. We'll be safe. I know a place."

He pushed away from her, wiping his face on the sleeve of the coat he seemed to have pulled on over a nightshirt. He might have crept off to find a private place for a good cry in his misery like the child he was—even the wealthy smith's house was only two rooms and a loft, shared by the smith's three sons—but Gentalir was old enough to know when he was being soothed with a lie. "There's no place to go. Even the Wanderers are gone."

"We don't know that. Just because they didn't come south this spring. Maybe they found better summer pastures. That's what we're going to do, go north and find the Wanderers." The resolution took root. It was a mark to aim for, at least. They would die, of course. Aunt Mara was already ailing. Winter was marching up from the south to overtake them. But they would die free and trying, not prisoners, not sacrifices to the prejudice and hatred of the willfully ignorant.

"I'll come," said Gentalir, rubbing his dog's head.

"Don't be silly."

"You're hurt. Aunt Mara's ill."

"That's no reason for you to die too." That wasn't what she had meant to say.

"I'm coming." He glared at her, then put his hands together, whispering over them with frowning concentration. A tongue of pale light curled up as he opened his palms. "There. See? That's why. Because I'm Kiron too. And my brothers know, and they're always saying they're going to tell Mother. Some day they will."

"Where did you learn that spell?"

"I watched Aunt Mara do it. She didn't see me; I was in the halfworld. And I heard the words and practiced them. My brothers saw me." He sighed shakily, closing his hands to extinguish the light. "And anyway, even if I wasn't Kiron somehow, I have to help. All those old heroes, the Hedenor and the Kiron who found us all and brought us here to the towns on the river long ago—they could have run away, like the rebel Kiron. They could have saved themselves. They didn't. They knew they had a duty to people that couldn't help themselves, to save them. Like Aunt Mara."

"Aunt Mara would say that you need to survive and maybe teach your children all that she taught you."

"And tell them I was too much of a coward to try to save her?" The look he gave her then was an adult one. "Can you get the chains off her?"

"I...I don't know," she said; honesty when she wanted the reassuring lie.

"I can't. She's too sick to do it herself. And if we use a hammer and chisel, they'll hear and wake in the house."

"I think I can." Alabeth gave up on persuading him to go back to bed, which was weak of her, but she was so tired and so alone. He warmed her inside, though it was wrong of her to feel she could lean on him, when he was only a child and needed her protection as much as Aunt Mara, as much as Nethin, a lost and deathly ill stranger, had.

She couldn't save anyone. They were all going to die. But they'd go to meet their own deaths in the wild, at least, not wait for murder.

"Aunt Mara can hardly walk. Let's take a canoe upriver as far as we can, before we start trying to head north. Maybe we can find a sheltered valley, someplace we can build a cabin, someplace we can find fuel and hunt through the winter. Then in the spring we'll try to cross the mountains." It was a stupid, desperate, hopeless plan, and Gentalir knew it as well as she.

"Shouldn't we go downriver? To where Rivermouth used to be? Then we could paddle up the coast and not have to go through the mountains."

She had thought of that. "They'll expect us to go with the current, to take the easier way, if they know we've taken a boat. If they search downriver first, we really do have a chance of getting away, if we've gone west instead. And I don't think there's a boat of any sort in Watersmeet that would do other than drown us on the ocean, even hugging the coast. Do you remember Aunt Mara's maps?"

"I only saw them once."

"The mountain range is narrower inland. And you know the Wanderers always come that way, not down the coast."

And the truth was she feared the very idea of the sea. If a great wave came, they were dead, without hope. She could at least pretend they had a chance to be prepared for winter and ice and mountain storm.

Gentalir nodded soberly. "Upriver, then. We can take the big canoe that belonged to my father. Mother doesn't use it anyway, but it's still sound. If you can get Aunt Mara, I'll load the canoe with things we'll need." He looked at her feet. "Boots. Coats. Blankets. Food. Everything in your house burned. Everything."

He understood the weight of that as well as she.

"I know. Get me a couple of bows and spare bowstrings, and as many arrows as you can find. Snares." Gentalir's father had been the leader of the village hunters until a snow-bear, come up from the south in the heart of winter, got him.

"Right." He hesitated, hugged her. "Powers be with you."

"And you. Take care, Gentalir."

The boy nodded, patted his leg for the dog to follow and slipped out. Stiffly, aching, Alabeth headed for the smithy.

CHAPTER FIFTEEN

CROW: DROWNED IN DREAMS

High summer, middle of Therminas-month, Gulf of Shai

Dying in the abandoned shepherd's hut, I called and my cousin heard. So simple as that. Death's reaching fingers swept away the vast distance between star and star; the chaos of the shadow road dissolved to nothing but a dream, no barrier at all between flame and flame, like two candles set close drawing together into one light.

"Crow!"
Crow!
"Is it over?" Crow asked, dazed and dizzy. A flying splinter of timber the length and thickness of her arm had struck her head when the last Yehillon ship rammed them, and though her helmet had saved her skull, she felt as though a hangover rampaged behind her eyes. She had come to herself in a heap by the forecastle door, with Mannie crouching over her. "Are we sinking?"

"No." Mannie laughed, and Crow felt the relief flooding her. "It's over, and we're not sinking. I thought for a moment I'd lost you though."

"I heard…"

Crow!

Headache pounded her, and she staggered to the side—leeward, leeward, remember that; never be sick into the wind—and threw up. A lot of people had been sick. The noxious alchemical smoke from the burning ship had taken the Nightwalkers that way, even though they had been prepared for it. Wearing wet scarves over faces had not helped after all, once the ring of chanting Makers had managed to set one of the Yehillon ships ablaze, which unfortunately caused their alchemical shot to explode and burn too. And once the alchemical smoke came billowing over them, tainted with some poison used in philosopher's fire, Maker-craft had failed. But they had been prepared for that too. The princess had planned…

"Imurra'lana?" Mannie's cousin, heir to the crown of Talverdin, was nowhere in sight.

"She's fine," Mannie said, cleaning her sword on an end of rope, which was the sort of thing that tended to annoy sailors, before sheathing it. She eyed the body of one of the Yehillon, who'd come scrambling over in a suicidal charge as the two ships clashed.

Thinking about heaving it over the side and deciding not to bother, Crow assumed.

"She went below to see the wounded."

The queen was going to be furious when she learned that her daughter, supposed to be commanding the defence from shore, had sailed on the flagship of the hastily assembled fleet, which was mostly human coasters and fishing vessels from Rensey, with a few new Talverdine ocean-going carracks and hulks. Once it was clear that the Yehillon ships intended to attack Dralla itself, not some deserted stretch of the spell-bound coast, the plan was to prevent the three Yehillon ships from getting far enough into the Gulf of Shai to destroy the defences of wind and whirlpool and hungry rock that defended Talverdin's only port. Mannie's father, Maurey'lana, had warned them the Yehillon alchemical cannon shot could do just that: lay their defences bare. If Prince Korian the navigator had not been weeks out at sea, he would have commanded the ships as a matter of course. But he was, and Imurra, trained as a knight from childhood but guarded as some precious flower, the heir of Talverdin, had been glad of it. Rash. She and Mannie and the captain of her guard had had a shouting match over it, but the princess had won.

So much death though.

"We've had losses," Crow said, cold statement. She had felt so many deaths. They couldn't all be Yehillon.

"The *Ratchal'nor* sank," Mannie said soberly. "Hit by what seems to have been regular iron cannon shot below the waterline. Some were saved. Not many. We need to import our own cannon or hire some gun founders and start making our own." By *we* she meant all of Eswiland: Talverdin and Eswy-Dunmorra alike. Or maybe Greyrock. You never knew with Mannie; even a witch couldn't tell who she thought she was.

"The Yehillon ships?"

Powers, if only the headache would let her think, let her listen. Something pounded at her, dragged at her heart...

"One burned, the one the Makers got before the smoke got us. One scuttled itself when we were about to board, though we picked up some survivors, mostly hireling sailors. Not that they thought a chance to burn Nightwalkers was a bad idea, Powers know, but still, not dedicated Yehillon. The third was the one that rammed and boarded us. It holed itself, though, and is sinking now. We've sprung a leak but nothing the pumps can't keep up with, and Imurra's taking the whole fleet in. Father said three ships escaped them at Hallasbourg, and we've got them all. It's over," Mannie confirmed. "Dralla's safe. Talverdin's safe." And then she caught Crow as she sagged and staggered.

Crow...

"Nethin!"

Crow had sought her cousin in her dreams. Her father had, she knew, but her father was kin to Nethin merely by marriage, bound by no tie of blood. Her mother Robin, who might have found him, spared no mite of strength away from her sister. Crow had hoped she could succeed where the Moss'avver, her father, himself failed, in this one thing. And at times she had thought she had found Nethin, but always she lost him again, drowned in darkness, a wild current swirling him away as their hands almost touched.

Nethin...

She fell.

✤ CHAPTER SIXTEEN ✤
NETHIN: GENEHAR'S GATE

Autumn in the Homeland

Darkness, and a noise like the sea, and consuming fire. I fled deeper into the darkness, but the pain followed, and thought began to fade as it devoured me, burning blood and bone. What awareness I had left wailed somewhere deep in my soul, shrieking like an abandoned baby, the last animal outrage at the loss of light and breath. I reached out to seize and hold what I could, crying for father, mother, any living soul at all to hold me, to make the agony cease, to speed it to its end...

And she was there, my cousin Crow, in the sea of darkness between soul and soul. I flung myself into her arms like a lost dog found, though we were nothing but minds, witch-hearts, souls, call it what you will, not arms or bodies or faces, not sight nor voice nor touching hand. Yet I knew her, and knew she held me, for a moment, safe, on Genehar's very threshold, Fescor's arms drawing me away into death.

But Crow clung the harder.

Witchery is not a magic of spells. It doesn't alter the world through pattern and ritual, tapping and shaping some power outside as Maker-craft does. Witchery comes from within. Witches can give only what they already have, give only out of themselves, and few have the strength in the blood to fight any illness or injury that would not heal itself more slowly, given time. Long ago my mother had saved me but could not save my sisters, and she was never strong in health after that.

But Crow was the daughter of two of the strongest witches living, a soul seething with restless strength and a frustrated, unfocused anger, a hawk that had not yet found her proper sky.

She flung that cold, clean sea gale against the fire, pouring through me, through the darkness, into the physical husk from which all self was fast unraveling.

⁂ CHAPTER SEVENTEEN ⁂

MANNIE: LIFELINE

Gulf of Shai, high summer, middle of Therminas-month

Hermengilde'kiro knew witches, understood the strength and the danger of visions and how to care for the vision-lost. If she had not been there at Crow's side, I'm not sure either of us would have survived. There are stories of soul-lost witches, bodies lingering, empty, till they waste away and one day cease to breathe.

"Nethin!" Crow cried and swayed with the pitching of the deck like a storm-tossed tree. Mannie caught her as she fell. Gray eyes stared into nothingness, wide, her pupils swallowing up the iris until she might have been Nightwalker herself, so dark were they.

"Get her below," a sailor said. "That blow to the head…"

"I don't think it is that." Mannie knelt now with Crow's head in her lap. "Visions. Dreams. She's a witch. But oh, Powers, she's not breathing."

A single breath. A long wait—too long. Another. Some small animals dug out of their winter sleep breathed that way. Not humans. Not even witches.

"She's cold." The sailor touched Crow's face hesitantly. "Hermengilde'kiro, is this usual?"

"I don't know. I don't…I don't think so. But I don't think there's anything the surgeons could do. Crow! Crow! Can you hear me?"

Crow had wandered in her dreams, hunting for her lost cousin, Mannie knew, but this was different, come on her swift and sudden and waking, utterly out of her control.

"Gwenllian'kiro?" The sailor took off his tunic and laid it over her. Mannie took one of Crow's hands in her own and rubbed it, till it clenched on her like a claw. She winced but couldn't free herself without hurting her friend.

Another sailor called to the man as a rope flapped loose.

"Go," she told him. "I'll be all right with her. There are men and women in worse shape below, and we'll be in port soon enough." The man nodded, left her with a quick squeeze of her shoulder.

The ship rose sluggishly as the next wave overtook it, and plunged down the trough, no longer the light, dancing thing it had been, heading out. Others, undamaged, scudded ahead. The bright-painted wooden warehouses of Dralla's waterfront seemed a distant haven.

Her mother had fallen like this more than once, gone empty and lost. The Moss'avver had fits of staring at nothing, all awareness fled to some other time and place, but he was used to it; he traveled such roads of his own waking will, sometimes. Crow was young, was inexperienced, was...was not breathing at all now.

Mannie's mother was terrified of her "bad spells," as she called them. Terrified one day she would be truly lost and never find her way back. In such fits the baroness spoke, disjointed and wandering even in her words, of roads and stars and empty winds, of being lost in darkness. Mannie, her father, her brother Ranulf, her mother's attendant Lady Ursula—they kept the younger boys away at such times—sat with Annot then, holding her, talking gently, paying out a rope of words, a lifeline to guide her home. Mannie could do as much for Crow.

"Breathe," Mannie ordered. "You great shambling swamp-born heron, breathe."

Crow breathed and kept breathing, deep and slow as though she toiled uphill. But any faint hope that the insult would bring her out—her brother Drustan called her Heron and Goose when he wanted to twit her about the size of her feet, the only insult that ever struck home with Crow—went unanswered.

The ship was struggling. Mannie felt it through the planking. Duty said she should be getting Imurra'lana off in the ship's boat. Two of the undamaged ships were keeping station behind, in case the flagship foundered after all, but the queen would definitely want Imurra off before it reached such a point. The princess's captain was one of the casualties below. Mannie was the only other person aboard with authority to face down the crown princess, though her cousin was not prone to taking orders from a girl she had lugged about on her hip as a baby.

Dralla seemed no closer. Was it safe to move Crow, to lower her over the side into some bobbing, shying small boat, to soak her in cold spray and, with Huvehla's grace, drag her up the side of another ship without dashing her to pieces on its hull?

Not until the flagship was actually threatening to sink. So much for getting Imurra'lana away. She wasn't about to leave Crow in order to argue with the princess anyhow.

"Crow, you have to come back," Mannie said firmly. "I'm right here. We're on the *Marrac'nor*, remember? The battle's over. We've won. We're heading into Dralla Harbor." Other pointless nonsense, telling her what she already knew, just to keep the words flowing, to keep the sound of her voice in Crow's ears. Crow's still face never changed; her grip on Mannie's hand never slackened, and the distant, drowned look in her unseeing eyes grew, if anything, duller, more lifeless. "Oh Powers, help me! Crow..." Mannie swallowed hard, held her, trying to shield her from wind and sea spray with her own body, and went on talking.

✣ Chapter Eighteen ✣
Nethin: Crow and Storm

Autumn in the Homeland

R ain. Storm. I burned. She lay not over me, not shielding me, but within. She was the storm and the rain, carried against the fire that scorched my veins. For a moment I felt she was burning with me, panicking, lost, dragged down into my death, and what self I had left rebelled that Crow should die too and tried to thrust her away, but the bloody Fenlander stubbornness, which a dozen generations of Dunmorran kings had not been able to break, would not let her lose herself. She struck out against her own panic, her own fear, found some cold, still core of her soul and anchored to it. Her breath filled my lungs. Her heart mastered my failing pulse, set it to her own rhythm, slow and laboring but unfaltering. And so she held me on the very threshold of Genehar's Gate, on the edge of death, as she fought the poison through vein and nerve, untouched by it herself. Crow was human. There was nothing of the halfworld in her blood. *Chiurra* was nothing to her but a harmless mineral.

But a drowning man could pull even a strong swimmer down with him. What will I had left remembered that. I stopped fighting, fighting her, fighting death, fighting the poison. I let it all go and gave myself up to her, so what little strength I had left flowed with hers.

Battle of the Gulf of Shai

I did not know Hermengilde'kiro as well as I knew her younger brothers. She was quiet, reserved, like her father, and perhaps a little shy. She and Lord Ranulf, the elder of the prince's children, were Crow's friends, while their younger brothers, Waldere and Dougal and Laverock, were mine. But I would have put my life into her hands unquestioningly, and through Crow, that day, I did. If Mannie had left Crow lying, run shouting for physicians, we would have been lost. But she held fast to my cousin, never let her go, by voice or hand, and kept that thread intact through the void and storm, drawing us back.

T ears welled in Crow's eyes, drowning the dilated pupils, trickling down the sides of her face into her hair, dampening Mannie's hand as she held her friend's head on her lap. The grip on her other hand never weakened.

"Crow?" Her throat was dry. She had been talking nonsense, she knew—gowns for her cousin Lovell's wedding—the lifeline of a familiar voice to draw the witch back from wherever she strayed. The passing sailors must think she was mad, those that spoke Eswyn. She brushed away the tears and bent close over her, close enough to feel her breath. "Crow, Gwenllian, can you hear? Are you awake?"

Stupid question. But Crow blinked, and her eyes wandered, then fixed at last on Mannie's, a handspan away.

"Kiss th'enchanted princess," she said and giggled as though she were drunk. "Wake her up an' you have t'marry…" A frown wandered over her face and fled, and she struggled to sit upright, letting go at last of Mannie's hand. Bruises were already blooming where her fingers had clenched.

Crow swayed, weak and uncontrolled as a calf first trying out its legs, and Mannie hurriedly got an arm around her. Crow's lolling head found her shoulder, and she sighed, letting Mannie take her weight. "He was burning," she said. "Burning up inside. Burning in his blood and bone. He's gone so far, Mannie. Stars we'll never see." Even her voice was faint and meandering, as if she were still half in a dream. "Mannie, what do I tell Aunt Fuallia and Mam?"

"Hush, Crow. Just…just don't worry, now."

"Someone has to." Crow stirred again and managed to sit up on her own. She fumbled a hand towards her sword, dropped when she fell the first time in the last moments of the battle, but her hand—she was left-handed, like her father—would not close on the hilt. She muttered and clawed the weapon towards herself, then abandoned the attempt, dragged her hand into her lap and beat it with the right. "Pins and needles," she muttered. "Bee stings. Ow."

"Here." Mannie took the hand—feverishly hot all of a sudden—and rubbed it. Fingers flexed and clenched, and the heat seemed to ebb until Mannie wondered if she had imagined it. Surely no living flesh could have contained such heat, and Crow had been so cold, not moments before.

"Better," Crow said.

"You don't *look* better. You look terrible." Crow did, her face gray under her tan, lips pallid, with a smear of blood across the temples and her brown braids unravelling. The blood was from Mannie's own face though. She realized it when she wiped what she thought was sweat with the back of her hand. Red smear, stinging under her eye. Nothing to matter. Clean it later.

"Feel terrible," Crow admitted. "You look nice, though you've got a bit of a cut. But nice. All disheveled and battered, with your hair tumbling down. You should wear leather more often."

"Crow!"

"Sorry." A ragged grin. "Mannie, beautiful Mannie—"

"You're delirious."

"Damned right I am. Flying. Better 'n Gehtish honey-wine, even. He's *alive*. Nethin's alive. He was dying, and I dragged him back from Fescor's very arms. I pulled him back."

Mannie didn't make the mistake of thinking she meant there, to the sluggishly rolling deck of the *Marrac'nor*, heading into Dralla Harbor from the Gulf of Shai. "Where is he?"

Crow sobered and looked tired, tired and ill. She had been through more than one battle that day, and Mannie thought that perhaps the sea fight had not been the worst.

"Far away," she said. "Yerku help us, Mannie, he's alive, but I have no idea how we can save him. He's so very far away."

✠ Chapter Twenty ✠

Nethin: Waking

Autumn in the Homeland

I hurt. I hurt beyond believing, an ache through all my chest, my ribs, that kept me from drawing any but the shallowest breath, a hurt that made it impossible to doubt I was alive.

I pushed myself up, or tried to, fell on my face, rolled over, got myself sitting upright. My left arm, the arm Orlando had stabbed with the *chiurra*-poisoned arrow, wouldn't answer but flopped and dragged from my shoulder, a dead weight. I pulled it into my lap. I could feel my own touch on the skin of the hand, but that was the only sign that it was any part of my body. A hole had been eaten in the sleeve of the shirt as if by some corrosive, and the edges of it were black and stiff with dried blood, brown as though singed. Beneath the hole, the flesh of my forearm looked as though it had melted and run like wax, reforming in ridges and swirls of white scar. When I touched those, they were hard and cold, and I felt nothing.

But I was alive.

Some part of me wanted to cry, to crawl into a hole and simply stop breathing, to cease to be. I was so tired, and I was tired of pain and fear. It seemed there had been nothing else since I woke in the coffin and would never be anything else again. But I could not lie down and die. The Powers alone knew what Crow had paid from her own body and soul to save mine, and, if nothing else, there was Alabeth, who had called destruction down on all she loved by bringing me home. If she was not already dead, she was a prisoner of Orlando, and soon would be. Giving up was not something I could do, if I was ever to feel anything but loathing for myself, in life or whatever came after.

The fire had died, but the ashes were not yet cold. How long? I didn't think I could stagger even as far as the river again as I was, so I would trust that whatever the contagion in this house, it had been cleansed by time and weather. It was too late for me anyhow, if it had not. Orlando's had not been the only sheepskin coat left in this place when the folk who lived here abandoned the house or died. Another hung from a peg. I struggled into it. Between my dead arm, and the coat being stiffened almost to a board by long hanging, it was no easy job. No weapons, not even a knife for their bread. No metal at all. Someone had come gleaning, despite the fear of catching something.

In a way, that was heartening.

I wrapped my feet in strips of rag torn from a ratty blanket, and put from me the thought of the people—man and wife, maybe—who had probably died in that bed, under that covering. The coat came down to my feet, and my hands were lost in the sleeves. I shoved the cuff of the left into the big square pocket, to prevent sleeve and arm both from dangling and flapping. A tall shepherd's crook was still propped by the door. Leaning on that, I hobbled out into the night. I didn't take the time to devise some spell to find Alabeth. I had been too long in Orlando's company on the shadow road. I knew the smell, the taste of his soul in my own. I was a witch, and I could track him in the wind. Upriver, and south of it.

The stone circle, the place Alabeth called Sand Ridge.

I had not gone very far back down the gully when the rider came at me out of the halfworld. The night-color of his hair was all glints of gold, and the horse's coat rippled like watered silk, smouldering bronze. I thought at first that the prince of the Yehillon was a shade, damned to wander and come to accuse his killer, but then I smelled horse and river water. I did not pause to think or to gather my strength for a spell. I simply swung the shepherd's crook as though it were a halberd. It was a weak blow, one-handed. The horse sidestepped, and the scimitar flashed and the top third of the crook flew away, leaving me with a short staff sliced to a sharply angled end. A better weapon, maybe, if I could get close enough to drive it into his ribs...He wore a shirt of scale armor under his mud-stained surcoat. So I just leaned on it, waiting.

He rode bareback, not even a bridle, only that long gaudy headscarf, twisted to make a rope halter, a single rein. Of course. Alabeth must have, in kindness, removed the mare's harness before she turned the beast loose. I would have been impressed, both that he had found the mare and that he managed to control her and even get her to swim the river with nothing but a bit of cloth around her nose, if I hadn't been so tired, so dully angry that after all this I was going to be killed again by another Powers-damned Yehillon prince. If only this man Aldis could have met Orlando first, settled whatever feud lay between them and left me with but one enemy.

He was as weary, as exhausted, as I. He didn't want to kill me. Too tired for panic, for even any strong anger...I had to listen to what I felt and realize, at last, as I should have done days before: this man wasn't my enemy. His deep-buried hatred wasn't for me at all.

"Oakhold sent me," he said.

✤ Chapter Twenty-One ✤
Alabeth: Watersmeet

The same

Alabeth says anyone sensible would have fled Watersmeet, given up the prisoner for dead and saved herself, along with all the weight of history and memory that she was the last to preserve. She says that not fleeing proves she is not sensible. I say it proves she is a hero. She says no, it proves she is lucky, because heroes are usually dead, most often from being heroic rather than sensible.

That doesn't mean they weren't right in what they chose to do.

"Aunt Mara?"

"Alabeth. You shouldn't have come back."

The old woman wriggled herself upright, coughing with the effort. She was lying on the floor of the smithy, away from the drafty door, at least, and someone had given her a blanket and found an old coat to cover her. But her hands were chained behind her back, the chain looped around the base of the anvil. No doubt they had thought that would stop her working any spell that needed a written symbol or some other tool, but her face was sunken and tight with pain.

"What's the point of dying alone in the mountains?" Alabeth knelt and tugged at the chain. The rusty night-color of it didn't mean it was corroded and weak, unfortunately.

"Where's Nethin? I hoped he was taking you to the shadow road. Couldn't he—?"

"Nethin's dead." Alabeth's voice cracked, and she sat back on her heels. "Aunt Mara, the enemy he was fleeing found us. I was heading up to the old shepherd's house. I thought it would be safe; nobody would go there for fear of catching the red rash, and I'd come back to get you. But that man was there, and he caught us, and—and he killed Nethin. He stabbed Nethin with a poisoned arrow, and Nethin just made a little noise, just a little whimper, and...and he was dead."

Aunt Mara said nothing. After a moment, Alabeth realized she was crying, silently.

"It's just as well," the old woman said, drawing a shuddering breath as Alabeth tried to take her in her arms. "It was fast, at least. Better that than what will come to the rest of us."

"Don't say that!"

"It's the truth. They'll stone me tomorrow. That's the truth. Stone me so that all the village carries the blame of it together, so that they get rid of the guilt of my living here. Nobody will speak up for me. They'll be too afraid, the ones who think it wrong. Afraid someone will accuse them of having Kiron blood too. Try to find the Wanderers, Alabeth. I pray they still survive somewhere beyond the mountains. I'm sorry. We should have gone with them long ago, but I thought I could change something here, make some difference. Save them from themselves and keep them from falling into the darkness... But the books are gone, Alabeth. The past is gone, memory's gone. It's over. There's nothing left to save. Another generation, maybe two, and Watersmeet will be as dead as drowned Rivermouth."

"We'll find some place we can live safe, at least. Together. You and me and Gentalir. Maybe it's all wrong, maybe we're not the last people in the world. Or maybe we will find the Wanderers. But I'm not going without you."

"Don't drag poor little Gentalir into this. He's already in enough danger for being so eager a pupil of mine. He doesn't need—"

"He's getting a canoe supplied and ready," Alabeth interrupted. "He knows he's in danger, Aunt Mara. He's Kiron-talented too."

The old woman turned her head sharply, straining to see Alabeth's face. "He is? I never guessed, but…" She let out a shuddering sigh. "Two of you. I wish I'd known sooner, to teach him what I've taught you…But he's hidden his gift this long. He can go on hiding it. You have to persuade him to stay, Alabeth. Give him a chance at life, at least."

So Aunt Mara didn't believe they could ever find the Wanderers, or that the Wanderers had survived whatever had painted the sunsets so brilliant last winter.

"I think he has the right to decide for himself," Alabeth said. "And so do I. We're all going, the three of us. We have a better chance of surviving together."

Staving off the inevitable, that was all she was doing. Her fingers traced the links around Aunt Mara's wrists. The old woman's head drooped wearily forward. Her hair was nearly as white as her skin. Her arms, strained behind her back, trembled.

"You have to help me," Alabeth said. She plucked a hair from Aunt Mara's head and one from her own. She added a straw that had been tracked in onto the beaten earth floor and wove all three strands through the chain around Aunt Mara's wrists. Water. The stone quenching trough was full. She took a dipper full and knelt down again.

"Aunt Mara, are you awake? I need your help."

"What? Yes."

"Good." She quoted the opening phrases of a spell, faltering in the first word. *Nethin.* She would never be able to speak the

High Court tongue again, without seeing his face before her. "We'll use this one. It's for breaking and mending."

"I'll just be a burden to you."

"You will not!" Alabeth shook her so the chains rattled. "Don't! Do you want to die?"

No answer at first, which was answer enough. Then...

"Everything's gone, Alabeth. You need to get away and live, however you can. Forget about me. Forget about the past, forget about saving the future. There's no hope of that now. All we worked for, generation upon generation, bringing the survivors together, trying to keep going, trying to save history and knowledge and science and Maker-craft. All gone. Burnt. Civilization has failed. Go to the Wanderers. I'm too old."

"If your ancestors had given up, *Princess*, no, *Empress*, last of the Hedenor caste, we'd have all died long ago, wouldn't we?"

"We failed. The new age we thought we could build never came. We were too few, too defeated. People have lost the will to be better, to look to some long climbing track and try to build the road to follow it. We should all have fled with the rebel Kiron. They were right, in the end, and the emperor was wrong. The only salvation was in running away."

"Well, we're running away now, so you can be some use, or you can act like a helpless old dotard and be a burden and be dragged along anyhow. Help me! If you don't come along to remember the past, how am I going to carry it on to the years to come?"

"What I've taught you, you have. What you don't remember is lost," said Aunt Mara. "What does it matter? There's no one for you to teach. There's no one left to care, to even hope for a better world."

Tears of frustration ran down Alabeth's face. Everything Aunt Mara said was true. There was no hope. There was no point. They were defeated; they had failed. They were the last dying ember of that world of wisdom and knowledge and beauty that had been. But if she stopped, if she just sat there, weeping, until the smith and the village elders came in the morning, it would die that much the faster, and somehow that was a betrayal of all the men and women who had tried to build here, to preserve something, to hold on to the tools to trudge back towards some world of light.

The Old Empire had had its flaws; Aunt Mara had taught her that as well. You could not marry out of your caste, or leave it for a different calling. Though there was a council of the caste-princes to advise him, in the end the emperor's word had been law—otherwise, perhaps, some warning of the danger of constant use of the shadow road would have been heeded. And yet even the children of laborers and street singers had been educated, even the poorest had had a voice in their family and caste-councils; folk had lived long in health and made beautiful things for the love of doing so. Folk in all castes had striven to make things better, more beautiful, more wonderful, to the honor of the Powers and their own skill, whether these were new songs, new buildings, or new varieties of apple. In a few years, when she and Gentalir were dead of cold or starvation or mountain bears, it would not matter to the times to come, whether she betrayed all those who had written their histories and tried to lay the foundations of a rebuilt world or not, because the times to come would not value the things she valued, would not know what they had lost and destroyed.

But it did matter, here and now, whether she betrayed herself. It must matter.

So she began the spell alone, without further debate. She sprinkled the water over the chain, sang the words under her breath, felt the power flow, a hesitant trickle, through the paths she had laid with hair and straw.

After a moment, Aunt Mara's voice joined hers, hardly more than a whisper, a creaking breath.

A link of the chain crumbled into flakes and shards of rust, and another, and another. It took only one.

"Drink a little," Alabeth said when she had chafed some of the stiffness out of Aunt Mara's wrists, and the old woman drank from the dipper, saying nothing. "Now, let's go. Gentalir will be waiting."

"Wait," Aunt Mara ordered. "Use your head, Alabeth. Get that basket."

The basket held kindling for the fire. Alabeth tipped it out, wondering what Aunt Mara wanted, wondering how long they had been. She pictured Gentalir growing impatient, coming back to seek them. Gentalir caught by his brothers pillaging the clothes-chest for coats, Gentalir and Aunt Mara and herself all together stumbling and falling under a hail of stones...

Hammer. Ax head. Broken knife. Knife blade without a handle. Chisels. Another ax. Steel arrowheads, a great handful. Two hoe heads. A haftless spade. Another knife. Tools brought here for mending, scrap for melting and reforging. The smith hoarded a great store of metal. Gold was worth nothing in the wilderness. Iron was the true metal.

"Now we can go," Aunt Mara said. "Don't clank."

Alabeth's arms burned with the weight of the basket, but such tools might be the difference between life and death, if they didn't sink the canoe with their weight first. They were lighter than they could have been, simply because she had not thought of them and Aunt Mara had, and the old woman's despair had been as heavy as the end of the world.

The black dog whined, its muzzle muffled in a fold of Gentalir's coat to stop it barking a greeting. The boy reached a hand and caught Aunt Mara's, all he could do while holding the dog quiet, but his eyes brimmed with tears. Aunt Mara hugged him, saying nothing, and they all turned to the canoe. Gentalir must have made more than one trip from his house; the bottom of the canoe held several bundles and baskets, and he was properly dressed. Thank the Powers of Chance and Night that his brothers were heavy sleepers.

Without a word, he passed them each a coat. Those would be missed in the morning, probably even before whatever food he had managed to plunder. When Alabeth plunged her hand into the pocket of hers, she found a sheathed knife. A brother's treasure, no doubt.

The dog calmed, they found a place for the stolen ironmongery and got Aunt Mara and the animal settled amidships before pushing the canoe out and scrambling into their own places, bow and stern.

Without a word, they turned the bow of the canoe into the current. Alabeth, forward, set the pace, allowing Gentalir in the stern to match her. Lord of the Waters, keep us safe, she prayed in the back of her mind. Let us pass safely, let us pass swiftly. Send us no storms and squalls, send us no hidden rocks, no trickster currents.

They needed to put miles between themselves and Watersmeet before daybreak and find some hidden place to lie up. Were there spells that could keep them hidden, in the halfworld or out of it? Would Aunt Mara even remember them, if there were? Alabeth's arms shook as she drove the paddle through the dark water. She felt weak—too weak. No food, no sleep, but it was the pain in her back, that box she had carried, that seemed to have sucked the life out of her. She felt like she had been a week in a sickbed. How long could she keep moving before her body simply failed her?

A blur of water and river sounds, of slow-growing gray dawn and the burning pain of exhausted muscles. She floated, sank, drowned in exhaustion, and they had gone...she did not know. She looked around. Not far enough, Powers help them, only a few miles, and dawn was overtaking them.

"What's that?" Gentalir paused in his paddling, and the canoe began to turn. She steadied it. They were keeping out of the current, close to the southern shore. She looked. He pointed towards the swelling rise of Sand Ridge.

Greenish light bloomed there once, and again. Rose and sank. She shivered. It seemed somehow to wake a worse pain in her back.

"Something bad," she said. "Keep going. Day's coming. The village will be waking."

The surface of the river quivered. The dog whined. Bushes ashore shivered and rattled.

A horse whinnied.

"What's *that*?" Gentalir hissed. He had probably never seen a horse more than once or twice in his life.

"Hush!" Alabeth watched the shore for movement. It was thickly grown with brush. Something moved in the willows, a vast shape, larger than a sardeer, large as an ice-bear maybe. Nethin's horse. Then she saw it clearly, following some deer track through the willows, twisting and turning. It broke into a trot.

Not straying about its own horsy business. It carried a rider. Riders. Someone had found it, and they were pursued. But even as she crouched lower in the canoe, as though that would save them from sight, she saw the muted glow of silver hair, a night-color like moonlight on snow.

"Nethin!" She only breathed the word, not quite able to believe it.

"Someone's found the horse and his body, Powers keep his soul," Aunt Mara whispered. "But where are they taking him?"

"That's nobody from the village." Gentalir whispered as well. "His hair is yellow!"

"Human." Alabeth remembered the word. "A person from Nethin's world. Not one of us. Not that Orlando, the murderer. Another one."

"Keep still."

They were drifting slowly backwards in the weak current close to shore. Alabeth drove her paddle into the water and took the canoe and all in it into the halfworld. It was just dark enough, still. Hadn't these *humans* done enough to him? Did they have to drag his body away after he was dead?

He moved. She was sure she saw him move, turn his head.

Of course, a rider wouldn't hold a dead body upright before him. He'd sling it over the horse's back, wouldn't he? Like a sack?

"He's alive!"

"It was only the branches moving in front of them," Aunt Mara said, but doubtfully. "Only the body being jostled. Wasn't it?"

"He moved. He's alive." Alabeth began paddling for the shore, and for a moment the canoe wavered and twisted in indecision, as Gentalir continued trying to hold them steady. Then he gave in and helped her.

"We'll be overtaken and caught," Aunt Mara warned, but that was all. When the canoe's bow nosed in to a muddy stretch of reeds, she steadied it while Alabeth and Gentalir waded ashore, dragging the boat up, away from the threat of waves. By beaching it in the halfworld, they had not marked the soft mud, which closed up behind them like water, nor battered down the mist-thin bulrushes.

"Wait here," she told the others, stringing one of the bows and slinging their one quiver of arrows over her shoulder. "I have to see…if he's alive, I have to help him. If I don't come back soon—go on."

The boy and the old woman didn't argue. They didn't protest. Gentalir took a length of oxhide rope and slipped it through his dog's collar to stop the animal from following her.

✠ CHAPTER TWENTY-TWO ✠
NETHIN: THE MERCENARY

Oakhold. Of course, I thought. That was the device on the mercenary's flowing surcoat, the great wide-branched, wide-rooted oak.

"Orlando said you were Yehillon," I said stupidly.

"Who's Orlando?"

"Who—? You tried to kill him. When you came onto the road."

"Oh, Roland. Giving himself Ronish airs again. You're injured, my lord. Your arm...?"

I ignored that. "Are you Yehillon? He is. Orlando—Roland, whatever his name is. He was terrified of you, and he called you the prince of the Yehillon. Though he said *he* was their prince, later."

A mirthless grin. "The Yehillon are welcome to him." He hesitated. I could feel his uncertainty. He did not want to say what he was about to say. "I was...bred—and I mean that literally—to be the prince of the Yehillon, my lord. I am not. Trust me. My oath, before all the Powers. I have sworn service to my lady of Oakhold. I am a knight and her vassal, not a hireling. My name is Aldis Alberickson, or Wolfram Katrinson. I'd suggest you not call me Aldis, because anyone who does is generally someone I need to kill. They keep sending assassins."

"Who does?"

"The High Circle of the Yehillon. I betrayed them, by escaping them twice. They know now they can't break me to their will, so they'd rather kill me and try again for a more tractable prince: Roland, or more likely a child of his, some poor boy with the Greater Gifts and fewer obsessions than he. So, Lord Nethin—trust me. The baroness of Oakhold sent me to save you, if I could."

"You're a warlock. Or you know the philosopher's secret arts."

"A bit of both. Will you trust me?"

"Alabeth," I said. "Orlando's going to kill her."

"Where?" he asked. "I tracked Russet and then worked a spell to find you. Should I recast it to find him or do you know?"

I shut my eyes. It was hard to open them again. "Sand Ridge. Where the circle of stones is, the gate to the shadow road."

He didn't ask how I knew, merely leapt down from the horse. I tried not to flinch back. I trusted him; I could see his heart, deeper than he would ever want me to know, but my animal body was hurt and feared his sudden move.

"You look dead on your feet, my lord," he said. "What has Roland done to you? Let me see your hand before we go anywhere. Is your arm broken?"

He meant the one I had shoved in my pocket, all too clearly nerveless.

"No. He had crossbow bolts with a poison on them. He says it has something called *chiurra* in it. Something that acts like philosopher's fire on Nightwalkers."

"*Chiurra?*" He was shocked, alarmed. "Where in Fescor's name did he get that? The fools of the High Circle let him..." Wolfram trailed off, shrugged. "Not poison only to Nightwalkers, Lord Nethin. It's your affinity for the halfworld that reacts to it, the same thing that Talverdin's guardian spells detect. I rode through the Greyrock Pass without a problem, except for dodging patrols"—that flash of a grin—"which wasn't really a problem. So human or not, *chiurra* will kill me as readily as you, and probably Roland—Orlando—himself as well. We all have the halfworld in our blood, Nightwalker or Yehillon, if we have the Lesser Gift. Roland's a fool to handle *chiurra*."

"He'd scratched his hand," I said. "I cured the infection, if that's what it was, and started it healing. He was going to kill Alabeth if I didn't. But then…then he killed me."

"He *what?*"

"He killed me." I was too tired to make up stories, to say *I almost died* when it wasn't true. "He stabbed me. Crow brought me back."

Wolfram exclaimed something that sounded like cursing, in a language I didn't know. Berbarani, probably. It's a good language for swearing in.

"My arm's dead though," I went on. "Not broken. Nothing you can do." I shrugged my left shoulder, all I could do. My nerveless hand flopped out of the pocket.

More Berbarani cursing. He took my hand, and this time I didn't flinch at his sudden movement. He chafed it. I could feel his touch, remotely. I couldn't curl my fingers around his, couldn't lift my hand away from his. His swearing grew softer, more intense and angry. Maybe it was actually prayer. His fingers pushed my coat sleeve up, explored the scar. I couldn't feel the pressure of them. In the darkness—and he could obviously see as clearly as I by night, human or no—the scar had color, a sickly, unclean white. Ugly scarring circled Wolfram's left wrist, but it was clean, had no poisonous night-color. A black horsehair was wound around one finger like a ring, and the Yehillon symbol, the pattern of the shadow road, the map, was tattooed on his right palm. It seemed some strange dream, to feel such trust, such relief that this man I thought I had killed had come to find me.

"Alabeth," I said yet again. But there was something else, something important he needed to know. I struggled to keep my thoughts in order. Waves of exhaustion were threatening to swamp me. I swayed on my feet. "There's a box," I said. "A wooden box. Orlando acts like it's something precious. Wolfram'lana, he talked of cutting this world off from the shadow road. Could he?"

At that, he didn't swear. He didn't say a thing for a moment, but I felt something boil up within him, a sick chill fear. Black eyes burned into mine.

"Did you handle the box at all?"

"Not really. Once."

"Did it feel—did you feel anything from it? Like the feeling of *chiurra*?"

"Maybe. There was…it felt…wrong. Something wrong in it."

"Come." Gentle as a father, Wolfram pulled down my sleeve and tucked my paralyzed hand back into the pocket. "A sling might be better, but that will have to do. And don't call me 'lana. I'm no true prince. Wolfram is enough." He made a stirrup of his hands and boosted me to the mare's back. "Russet's strong. We'll get across the river together. The current's weak here, and if you hold to her mane, you should be fine. If you are swept off, don't panic. Get clear of her, and I'll bring you ashore."

His armor would be a drag on him, but at least it wasn't plate. The sheepskin coat would pull me under, weak and one-armed as I was, if I came off the horse. I should take it off. I didn't. I wound my good hand in her mane.

I wondered if he had bespelled the horse; she followed him into the river so willingly. The water was ice-cold, rising up over my feet, to calves, to thighs, as the horse waded in and then lurched, swimming. The long coat was rapidly soaked, and I lost sight of Wolfram, but then he was there again, taking Russet's head as she scrambled up the southern bank of the river.

He found a rock and mounted behind me. He was exhausted too. I could feel that, under his fear. He had come off the shadow road only hours before, and I could feel its corroding, life-draining influence still clinging to him.

I shivered, but the horse's body warmed me. Wolfram leaned close, not quite holding me like a child, but ready to do so if I began to fall.

"If we're attacked, get your leg over and slide down, roll away," he said. "If you're not fast enough, I'll drop you. Try to roll as you land, get away from the hooves." I nodded. He couldn't draw his scimitar with me before him. He should have taken me up behind, but he too obviously thought I was about to pass out.

Maybe he was right. Time came and went, and only the rhythm of the horse, trotting, walking, cantering, tied the early morning hours together for me. It was night, and then the sky was the color of blue-green glass, with fingers of red haze reaching over us from the east. Storm coming, if weather-lore ran true here.

"Are we going to save Alabeth?" I asked at one point, as the horse trudged along another gully, looking for a way up and westwards. Will we be in time? I meant, but Wolfram's answer, his grim feeling of being already defeated, chilled me.

"I'm going to stop Orlando from destroying this world."

That woke me up.

"How?"

Wolfram did not answer, but after a moment he said, "I should let you down here."

"No," I protested. I found arguments. "You might need another Maker. Eyiss knows, you might need a witch."

He said nothing, but he didn't tip me off into the brush.

"How will he destroy the world?" I demanded, which is what I had actually meant. "What do you fear is in that box?"

"Lodestones. *Chiurra*. Chalk and charcoal. The requirements for a ritual," he said. "Something built more of the philosopher's secret arts than of magic requiring the Great Gifts, warlock magic, though it requires that too, but no more than what any average warlock possesses. Look, what do you know about my father?"

"Your father?"

"It's relevant." We were riding away from the river, no longer heading straight for Sand Ridge. The western slope of the gully was too steep, the stone too loose, for the mare to climb.

A flare like lightning lit the sky over Sand Ridge, and a wave of nausea washed through me. I swallowed hard, and Wolfram reined in a moment. Nothing followed it. He muttered in Berbarani, then guessed, "He's not ready yet. Something escaped him a moment, is all. Damn this shale." He shook his head, urged the horse on as fast as she could go over the tilted slabs of stone, and in the last of the night that still lingered in the gully, he took us into the halfworld.

"My father...," he prompted.

"Prince Alberick," I said. "I know the Warden of Greyrock killed him in some great battle that damaged the very fabric of the world where it took place. Nothing grows there. There's just a...a dead pit in the ground. My father thought I should see it, last time we visited Cragroyal and Oakhold."

"Well then. My father Alberick was the greatest of the princes of the Yehillon. He had the greatest of the Great Gifts, which means he seemed to be a Nightwalker."

"I know," I said.

"Family history," he agreed. "Have you heard your elders discussing their theories about the origins of the Yehillon? They—we—were Nightwalkers, once."

"I've overheard things. And I had started to figure that out myself," I said. "The people here have stories about their Maker-caste. Some who fled after what they call the Disaster, the Calamity, and others who were sent to bring them back, but never returned." I sketched for him briefly what I had gathered from Alabeth, that use of the shadow road, or overuse, or misuse, had somehow damaged the foundations of the world, causing great volcanoes and earthquakes and furious waves, dimming the sun and poisoning the very winds, throwing nature into an age of cold and spreading winter that had lasted now over a thousand years.

He seemed to grow grimmer as I spoke, as if I were confirming something he feared.

"Those Kiron-caste warlocks who fled and those sent to bring them back would be your ancestors and mine. But my father had more than the Great Gifts. You'd call him one of the great Makers, a warlock more powerful than what has been seen in generations, like Prince Maurey. And you, I guess."

"But he was human," I said. "He couldn't have really been a Maker."

Wolfram snorted. "What do you call me? Do you think the philosopher's secret arts could open the shadow road or get a human through the guardian spells of the Greyrock Pass?"

"What do you call yourself?" I asked. Black eyes. He looked more a half-breed Nightwalker than I did.

"An ex-mercenary," Wolfram said blandly. "A liegeman of Oakhold. My lady Annot's vassal. Shall we both agree to call ourselves warlocks? What you did, Lord Nethin, the spell to open the shadow road, that is not a spell that one warlock alone should ever be able to work. Or even two. I don't quite have my father's gifts, but I am still stronger than any in Talverdin but you and Prince Maurey. The shadow-road spell is meant to require a great circle, a score of singers at least."

I remembered sitting by the river with my father. The sharing of secrets. "Witch-blood," I said.

"Yes. I thought witches were a story for children on a winter's night, but the Moss'avver convinced me otherwise."

"You've met my uncle then."

"Oh yes. And, Powers give me strength, your cousin."

He wasn't talking about gentle, scholarly Drustan.

I almost laughed but shivered instead. Powers, give Crow strength. Don't take a toll from her to redress Genehar's balance, I thought. Let my arm be price enough.

Wolfram thought my shivering was cold, which in part it was, and pulled me closer against him. We were both soaked, he entirely, I from the waist down, and the horse was just as wet. She still radiated heat, though, and with my back against Wolfram, shielded from the wind, I was probably warmer than he was.

"My father," he went on, "had a Gehtish father, and Gehtaland is like the Fens, full of witches, no?"

"I don't know about 'full of.' They have witches."

"So probably he had some witch ancestry. Certainly the Great Gifts he displayed were far beyond what any other prince had, even ones with the curse—the appearance of being Nightwalker. I suspect—and the Warden says—he had abilities of which there is no record, though even the Warden won't say what those were. Anyhow, maybe because Alberick was so far beyond what was known, he delved more deeply into our past than any before him. He discovered things long forgotten—"

"By stealing the Baroness's research," I said.

"In part, yes. But much was his own. And he developed new ideas too. Don't think I admire him. He and the Circle abducted my mother and forced her into marriage with him, because their genealogies said that was an ideal mating to produce one with the Great Gifts. The Circle let her die once I was born— since my father was dead, her usefulness to them was over. I doubt Alberick would have treated her any better had he lived. He killed anyone who opposed his will, and she had come to loathe and fear him. Her blessed uncle Gerhardt had turned apostate and traitor and left the Yehillon. He came back to rescue me. He made sure I was trained in all I'd need to know…till they killed him and took me back. But Alberick, Alberick was a great scholar and master of the philosopher's secret arts. And a great…warlock. So I dare not dismiss what his work uncovered. And if Roland has stolen what I think he has stolen…I thought I kept them well-hidden, but Roland was always sly, clever, more cunning than I was willing to give him credit for when I was a boy, maybe. He may have made copies. He certainly seems to have copied the shadow-road spell."

"It was corrupted. It wouldn't have worked. The Homelanders only used it to flesh out my father's spell."

I felt Wolfram shrug. He honestly did not take any pride in his father's achievement.

"In addition to new weapons, and the attempt to recreate the spell to open the true shadow road, my father theorized that it would be possible to tear a world loose from the shadow road. The true shadow road. He was the first in who knows how many centuries to realize that calling the halfworld 'shadow road' was a mistake, a misunderstanding, a corruption of a term meant for something else. He speculated on loosing our world, so that no invasion of Nightwalkers might happen in the future. He suspected they came from another world, and might come again. So in addition to trying to recreate the spell to open the gates of the shadow road, from forgotten scraps of ritual and tales, he created a new spell, to sever a world from the shadow road, cut it off completely. But he never used it. He began to suspect that to use it would destroy not just the link with the road, but the world itself. The shadow road is inherently unstable, corrosive. You know. You've traveled it. But if Roland found the notes and the instructions for that ritual…"

"If your father was right, this world could be destroyed? Worse than what has happened already?" It seemed selfish to add *with us in it?* But I wanted to. "Can he, really?"

"Not if we're in time." I could feel that Wolfram was grim and angry—and full of sorrow. As though under all the hate and anger, he cared about Orlando despite himself. As though they were brothers, cousins, some near kin that couldn't help caring. Raised together, I guessed even then, from the little he said. Maybe the only other young person he had known, the only person who hadn't been one of his captors.

"He has Alabeth."

"My lord, I do believe my father was right. I've studied his writings. This won't merely cut the world off from the shadow road. It will cause it to tear itself apart—as you say it has already begun to do. Long ago."

*The stone skin of the world erupts in fire, cracking into rivers and roads of molten rock. Forests slide into lakes of fire. Seas pour into gaping maws of boiling stone…*I shook my head and did not tell him what I saw. I could not find the words.

He would not save Alabeth if doing so gave Orlando the time he needed to complete his ritual: that was what Wolfram was saying. She would not be a useful hostage. He would not put her above her world. I wanted to protest, to say that the world was not worth saving and Alabeth was, but I could not. I knew he was right and I was wrong. I knew what my father would choose. I sank into dull, defeated exhaustion, maybe even dozed, sheltered by his body, warmed by the horse.

Wolfram's painful grip on my shoulder woke me. We were in the halfworld, doubly hidden behind a towering stone.

Orlando was not in the halfworld; thank the Powers for that. I could tell by the fact that he could rip up handfuls of some fluffy-seeded plant. In the halfworld, the weeds, not anchored in long years, would have been as mist to his hands. For a moment I could not tell what he was doing—not gardening—but he had clearly been busy. He had enclosed the whole circle that the fallen and half-buried stones had once fenced with a line of black. It was lichen burnt in place, I realized. The interior was traced out in figures also made of lines that had been burnt. I could make out an eight-pointed star composed of two superimposed squares, and several curving scorched-black bands. He must have more than a little Maker's skill with fire, to control it so well. All of the bands, and the points of the circle, were filled with what looked like calligraphy, scrolling letters and symbols I could not read, drawn in pale powders. The rising wind raised

little puffs of dust from them, but it was still not strong enough
to erase whatever was written there.

Then I realized that outside the point of each star a patch
had been weeded clear of the shallow-rooted weeds and lichen.

Wolfram hissed, and I felt the shock of his recognition.
This was what he had been fearing then.

"Down," he said, and I nodded understanding. Remaining
in the halfworld, I slid to the ground, silent on the lichen and
wiry grass. He handed me a long, slim dagger; then, leaning
forward, a hand on either side of Russet's neck, Wolfram began
murmuring a spell that would keep her in the halfworld without
a Nightwalker to hold her there. I edged around the stone,
leaning on it for support. My legs felt as though they might fold
up under me.

I had been looking all that time, searching the shadow
of every stone. There was no sign of Alabeth.

✠ CHAPTER TWENTY-THREE ✠
NETHIN: FIRE AT THE GATE

All I felt was a leaden grimness, not outrage, not anger. Orlando had killed Alabeth already, stabbed her with one of his poisoned crossbow bolts and tossed her body aside. I had tried to help Aunt Robin purge a very different poison from my mother's blood and had no idea whether I had succeeded, but I was not Crow or Korby, able to drag a shade back from the threshold of death. Alabeth's shade was beyond my saving.

Wolfram, afoot now, stepped away from the stone, and as he went, he vanished.

I was already in the halfworld. I blinked. The world was still all shades of gray, colorless. I knew I hadn't stumbled out to the everyday plane in my exhaustion. I was in the halfworld and Wolfram had vanished. *The deeper halfworld...* I had heard rumors. The Warden walked where no other Nightwalker could. The Warden walked through stone. But stories like that collected about a man like Maurey'lana. Now I wondered.

Orlando squatted by the patch of bare sand he had cleared, and scraped out a shallow pit. He opened the lid of the larger wooden box. I didn't see the smaller, the one that had held the arrows. If he had lost it, we had fewer weapons to fear. He reached in with, of all things, a pair of tongs. The object he lifted out looked harmless enough, an irregular lump of stone or perhaps hard clay, but in the halfworld it glowed greasy white, and even with the tongs Orlando held it at arm's length as he nestled it into the sand. From six other points of the star, columns of flame burst briefly from the shallow pits in answer to the addition of the seventh lump. That accounted for the flare of firefly-green lightning we had seen before, but even as I thought that, I pitched to my knees, rocked with a wave of sick dizziness. Even the horse, spell-fast in the halfworld, made a distressed noise. Wolfram appeared briefly, on hands and knees. Then he vanished once more.

Orlando heaved up the chest and staggered with it to the next point, the eighth and last point of the star. It was already marked by a chunk of shiny black rock, as was each other point. He squatted down and began digging and weeding again, just inside the tip marked by the lodestone. There was no sign of Wolfram. Then he appeared, not more than a yard or two farther away than when I last saw him. He stood, swaying, a perfect picture of a man about to faint. I started towards him, but as I stepped across the scorched and ashy perimeter I pitched forward, nearly falling onto my face. I caught myself awkwardly on my one arm, retching. I felt as though I had stumbled into some clinging, filthy web, which reached tendrils over my skin, down my throat, burrowing into my nostrils, my ears, my eyes, like roots, growing, choking…I was buried, rotting beneath the soil, and the hungry hillside was feeding on me.

I forced myself to sit back on my heels and wiped my arm over my face. Knowing there was nothing visible, nothing tangible touching me did not lessen the reality of the feeling. Something was growing, binding all this circle into a mass, and in the halfworld, I was on the edge of being pulled into it, made a part of it.

Wolfram again, on his knees like me. No longer calm, grim, masterful, he was fighting against a suffocating panic. I began to crawl towards him, moving like a three-legged dog. He saw me and waved me back. I shook my head and came on. By concentrating on movement—arm, knee, knee—I could shut out the urge to choke and spit and the feeling that some foul fungus was spreading through me as though I were a rotten log. Wolfram was having a harder time. I put my hand on him. His heart was racing.

"It's not..." I couldn't say *not real*. "It's not physical yet, not solid. Just fix your mind on something else." I could feel his panic rising. Buried alive, mouth full of sand...for a moment I could feel, in his memory, the horrible grit of it pouring into my mouth, eyes clenched shut, ears filled, nostrils filled, the weight of it. Sandstorm. Avalanche of sand, a dune, rolling, traveling; the halfworld was no protection, not against the weight of aeons in the grains of stone that rolled over the collapsed tent out of which he had been dragging the others. "Stop that!" I snarled. Buried alive. He had no idea. I let go his shoulder, reached for his hand and pulled him as I lurched to my feet. Eyes shut, I forced myself deeper into his awareness. He hadn't died then. He needed to remember that. The frantic hands, digging. Remember air, and the shelter of a tent that hadn't collapsed, into which they crowded, safe, to wait out the storm, lord and family, servants and guards, camel drivers and all. *A hand finding him, drawing him to safety*. I gave him that memory, and he clung to it, along with my hand, and staggered to his feet after me.

"Phaydos, Phaydos, Lord of Sun, bring us day, give us light..." He was babbling a Hallish prayer. It changed into, "All right, all right, my lord," and an irritated, shamed shaking free of my grip.

"All right now?" I asked and ruined my appearance of being calm and cool by gagging again.

"No," he said with bleak humor. "Powers, but this is foul. And it's worse in the deeper halfworld. I can't stay there. I can't breathe there. Really. It's not just in my head. The deeper halfworld is starting to burn, and the smoke is poisonous."

Even as he spoke, a tendril of smoke coiled from one of the pits, flowing out, branching. Others began to rise. A flare of fire.

Orlando had finished at the eighth pit and placed his lump of whatever that stuff was in it. Raw *chiurra* mineral, maybe. He put the tongs in the box and took out a jar. Lurching to his feet, he began to walk the perimeter of his circle, tossing handfuls of a dark powder before him, singing, invoking the names of the Powers, though other meaning escaped me. Orlando's face was a sickly gray, and his lips cracked and bled, as did his hands, as if he had been burned. Cold fire rose from the pits and began to pulse, slowly, like a giant's heartbeat. The tendrils of smoke flowed and spread and traced all the lines of ash he had made. The earth shuddered and went on shuddering. It was like the vibrating ribcage of some vast purring cat. Wolfram took a step away from me, but I followed. We might have been fighting our way through tar. The air clung and held us, poured into us, choking us, binding our limbs. In the ordinary world, Orlando had no such trouble moving. His stumbling awkwardness was the failure of his own body.

"Out," said Wolfram, his very words slurred and choking, "out of the halfworld. And then be sensible, my lord, and get out of this circle."

But then he fell, and now I could see, dim and misty and not quite there when I looked directly, the smoke, the ropes of sand pouring over him, crawling into him, seeking that seed of the halfworld in him, battening on it like a sucking lamprey. I could feel new strength in the horrible probing roots that forced their way down my throat and plunged through my eyes. I choked on a scream. I was about to fling myself from the halfworld when some last thought remembered it was dawn. The sun had risen. There would be no darkness by which I could return, and Wolfram was being bound into this spell; Wolfram was fighting—I felt his intention—to leave the halfworld, but he could not. The spell was making him a part of itself.

I grabbed him. I had vague notions of spells of unbinding, but they all fled me as I fell into his fear, and instead I seized him, wrapped him in my anger and ripped, as Orlando had ripped up the weeds. We tore free of the halfworld, and sand and dust rose in spiralling dust-demons about us.

Here Orlando's spell could not be felt, but the poisonous, heavy heat of the *chiurra* could. It battered at me, but pain was nothing. I had survived death by this. Wolfram rolled over, found his sword and said, "Run," even as he came to his feet, already running himself, not out of the circle but across it.

Orlando saw us and shouted. He ran himself, not away, but completing the last gap of his circle, flinging the last handfuls of that dark powder, singing. And then he leapt and rolled and came up with something he must have found on the hill and carried back to the gate: his hand crossbow. Of course he had carried a spare cord for it in that box of arrows, and of course he had thought to bring bolts and cord with him when he abandoned the smaller box. He was madly obsessed, but he wasn't a fool: he had taken precautions to defend himself against deadly interruptions. He didn't know that the villagers wouldn't all turn out seeking to rescue Alabeth and me.

The bow was already spanned, the trigger held with some sort of catch. He took aim at Wolfram. I stooped and grabbed a stone, throwing it with my whole strength, shouting as I let fly. The wind rose to a wail, but I hardly noticed. It was enough to split Orlando's attention, to start him turning even as he released the trigger. I heard the sharp crack of the bowstring and the hiss of the bolt past my head. Orlando turned as if to run, realized he could not outrun Wolfram and finally drew his sword. His terror died as he did so, and an exultant calm took its place. He laughed.

"Kill me, Aldis!" he shouted in Hallian, assuming a guard position suitable for the Ronish style of swordplay, one hand tucked behind his back. "I die a hero. My work is done, my blessing in the halls of Geneh is assured. I shall sit at the right hand of the Lady of the Dead, a prince among all the princes,

Blessed Miron's true heir, Alberick's true son that should have been. Think of that, *wallachim*, when your shade flies lost and wailing in the empty void, rejected by Fescor and Geneh forever, as you rejected your destiny."

He was dying, I thought, and he knew it. He had handled those poisons, the raw *chiurra* and others too long. His body was corrupted.

A minor consideration when we stood at the heart of a spell that would rip this world from the umbilical that bound it into the web of worlds and shatter its already weak foundations.

Wolfram was not going for him after all. The nearest point of the star was his target. I stood by one of the lines of ash, so I kicked at it, breaking the line, digging down to bluish sand with my rag-wrapped heel. Nothing altered in the flow of force. It was too late for such measures. The lines of alchemically created smoke, the invisible lines of the lodestones' longing and the fire of the secret arts of the philosophers now carried the spell.

Wolfram staggered. I could feel the pain eating into him, into Orlando too, *chiurra* setting fire in the marrow. Even at this distance I felt the malevolent heat of it reaching out to my blood. With a hand swathed in the hem of his surcoat, Wolfram reached for the chunk of mineral, but against his will flinched back. It's hard to stick your hand knowingly into a fire no matter what the need. He tried again, this time using the blade of his scimitar, but even standing so close was draining his strength, making him weak and clumsy. His hand trembled, and he lost his grip on the hilt. Finally he tried what he should have tried first and began some spell to disrupt Orlando's, but the threads of words he tried to weave were frayed, and they were sucked away into the lines of pale fire in the air.

One of the standing stones fell with a dull thud that I felt as much as heard.

Orlando, not realizing that Wolfram's spell was futile, maybe even thinking the falling of the great stone was some act of his enemy's meant to disrupt his ritual, charged him. I shouted. Wolfram saw him coming and rolled away from the point of the star, scimitar in hand once more, and met him rising. An outraged fury burned away all Orlando's fear of close-quarters fighting, his cowardice, when set blade to blade. He was mad in defence of his great ritual, the idolized Alberick's masterwork, his chance of martyrdom in cutting the homeland of the Nightwalkers off from the wider worlds of the stars forever. He was no unskilled duelist either. But his technique belonged to the practice hall. Sick as they both were, he held Wolfram off, briefly. Oakhold's knight was wary of closing with him, and I remembered stories of Yehillon assassins who painted their blades with some paste that ate into Nightwalker flesh.

"You're a fool, Roland," Wolfram said, speaking Hallian. "This Geneh-damned spell of yours is an abomination. Even my father wasn't mad enough to use it. He knew what it would do. It may cut a world off from the shadow road, but it will destroy that world too. Destroy the shadow road itself, maybe. What will that do to all the other worlds bound by the road? Did you ever stop to think? Did you work out a way to abort it, before you began? In case? We need to stop it. Even you can't want to destroy this entire world, Roland. Not even my father would…"

That probably wasn't true, from everything I had heard about Prince Alberick. I doubted it was true of Orlando.

"The true world lies safe in the hands of the Powers," Orlando said. "If this world perishes utterly, all the better. Only the enclave on Eswiland will remain to be destroyed, to purify the worlds of all existence of the Nightwalkers and their evil."

"It's all lies, you know. Our ancestors were Nightwalkers too. We all come from here. Why do you think all the inbreeding orchestrated by the High Circle throws up Nightwalker black eyes, and full Nightwalkers, every few generations? Prince Alberick was a Nightwalker. I'm a Nightwalker. You're a bloody Nightwalker, for all your brown eyes."

If Wolfram was trying to distract him, it wasn't working. Anyhow, the spell wasn't one that needed the caster to maintain it, once it was given life. Orlando lunged and thrust, and each time, Wolfram either swept his blade aside or simply wasn't there. But he was retreating. No, he was drawing Orlando away from me, giving me time…

You can't just cry "Stop!" to a spell, and breaking a philosopher's completed ritual was something I had never even heard discussed.

I could barely understand how it all held together. It only looked like Maker's work; it was something created by the secret arts of the philosophers, in which ritual and discipline were more important than Maker's will or understanding. A spell of my own, to turn it aside? I took up a handful of ash, but the wind, gusting madly, whirled it away.

Wolfram's dagger. I had dropped it one of the times I had fallen. I turned back to look for it. There, where I had first stumbled. I snatched it up. Where now?

The center of the star. Instinct, a sense for the pattern of power, told me that was right. I ran for it, unsteady on the shaking ground. The last time I fell I stayed down. Plunging the dagger into the earth, I started to cut a pattern, a circle. And another. Another. Seven circles around a central point, cut down through the lichen and thin, dry soil into a layer of bluish sand. I joined each to the next with a carefully aligned stroke, making the pattern of the Coronation Shrine, the Yehillon symbol. I shut my eyes, the better to summon up the memory of the spell I had learned, what seemed so long ago, in that haze of drugs. Rocking back and forth, I began to sing. Into the framework of the gate spell I wove a different intention though. I tried to force Orlando's lines of power apart, to fray them loose from their roots in the substance of the shadow road and the halfworld that was somehow akin to it, as snow and fog are kin and yet of very different natures.

But I was tired, so tired, and weak, and I could feel the spell faltering, staggering like a wing-wounded bird, unable to mount the air.

A hand gripped my shoulder, then slid over, resting open-palmed against my neck, skin to skin. My eyes snapped open and I looked up.

"Sing," ordered Alabeth. "I will follow thee."

I was too stunned to disobey. Alabeth, alive and free. The beauty of her face, her frown of concentration, the bright clear dawn joy in her, to see me there. I hadn't been paying attention or I would have felt her approach, as she couldn't have been in the halfworld, not once she crossed the perimeter of Orlando's spell. Crow would jeer at me, a witch letting someone sneak up on him.

I nodded. I wanted to reach up and take her hand, but I had plunged the dagger into the center of the Yehillon pattern I had drawn, and I needed to hold it there, keep that connection with the very earth of this world. Hand to hand. That was how the mages of this world had always worked their magic, the combining of power that we had only recently rediscovered.

I began again, eyes open this time. Wolfram fell. He was weaker, sicker than he let on, from his passage through the shadow road. He kicked Orlando's feet out from under him as the Yehillon closed in for the kill and was on his own again. Wolfram was a master of his weapon, I could see, but just about done in. I could feel the miring weariness dragging on every muscle, the exhaustion no heat of battle-fury could stave off for long. But Orlando was no master. He was also unwell, and his first exultant fury at having his enemy before him had passed. He felt of fear now—old fear. He had always feared Aldis. They had learned the Ronish sword together, as youths—Wolfram had never let on that he was already a master, tutored by the best in every city he and his uncle had passed through— and Wolfram's chill focus terrified Orlando now as it had

Roland then. I could sense that he believed Aldis would kill him, and that he had always believed that. He had believed it his destiny to defeat the traitor Aldis and take his place, and yet he had always believed, too, that he would fail. That Aldis would kill him, as he could have, at any time, when they fenced together as students. It left him afraid, already handicapped, every time he drew his blade, no matter who the opponent. He always saw his death. Witches read emotions, not coherent thoughts. Hearts, not minds. And yet I knew all that, watching the two of them. Vision, maybe. I could see them, somewhere inside—two blond boys, close kin, locked in hate and something that was a crooked sort of yearning to love.

I watched, and watched inwardly too, and somewhere I even pitied the boy Orlando had been, never good enough, while the one he could have idolized and adored as an older brother discarded his honor like so much rubbish and betrayed them all. And I sang. I wove my shadow-road gate into Orlando's ritual, drew the roots of that mass of destruction to latch onto it, to twine through it, as Alabeth's sweet voice twined through mine, picking up phrases, repeating them with a fine sense of balance and timing, letting me draw out her strength and use it to bolster my own. Not only hers. She had been joined by others. Aunt Mara and a third Maker, hand in hand, a chain of power, though only Alabeth sang.

And then I let my almost-gate fade and slowly, so slowly, die. I fed its dying up the tendrils of Orlando's spell I had stolen. Like a tree when some blight attacks its roots, Orlando's working wilted for lack of vital force, and the blight spread from the roots I had damaged to the great knotted web as a whole. The force that had been pushing, ripping, insidiously prising the world free of the greater web of worlds, faltered. The pulsing of the firefly-green glow of the eight chunks of mineral grew erratic, no longer synchronized to a single heartbeat. The lines of smoke, the lines of force pulled by the lodestones, began to fray.

Orlando looked around. "No!" he screamed, and he flung out a hand towards me, launching his voice, high and shrill, into the opening of a curse.

Wolfram stopped playing, stopped delaying and waiting for surrender. He had not wanted in the end to have to kill his enemy, despite all the hatred he focused on Orlando as the most devoted and blind of Yehillon. Roland was still the only companion, the fellow and not the captor and tormentor, of his youth; but as that curse spewed impotently at me, the scimitar swept in a clean arc and Wolfram cut Orlando down mid-word.

I felt the third Maker of our chain flinch. A child. Alabeth's fingers clenched on my neck. All three were afraid. They had no idea who Wolfram was, but with the rising sun kindling light in his hair, he was clearly not one of their kind. Alien. Dangerous. Perhaps my enemy as well as Orlando's. I could not spare a word to reassure them. Wolfram began to walk around the eight-pointed star. I widened my eyes at him, shook my head. No, no, I willed at him. As with the proper gate spell, the layers of the world were mixing, or we were hovering between them, and he was like a lodestone himself, drawing the halfworld about him. Perhaps I was too, but I wasn't wandering through the lines of force my singing was trying to seize and diffuse.

He saw—no, there was nothing to see—he sensed, somehow, the danger. Stopped and stepped back, just before he would have tangled himself into my spell, been caught maybe, into Orlando's mess again and dragged away. He followed a slow, maze-like course out of the star, frowning in concentration, his eyes half shut. I wanted him over here. I needed him. Even with the help of the other three, I was too exhausted. I could feel how weak my grip on the words was. I was creating this spell as I went, my mind racing barely ahead of my lips. If I faltered, if I failed to find the right words in time, disrupted the rhythm, the flow and balance of the spell, it would all start to disintegrate, and Orlando's working might stabilize. We could be pulled into it, devoured by it, as it carried on its purpose and wrenched this world from its place in the balance of the cosmos. Though that probably meant merely dying sooner rather than later, as the world tore itself apart in ruin.

I raised my chin, jerked my head at him, the most I could do to beckon him. He ignored me.

Yehillon. Traitor after all. A traitor thought of my own. If I could not trust him, after this, after touching and knowing his mind as I did, I could not trust myself. But I needed him, and he was pacing the outside of Orlando's ritual circle.

Wolfram stooped. He lifted something. One of the shiny black lodestones. He took a handful of sand, sprinkled it over the stone, his lips moving, frowning in concentration. And then he hurled it away, far out of the old gate circle.

The burden pressing on me grew lighter. I took a deeper breath. I had not even realized what a weight I was carrying. I nodded to his questioning look. *Yes.* That worked.

He carried on around the circle, neutralizing each of the lodestones with the substance of this world, freeing them from the philosopher's ritual. I sang the last constricting strands of Orlando's web apart, and his spell withered to ash and fell away into nothing. The world settled into its place again and fell still.

I shut my eyes, dizzy, ears ringing. After a bit I realized I was leaning on Alabeth, and she had her arms around me. That was good, that was nice. Her hair smelled like river water. I could stay there, quite happily, probably forever. Far better than trying to move ever again.

Snuffing loudly and wetly, a dog stuck its nose in my ear.

✠ Chapter Twenty-Four ✠

Alabeth: Graveside

Autumn, a week later

I visit the graves of my sisters with offerings of bread and oil and wine on the anniversary of their deaths—a human custom. I think of them as grown women, wonder who they might have become, had they lived. They are real people in my head, both as the little children I remember (so much taller and older than my toddling self), and the women they grow into in my imagination. But they have names and faces, and the memories of them are real: picking strawberries, paddling in the river, squabbling over a hobbyhorse, wrestling with puppies. To have lost them without knowing them, without having even their names...Alabeth says she does not often think of her family, but that does not mean their loss is not, sometimes, a sudden ache and painful hole in the heart. When she holds her son and sees features in his face belonging to none of his living kinsfolk, she wonders, Is that my mother's nose, my father's chin?

Overhill was a town of ruins—thatch rotting, stone walls newly fallen—as if someone had lifted and shaken the hillside. Facing it across a small valley were older ruins of fire-blackened stone overgrown with thorny harda-vine, the hall of the Kiron. The mountainside above showed a naked scar where its face had slid away. Somewhere inside that mountain were entombed many of the miners of Overhill.

In a pit also overgrown in harda-vine were the bones of her parents, mother and father, maybe brothers and sisters, who knew? Aunts and uncles, cousins...horses and dogs, the ashes of books. Murdered. Alabeth had no prayers to give them, not here. Here she only wanted the feel of a knife in her hand or a long clean sight along a straight arrow, and that was not what Aunt Mara had taught her.

She shook her head to shake those thoughts from her mind. Her back pulled when she did so, blisters healing. That brought a flush of heat in memory: Nethin and his friend Wolfram singing together, three cool hands on her back and cloths steeped in water and herbs from Wolfram's supplies.

"He saith it is no worse than bad burns from the sun," Nethin had said. "The poison thou carried in the chest hath done this, but thou hast taken little lasting harm. A faint scar, mayhap. No worse. It is clean. It healeth already."

Certainly, she hardly felt it now, except when she twisted too far and both the blisters and the bandages, wrapped around her trunk to stop her shirt chafing, caught her at the shoulder blades.

But she had not come here to brood over the grave-pit where all her kin lay. She and Wolfram had been sent as scouts.

Smoke rose, not from the mountain but from what had been the main street of the town. A black raised scar, limned in scarlet, ran down the street. It spread and overflowed into the stone-walled yards, engulfing the walls its labor pains had tumbled. Last night there had been thunder, a sifting snow of ash over their camp at Sand Ridge, the lightest of flurries, and a glowing sky across the river. She and Gentalir had been prepared to flee then and there, but Nethin, eyes hazed with sleep, had said, "Wait." Wait, he was not ready, which would kill them all. The shadow-road spell took great mental preparation, great inner strength. This upheaval on their horizon was only a little restless stirring, no great eruption. How he knew he would not say, only insisting that sometimes he knew such things.

Wolfram backed him. Wolfram said he had seen volcanoes, or so Nethin, translating, claimed, and that this was only minor fretting, nothing to flee, yet. Wolfram certainly seemed settled in his mind by Nethin's words. Although Alabeth, and she was certain Gentalir and Aunt Mara, did not sleep again, morning seemed to be proving Nethin right. Only fretting. But a few days of such restless fretting and all Overhill would be entombed in basalt, taken into a mountain's heart.

Now the fissure rested. Tendrils of stone that had flowed red-hot to strike hissing into the stream half dammed it. Black now but not yet quenched, the rock still steamed in the water.

Ash spat into the air. Stones the size of fists pounded the valley. A hot wind stinking of rotten eggs blew clouds of fallen leaves around them, and the scarlet edge of living stone began to spread, to grow, a tide at flood, an apron of fire running for the streambed.

Wolfram whistled, demanding her attention, and Alabeth, with a last look at the Kiron grave-pit of weeds, turned away. They had seen what they had come to see.

"We see. We go."

"We go," she agreed. No point saying more. The yellow-haired man had only a few words of High Court, though he seemed to catch more of it than he managed to speak.

Afoot, they left Overhill behind them, heading for the river and the canoe, dutiful scouts reporting back.

She knew what Aunt Mara was going to say, and she was afraid, sick afraid. It was not a full day's journey over the old coal road from Overhill to Watersmeet. The spur of mountain between would be no great barrier between the volcano and Watersmeet, no salvation, if the grave of Overhill erupted in something more violent than last night's dusting of ash. Aunt Mara would not leave without warning Watersmeet of the danger that now lay so close to them.

CHAPTER TWENTY-FIVE

NETHIN: BROKEN WORLD

Autumn, the Homeland, the next day

"They will not succeed," I said to Aunt Mara. "The folk of Watersmeet will not listen. Not yet. Only a week since they were going to execute thee by stoning, and they would have killed Alabeth and me if they had caught us. Gentalir saith his own family would have turned him out and driven him away had they known him to be mage-talented. We should never have let them return."

"We must try," Aunt Mara said. "And better Gentalir speaks to them than you the stranger or I the corrupter of their youths. They are ignorant. Their wickedness, their hate and even their murder, all arise from their ignorance. They can learn better."

I shook my head. "The last Nightwalkers of the Homeland." But I said that in my own tongue. "Are you happy, Great-grandfather?"

We sat on the hillside of thin, sun-warmed grass, bleached with autumn, leaning against one of the outermost stones. Though only Aunt Mara and I remained—the cripple and the ancient, I had said, making a joke of it—we were safe enough. No one from Watersmeet had ventured near in the week since Aunt Mara escaped them; none would come today, she was certain, especially after the eruption that had begun the night before last. The northwest was quiet now, only the haze of the sky, the little drifts of gray upswirled in every breeze, confirmed what Alabeth and Wolfram had seen yesterday with their own eyes: a new volcano being born.

Large or small. We had no way of knowing what it would grow into. A brief unease, already over, or prelude to some violent cataclysm? I knew what I had dreamed: slow restlessness, slow creep and snow of ash. Time. Even yesterday I had not felt strong enough for what I had to do. It was not cowardice, I thought, but reason. Knowing what it would demand of me. To begin and fail would be to damn us all.

My poor health was what had kept us camped on Sand Ridge for a week, and even the days of rest, sleeping and eating roasted fish and baked botati tubers, would not have been enough to let me face the shadow road; but when I never seemed to recover and kept sliding into sleep—fainting, to tell the truth—Wolfram had finally, two days ago, worked some spell of healing, one I had never learnt. He wrote symbols all about me, traced lines over my heart and head with water and the ashes of certain plants. The spell seemed to make him nervous, but the sound of it had the Warden's voice in it, his careful, balanced phrases, the way every line seemed as though it was written for some great, deep-voiced choir. I put more faith in it than Wolfram did, and maybe that helped. Wolfram said that my exhaustion and my inability to stay awake for long were caused by the lingering poison in my blood, as much as by the life-sapping nature of the road. Plain old poison, from when I was drugged in the coffin, not the deadly *chiurra* compound that Crow had washed from me. So now that Wolfram had treated me for that old poisoning, my eyes did not go heavy and close of their own accord, and if my thoughts drifted and I glimpsed visions hovering when I did lie down to sleep, well, I was a witch. Perhaps that was normal.

My arm was still lifeless, but Alabeth had made me a sling, so at least it did not flop and dangle. It seemed more an injured limb and less some hideous foreign thing tacked onto me in place of my own.

No more delays. I was still weak but strong enough. I would have to be. We could not camp in a snow of ash and the threat of Watersmeet's hatred forever. They could so easily decide that our deaths were what it would take to stop the volcano. And yet, it was not so easy. They were our kinsfolk, even mine, even Wolfram's. And they were huddled in the shadow of death by rock and fire and ice.

✣ CHAPTER TWENTY-SIX ✣
ALABETH: RETURN TO WATERSMEET

While Aunt Mara and I waited, Alabeth and Gentalir returned to Watersmeet, guarded by Wolfram. Alabeth confessed later that as much as the physical danger to them all, she had feared what it would do to Gentalir to confront his family with what he was.

"Y ou can't stay. Don't you understand?" Gentalir's voice rose. Another moment and he would be screaming. Alabeth put an arm around his shoulders and glared at the smith, at the whole crowd of them, all the villagers of Watersmeet, all the folk she had known all her life.

"We're not your enemies," she said. "We're telling you the truth. Great Powers above, don't you see it? You can't be so blind. You've seen what's happened. You can't stay here."

"And who's to blame for that?" demanded the smith, swinging the big hammer she didn't quite dare threaten to use.

Gentalir tensed. After her first outraged tirade, calling him a snake, a canker in the heart of her family, a Wanderer changeling, his mother refused even to speak to him. Alabeth squeezed his shoulder.

"The Kiron never meant to injure the world. Lord Nethin never meant to come here at all. He was forced against his will. What's happening isn't his will, but he caused it; he knows that. He meant you no harm, and he's trying to help you, trying to save you all." *Murderers of my parents.* But Alabeth did not let the words out. These folk, most of them, had not been at Overhill when the last Kiron community was destroyed. They had not thrown the stones, wielded the axes. Not that time.

"Kiron lies. Get out of here. You should have been burned with the ones that spawned you. This would never have happened if we'd driven the old woman out as we ought to have, years ago."

Some of the men and women clustered behind the smith shuffled uneasily. But none of those shuffling and whispering and glancing away spoke up.

All that stopped the smith and her hammer, the others with their spears or forks or axes, was Wolfram. He had found Russet's discarded harness and wrapped his headscarf over his bright hair. That unnatural yellow tangle hidden, black eyes bright and hard as coal, he might almost have been one of the Kiron warrior-mages of legend, save that both his horse and his skin were too brown. But Watersmeet feared him. He was a mage of astonishing strength, like Nethin, and had turned aside the villagers' arrows, when Alabeth and Gentalir first paddled the canoe back to the landing stage.

They weren't utter fools. Wolfram had already swum his great horse over in the early dawn and had been waiting in the halfworld when they arrived. Now he loomed, a silent and menacing guardian, like a shade dragged from the Golden Years.

"Remember when purple ewe-bane started growing down in the east summer pasture? You didn't know what it was, Oalla." The young village shepherd hunched her shoulders and backed away behind her cousin. "None of us did," Alabeth went on. "It's a high mountain plant. We didn't know." Aunt Mara's books would have told them, but nobody thought to bring a branch to show her, until it was too late and the ewes had mostly miscarried. "You didn't know it was dangerous, Oalla. Nobody did. It smelled wholesome. The sheep liked to eat it. But we lost so many lambs, until we figured it out. Didn't we? The shadow road is the same thing. The Kiron caste did not know. The princes did not know. The holy emperor himself did not know that opening the gates stressed and twisted the world, like, like iron overwrought, overbeaten, that grows false and brittle. It was no evil in them, no ill will, no wickedness. It was a terrible mistake. And then they disagreed over how to cope with it, after the disaster they had caused. Some princes of the Kiron wanted to use the shadow road one last time, to find a new homeland. The emperor forbade it. But they went anyway."

"The emperor was wrong. They were right," cried Gentalir. "And they've come back for us. Don't you see? You'll all die if you stay here, even if nothing more happens at Overhill. It just keeps getting colder."

"Winter's the least of our problems now, isn't it?" shouted one of his brothers. "Thanks to you and what your mage-working has called up."

"I didn't—"

Alabeth gave Gentalir a warning squeeze. "Don't," she whispered. "Don't argue like a child. Be wise." She took a breath. "You've condemned us to death for something that isn't our fault—not mine and Gentalir's and Mara's, not Lord Nethin's, not the fault of anyone living. You've turned your backs on what can save you. This is your last chance to escape. Come with us. Come see Lord Nethin's home, the kingdom of the Nightwalkers. Start new lives in a kinder land."

"By traveling the shadow road?" Gentalir's mother snorted. "And when the Kiron there destroy that world, will they migrate on to another? Like a plague of redworms, leaving nothing but barren fields in their wake?"

"They don't use the shadow road. They didn't even remember it, until some wicked folk found it and forced Nethin to open it again. Once we're there, it will never be used again. Nethin swears it."

"Kiron lies."

The earth shivered, just enough to feel in the soles of the feet. Everyone looked around nervously.

Smoke rose from behind the high ground to the west, the direction of Overhill, almost lost against the piled and curdled gray of the clouds, unless you knew it was there.

"You've brought a new age of Calamity on us," the smith said.

They had.

Alabeth didn't want to disagree, because in her heart she felt the same thing, but such small smokes were common in some parts of the world, or so Aunt Mara said. "If the mountains were going to erupt the way they did in the Great Calamity in Veralin province, they'd have done so already, and none of us would be standing here chatting, would we? Probably Overhill is going to do nothing more than smoulder for a few weeks and fill that valley with black stone. But that doesn't mean you can stay sitting in its dooryard waiting for the ice to take you."

"Who can say what it will grow into?"

"That's what *I'm* saying!" Gentalir cried. "Mother, come with us. If you say you will, they'll all come. You know they listen to you. Save them."

The smith turned her back, grabbed the next youngest of her boys when he took a step forward and jerked him with her.

"Get out," she said. "Out of our village, out of my sight, out of our world, and be glad you leave with your lives." She shot a baleful look over her shoulder at Wolfram. "Take your foreign mages and your spells and your talk of the old days, and never come back. That one is no son of mine any longer. *Kiron.*"

"At least leave here!" Alabeth cried. "Go downriver, get away from that smoking pit at Overhill."

The smith spat. "The day I take a Kiron's advice..." She walked away from the river, past the ruins of a house burnt in the bad earthquake, into her smithy, her sons with her. Everyone else followed, scattering, some in haste, some slow. None looked back.

"You don't have to do what she says," Alabeth called after them. "You can come, anyone who wants to. Oalla…" The shepherd shook her head and ran, as if afraid her name on Alabeth's tongue might condemn her.

"Mother!" Gentalir screamed, but Wolfram rode between them. He said nothing; words seemed to fail him in this. He only reached down and put a hand on the boy's head.

"Takest thou him—at—*to* lady," he told Alabeth. "I follow. I guard."

She nodded. Gentalir was crying in great, shuddering sobs. It was one thing to nerve yourself to stand up for what was right, to abandon your family to save the life of someone you loved, unjustly condemned. But to have your own mother reject you to your face…

There wasn't anything at all anyone could say. She put her arms around the boy. The black dog whined and stood on its hind legs, licking his tears.

"Come on, Genta," she said. "We'd better go."

Gentalir nodded, snuffling, wiping his face on his sleeve, on his dog, refusing to look up from its fur. "I'm all right," he said, but he choked on the words.

She led him away to the canoe. She had expected nothing better from them. So why was she choking, a lump in her throat she could not swallow?

✤ CHAPTER TWENTY-SEVEN ✤
NETHIN: RETURN JOURNEY

"What shall I do in thy new world?" Aunt Mara asked suddenly, bringing me back from thoughts of the shadow road, the spell already beginning its slow dance in my mind. "I have nothing to teach Alabeth and Gentalir there. All the little knowledge I have hoarded and saved is nothing to what thou art able to do."

"I am not an ordinary mage, and neither is Wolfram," I pointed out. "Judge not the strength of our Makers by us. Perhaps thy magecraft hath preserved workings our Makers have forgotten, as we have what thine hath lost. Certainly we had forgotten the way to work together, until recent years. But besides, thou hast vast knowledge that we have not. Thy histories..."

"Burnt. All burnt."

We sat shoulder to shoulder, old friends of a week. I tapped her forehead, as if she were a friend my own age. "Thou must write the histories of this world anew, lest we in our world forget yet again what our rebel Kiron ancestors knew, and unwitting, destroy ourselves."

"Hah." She said nothing more, but I felt a darkness, like a cloud that had hovered within her, lift. Like the croup, not yet lung fever, that Wolfram and I had driven out of her once we had begun the healing of Alabeth's burns.

Aunt Mara took a deep breath, savoring her ability to do so. "I am not so very old after all," she announced. "Though too old to see my world come to this."

"I'm sorry."

"Thou'rt blameless. Thou wast no more than the pebble that starteth the rockfall."

We both sat silent. Then the hill shivered beneath us.

"The shadow road overthroweth nature," said Aunt Mara. "The fabric of the world twisteth. Who can say what currents have been stirred up beneath."

My ancestors, the rebel Kiron who found a haven in Eswiland and became the Nightwalkers, knew what they were doing when they let knowledge of the shadow road fade away. They turned the old Eswilander open-air temples into gates— perhaps they hoped that in the future they might go back and lead more of their folk to the new world—but then they let it all be forgotten. Wisely so.

I wondered how many times one had to open the gates to the shadow road before the world began to grow weakened, like metal twisted too many times. Twice? Three times? Three hundred? I thought of Dralla smashed by mountainous waves; and Hayonwey buried under hot ash; and poisonous winds sweeping over Eswy-Dunmorra, carrying slow death; and I still knew I would open the gate to go back.

Snow began to fall—big, white goose-down flakes. There was ash in it. I tasted it, smelled it in the air.

"They come," said Aunt Mara, and I looked back to the river. The canoe, with Wolfram now in the stern, drove in ashore. Russet waded out a moment later and shook herself, droplets flying from her mane. Wolfram was right there with a blanket, but the poor beast stood, head hanging, worn out. Even from here I could feel Alabeth's anger, Gentalir's utter misery. He looked as beaten as the horse.

"They wouldn't be persuaded," Wolfram reported when Aunt Mara and I walked down to them. He simmered with anger too. "The boy's own mother, isn't she, the smith? I don't know what she said, but no child should ever have to hear that tone in his mother's voice." He stalked away, leading the plodding horse. "We've done all we can, my lord," he called back over his shoulder. "They'll have to face what comes as best they can on their own."

"Perhaps if I had not gone...," Alabeth whispered to me. "Perhaps they would have listened, if it had been Gentalir alone."

"No," Aunt Mara told her, putting an arm around each of them, Alabeth and Gentalir. "They have been refusing to listen for years. Thou can'st not blame thyself. Nor Gentalir himself." She began to speak to the boy in their own language. I followed them back to the camp.

We put out the fire on which we had cooked our last meal. We loaded all the baggage we would take—mostly waterskins and botati tubers, which were fair eating even raw—on the long-suffering horse. "Thou must keep the dog tied," I warned Gentalir. "Thou hast no idea what we face, and how difficult it may be for a beast to endure. The horse is a calm horse, but a dog hath more...more imagination. If she should take fright and run away into the lightning..."

Gentalir, face bleak, tightened the dog's collar and tied the leather-rope leash around his wrist, knotting it so that I supposed we'd have to cut the dog free of him once we made it home.

"Wait for me," I ordered.

Seven circles around the central stone, lines ax-scraped down through the thin grass and lichen into the multicolored sands beneath. Gaps left for the gates, the pattern of turnings, the opposite of the maze that had brought us here, the Yehillon symbol reversed. It was burned into my mind. I had not needed Wolfram's tattoo to guide me, though I had referred to it nonetheless, cutting this path yesterday.

I could feel the spell hovering in my mind, awaiting words and will. Felt dizzy, memory of drugs stirring in my blood.

"Whenever you're ready, my lord," Wolfram said, at my shoulder. I had not felt him approach. I needed to pay more attention to my witch's senses. "You lead. I'll follow."

I nodded. My stomach wanted to throw up, but I ignored it. It was fear, only fear, and the way home lay through the fear. There was no going around.

"I'm ready."

We went back to the others. Aunt Mara perched on Russet amid the bags of food. Alabeth and Gentalir, dog pressed against his leg, stood on either side. Alabeth held the mare's reins. I touched each of them, taking a hair: Alabeth, Gentalir, the dog, the mare. Aunt Mara saw what I was about and wordlessly broke a white hair, handing it down to me. I wound them all around my finger with one of my own, one of Wolfram's. It wasn't necessary, it was hardly even magic, a mere charm for luck and blessing, but I knew I would feel better for it. Safer. And if our strength was united, we might stand better against the road, endure its life-sapping cold more strongly.

Alabeth leaned forward and kissed my cheek, said nothing, but blushed. Gentalir, wanly, smiled.

I took a breath and began to sing.

✳ CHAPTER TWENTY-EIGHT ✳
ARROMNA: SEEKING THE LOST

High summer in Talverdin, early Melkinas-month

All the time I was lost, Arromna'den had been waiting, ready to rescue me, if only I would show up to be rescued. I wish I could have obliged her sooner!

"I tell you they're gone, dead and gone. The whole thing was a spectacular failure." The apothecary's face twisted unpleasantly. "Ask your precious spy. You shouldn't tamper with the Powers-damned shadow road. You'll kill us all."

Arromna'den said nothing. When her message-raven reached Sennamor Castle, saying she had at last discovered what the Homelanders were up to and that Nethin'kiro was found and in danger of his life, a whole company of rangers from the east, including her brother, Captain Serrey, as well as a troop of the queen's knights from Dralla, had been dispatched to the Coronation Shrine.

Dispatched, but not in time.

By the time help arrived, Arromna was hiding out in the wilds, keeping watch on the Coronation Shrine, hoping against hope to see the lightning flare and Nethin'kiro returning, safe and unharmed. The mountain rangers found some of the Homelanders trying to go to earth in the hills, while the knights arrested more who were on the road back to their homes, hasty and oh-so-innocent travelers. Sarval'den and Eslin the apothecary had been taken at the House Langen hunting lodge Sarval had appropriated, by House Langen guards serving the head of the house—who was not best pleased with his cousin Sarval. It was Lorcanney'kiro, the head of House Langen, who had first suspected that the Homelanders were plotting something more than their usual complaints in the council. He had asked the queen to have her Office of Inquiry put a watch on Sarval, which led to Arromna's masquerade as a House Langen guard, seconded to Sarval's service. Sarval had always been nagging for more guards to do her honor and pamper her dignity. She never questioned it, when Lorcanney'kiro Langen finally assigned her another.

Once arrested, Sarval was tended by the knights' surgeon and taken in a straw-cushioned cart down to the governor's gaol in Dralla, though no one expected her to live long enough to face trial and probable execution. Burns covered half her body: a curse inflicted on her by Nethin'kiro, her Homelanders claimed, before they realized Arromna was there to contradict them.

Arromna looked around the shrine. There was no sign left of the horrors of that night, only the trampled grass, where the knights and rangers had searched, pacing the pattern given in the spell as though they might find Nethin'kiro hidden down among the grasses. She still seemed to see the boy, though, so frail and yet unbroken, like steel, vanishing between the stones. "Come on," she told her brother, turning her back on the shrine. "I can't stand staring at this place. It just makes it worse." She and Serrey wandered away. The captain of the knights, gray-haired Taynalla'den, no mean Maker, was nerving herself up to have all the Makers there attempt together the spell Nethin'kiro had been forced to learn. They had captured it when they took the hunting lodge, saving the papers from the fire only just in time. If they could start…whatever it was that had happened, perhaps the young lord would be freed, if he were trapped. Or perhaps at least they would understand what had happened to him.

"Did the spell fail?" Serrey wondered.

Arromna considered. "I wouldn't have said so. They vanished into it."

"And a human?"

"I can't explain the human. He just showed up."

"You should have had more backup. The Office of Inquiry…"

"…won't make the mistake of underestimating the Homelanders again. If we didn't get them all. But I think we did."

"Except Roshing'den and that Ronish half-breed Orlando."

"Veyros forgive me," said Arromna. "I should have taken Nethin'kiro and run into the mountains the first night they had him at the lodge. He was just so ill though…But I should have risked it."

"We should have traveled faster."

They fell silent again. The place felt haunted, at least to Arromna.

Captain Taynalla, directed by the apothecary, who walked at her side with hands bound, was pacing yet again through the maze marked by the many stone circles of the shrine.

A stir went through the rangers' half-dozen dogs, and their handlers took up bows and slings.

"Horses," said Serrey, cocking an ear. "Coming up the processional way." He strode in that direction, Arromna and the second-in-command of the knights falling in at his side. Sentries were posted lower down. Though it was unlikely any Homelander strays would ride up the main track, Serrey and Captain Taynalla weren't taking any chances.

Two riders, black horse and white, were escorted by a mounted sentry. The rider of the black Kordaler stallion wore a cloak of plaid, blue and russet and white, and her shield was striped the same colors. The other's shield bore the Dunmorran rock and castle of Greyrock on blue, with the unicorn of Talverdine House Keldyachi, the royal House, small in a corner.

"Ah," Serrey said and waved. The escort waved in answer and headed back down the track. The other two came on, the black horse in the lead, the white following.

"Hermengilde'kiro, Gwenllian'kiro." Serrey bowed. "It's good to see you both again. Is there more news from Dralla?"

"Captain Serrey." The Warden's daughter bowed in answer. "All the Yehillon ships were sunk or taken, yes, but we're not here as couriers, and you'll have heard that from Taynalla'den. There haven't been any more attacks. No, but Immura'lana finally released us to join Taynalla'den. Nothing short of a royal order and someone sitting on her head keeps a half-dead Fenlander in bed, you know. We came as soon as the princess's physicians decided Gwenllian was fit to ride, so...Serrey'den, have you found Nethin'kiro?"

"He's not here," Gwenllian said, before either of them could answer. The Fenlander was gray around the eyes and moved stiffly, dismounting from her tall stallion. Wounded in the sea battle two weeks before, Arromna assumed. Word of the victory had passed around the entire kingdom by message-raven, and the knights from Dralla had been full of news of it. "But he's coming, Mannie. I can almost hear him..." She swayed. Hermengilde'kiro joined her on the ground and put an arm around her waist. "Told you, you should stay in bed another day," she murmured in Eswyn, "thick-headed Fenlander."

Captain Taynalla strode over, calling a greeting, but Gwenllian—Arromna remembered, from postings at the watchtower in Kanifglin, that she called herself Crow—left her horse standing and pushed by, heading for the shrine. Arromna went after her.

"You saw Nethin?" Crow demanded as Arromna overtook her, almost running. "You were with him. Tell me."

"He's ill. Poisoned."

"I know that." The young Fenlander flexed her left hand as if it ached. "But how do you?"

"He was drugged when they captured him, weeks ago, Gwenllian'kiro. But I swear to you, in Vebris's name, I did not know Sarval and Roshing were his abductors. I did not know he was the heart of their great secret. But I shouldn't have waited once they had him at the lodge and I discovered him. That was a misjudgement, and if he's lost I will—"

Crow cut her off with a wave. "Guilt later. You mean he was poisoned before."

Before what? Arromna wondered.

"Powers, that apothecary should lose his head."

"He probably will." Arromna remembered that the young lord was not the only person in Crow's family to have been poisoned by the Homelanders. "Is there any further news of Fuallia'den and Romner'kiro?"

"Recovering. Slowly. Aunt Fu was expected to die, but Mam and...Mam pulled her through."

Crow didn't walk the maze. She cut straight across, heading for the standing stone at the center. Eslin, left where he had been when the captain of knights came to meet the newcomers, made a strangled squealing noise and fell on his knees between his two guards when Crow halted to look at him.

Possibly the first full-blooded human he'd seen in the flesh, Arromna considered. And Crow, her pale brown hair in long braids, pewter eyes burning in a battered face, brigandine scuffed and stained for all that it was clean and new-oiled, looked like a nightmare who could have ridden in Bloody Hallow's train. Except Hallow had conquered and massacred the Fenlanders too. The Homelanders did not study human history though.

Crow drew her sword, not the weight of her father's legendary greatsword, but still a heavy hand-a-half weapon. Two-handed, as if about to commit execution, she tilted up the apothecary's chin with the tip of the blade.

And she was her father the Moss'avver's daughter.

"Crow, no." Hermengilde'kiro was right there at Arromna's shoulder, and she hadn't heard the lady following them. Even in mail, she moved like a cat.

Crow gave them both a reproving look. Her father's daughter, yes.

"My cousin," was all she said, looking back down at the man. Crow sheathed her sword with a scrape and hiss of hungry steel and moved on. The shivering apothecary had wet himself.

"Now that," said Hermengilde'kiro, "was not nice."

"I don't feel nice," Crow growled. She cast back and forth along the circle, a hound seeking a scent. Paths had been trampled through the pink and white yarrow, great clods kicked up where horses had galloped. One set, still visible from that night and carefully avoided since, simply ceased. Crow frowned but didn't ask about the tracks. She put her back to the central stone, folded her arms and shut her eyes.

"What—?" Hermengilde began to ask. Crow kicked her ankle. Hermengilde raised her eyebrows at Arromna and settled down on her heels, indicating with a hand that the ranger might as well make herself comfortable too.

Captain Taynalla headed back towards them, the sheaf of charred papers now in her hand. No doubt she was about to recruit Hermengilde'kiro for the attempt at the shadow-road spell; the lady was known to be a strong Maker, though whether she had any of her father's abnormal abilities, rumor did not say.

White sparks spat over the stones.

Crow opened her eyes.

Lightning, stone to stone, and a rent in the air, beyond which was...madness, Arromna thought. Stars torn into whirlpools, rivers of rippling darkness pouring like waterfalls. She could feel herself falling, as though the earth on which she stood had vanished. Floating, drowning, no up or down, no surface to strike out for. The halfworld was all about her, without her ever having stepped into it, but streaks of color danced like the northern lights.

Then there was daylight, the scent of warm turf and distant sea and trampled yarrow, the reek of horse, overwhelming because for a moment she had smelled nothing at all. Dogs were yammering in a frenzy, and a higher-pitched yap right behind sent her shying sideways, hand on her knife. Her heart pounded as if she'd been running frantic for miles.

Crow shoved past her as she turned, drawing her sword, remembering what they all should have, that Roshing and Orlando were with Nethin, and they could still cut his throat. But the Fenlander was shouting in some alien human tongue, and Hermengilde'kiro had lurched to her feet, grinning and startled, neither making any move towards their weapons.

Neither Roshing nor Orlando. Bemused, Arromna fended off a small black dog, which was hurling itself indiscriminately at everyone within reach.

✾ CHAPTER TWENTY-NINE ✾
NETHIN: HOMECOMING

The height of summer, early Melkinas-month

I will not write of the road home. It was long and cold and dark, but at least no one was threatening to kill me. Gentalir wept sometimes, and Aunt Mara too, quietly and privately, and their grief dragged at me till I learned to wall it off from my own heart. They had a right to mourn. Of the three from Watersmeet, only Alabeth did not feel torn, battered and rejected, half her heart left behind. There had never been anything there for her, while ahead…I could not let my thoughts run too far on. I held the road together about us and walked more than half in a dream. It was Wolfram who called the halts for rest and food, Wolfram who kept me aware of where I was when I began to slide into dreams of gentle mist and the dark threshold of Genehar's Gate.

I hardly realized when we arrived. I was thoughtless as a fish heading upstream. I simply let go the stirrup leather to which I had been clinging—the mare was carrying Aunt Mara and walked, head hanging, as worn and sapped of strength as the rest of us—and turned to step through, releasing the shadow road to fray and fade behind us. I had no thought of what we might find. Wolfram and Alabeth both moved to put themselves before me, but Gentalir's dog bounded ahead, jerking the boy after her by the leash he had never untied from his wrist, even when we slept.

Sunlight blinded me. The uproar had me awash in panic before I sorted out voices and faces and the battering of minds blazing high with emotion.

I staggered, seized and mashed into Crow's bosom, which might not have been such a bad thing, except for the rivets of her brigandine. I couldn't follow her purling Fenspeech, but when she switched to Eswyn it was insults. *Bleached runt of a warlock...* From Crow, that was love. For a few moments I let her hold me. Safe. Home.

She let me go when I started to squirm. "Powers, you show up too late, and then you suffocate me." My voice was hoarse, barely there at all. I held her off at arm's length. She grinned through her tears. I suppose I was crying too. Eyes full of water anyway. "You crying?" I asked.

"No. You smell, and it's making my eyes run. Powers, Nethin-brat, when did you last take a bath?"

"What month is it?" I started to pretend I was counting on my fingers, one-handed, which is when she sobered and put a hand on my left arm in the sling, looking a question. I shook my head. Neither of us said anything, but I leaned into her again, and her arms around me this time were gentle.

"Glad you're not dead, cousin," she said into my hair. "Better introduce us to your friends. And are you likely to have company following?"

"Roshing and Roland are dead." Wolfram spoke over my head.

"And here I'd been hoping you were a figment of my imagination. Where'd you find the Wolf, coz, and why didn't you leave him where you found him?"

"Crow—," Mannie protested.

Crow gave me a wry grin, shrugged. "Well, introduce me to the others then, Nethin. Mannie wants that one to herself."

"Crow!"

I watched Wolfram and Mannie out of the corner of my eye as I set about the introduction of Aunt Mara, Alabeth and Gentalir to Crow, Arromna and a graying royal captain whom I didn't know myself.

Mannie and Wolfram didn't seem to have much to say to one another, and they didn't touch, but they came alive together, somehow. When they joined the rest of the ever-growing crowd, they stood shoulder to shoulder. Wolfram seemed to be trying to fade away into her shadow, a faceless guard, a mere knight of her mother's service. I had a feeling he would have vanished entirely by the time anyone in authority decided to ask about his black eyes and the way he had ridden through the halfworld and into my spell.

It was Mannie, finally, who brought everyone back to some sense. I was swaying on my feet, struggling to frame answers to the hammering questions of the two captains and Arromna'den, who turned out to be a former mountain ranger now serving with the queen's Office of Inquiry.

"That's enough." Mannie's voice was quiet. She had no right to command the captains, but they left off. "Forgive me, Taynalla'den, Serrey'den, but Nethin'kiro's dead on his feet, and the rest aren't much better. There's no one following them from the shadow road, no Yehillon but the prisoners in Dralla."

I felt Crow's flash of amusement at that, and her eyes found Wolfram.

"You've accounted for all the Homelanders, Arromna says. The details will take a month, not an hour, and *they* can wait. Is the nearest shelter that old House Langen hunting lodge, or is there anything closer?"

Other than a few hill shepherds' summer huts, which offered little more than a roof and a fire, there was not. I would have been quite happy simply to stretch out in the warm grass and sleep, knowing that at last I was safe, but everyone else seemed to think I needed a bed and a physician, so they sorted out horses for us all and headed back towards where the green hills rose into the knees of the mountains. Taynalla'den sent message-ravens to Sennamor, carrying the briefest sketch of a report: *Nethin safe, Roshing dead, Sarval arrested.* Thence—I was half thinking in the formality of the Maker's tongue still—news would be flown to my parents at Hayonwey. I had the feeling they would know sooner. Aunt Robin was still at Hayonwey, and Crow could let her know. Perhaps I could, if I knew what I was doing.

Hot sun and the swaying of the horse. I'd ridden as soon as I'd walked. Now I slept, rocked with the horse's rhythm.

My mother, hair sunlit silver, wrapped in a great blue cloak of my father's. She is sitting on the thymey ground in the rose garden my father made with her, when he first brought her to Hayonwey. Two of my father's men-at-arms lounge nearby, not taking any chances. Four bluehound puppies, still at that splay-legged beetle stage, struggle about, tussling over their dam's tail, pouncing at Mama's wriggling toes, nipping at them.

She looks up. She is thin, but she has always been thin. We don't need to say anything. She smiles, and I feel the great black horror that has been pressing down on her lift, float away, dissolve like river mist in the climbing sun.

"Fu?" Aunt Robin calls. "Fuallia! Show some sense. At least get off the damp ground."

It's our dream. She doesn't see me. But Mama takes her sister's hand. "Nethin's back," she says. "He's safe. He'll be home soon."

"Soon," I agree.

"Nethin." Crow's presence, drifting into my dream. I float on a river, a channel through high reeds. So quiet, the scent of earth and water. "No, not here. Cast around."

I nearly wake, but don't, quite. Rhythm of the horse, a boy's giggle, Alabeth and Gentalir commenting on one another's riding skills, or lack thereof. Sun beating on my back. Scent of bruised turf, and warm dusty stone and mountain thyme.

Hoofbeats on the hard track, a sheep track, winding up a narrow valley towards the game path we ride.

I opened my eyes.

Our track skirted the rising face of the mountain, blue-gray slopes rising now, looming into the north and east. To the south, a pinewood spread, marching downhill. A narrow, deep-trodden sheep track branched off from our way and snaked into the dappled shadow. I turned the head of the white gelding I rode.

"Keep on," I told Taynalla'den. "I'll catch up."

"My lord—?"

"Let him go, Captain," Crow said quietly. "I'll wait. There's no danger."

"Go on with the good knights," I remembered to tell Alabeth, Mara and Gentalir, to reassure them I was not abandoning them. "I will rejoin ye presently. Lady Hermengilde and Captain Taynalla have the Maker's tongue; ye may speak with them, and Wolfram will be with ye."

They went on, at least a little ways. Crow waited, lying back to watch the clouds while black Pike grazed by her feet.

Years of fallen pine needles made a muffling cushion to hoof-falls. The air was sweet with the spice of pines, and the wind whispered half-heard music. I came to where the tall trunks opened out again into sunlight as he approached the woods, riding unescorted. Romner always did ride alone, a bad habit I'd picked up from him. I reined in the horse and waited.

My father. His face was old, haggard, thin, beard and temples streaked with gray. And he did not look in the least like his grandfather. Roshing never had such peace in his eyes.

"Your mother sent me," he said, and then without dismounting we clasped each other close and hard, the horses shuffling and uneasy, strangers to one another, but our knees survived it.

The hunting lodge had been cleared of Homelander prisoners, and my father, Wolfram and I took over the lord's bedchamber.

I bathed, and my father washed my sadly cropped hair as though
I were a little boy again. I was too tired to figure out how to
manage it one-handed, though I was going to have to learn. And
though there was food, lots of food, down in the main hall, and
I knew I was ravenous, I fell into the feather bed and into sleep,
deep and dreamless. I woke only once, hearing the low murmur
of voices. Wolfram was talking with my father. I thought, on the
edge of waking, that I had heard the faint hum of the crystal-lined
speaking-stone, and perhaps the Warden's voice, but whatever
Maurey'lana had said faded from memory and the only words
belonged to Wolfram and my father over by the door, murmuring.

"Straight to Rensey?"

"The Warden's right. It may do something," said Wolfram.
"We can execute them all, and the survivors on the continent
will start again, form a new High Circle, find a new heir.
The High Circle captives from Hallasbourg will certainly be
tried and executed; as Queen Ancrena's allies, Dugald and
Eleanor can regard the intended attack on Talverdin as one
on Eswy-Dunmorra, and act accordingly. But as for the rest…
if Alberick's son stands before them, to tell them what we are,
how they've been used and perverted by misunderstanding
and malevolence…who knows? It may at least send them away
shattered in belief and confidence. I always meant to prove
it to them, someday—what we were. I know better now; I'm
not a boy, and I know it could never be so easy. But it will shake
them, confuse them…make them lose their way. Outside the
High Circle, they worship their princes. They'll want to believe
and disbelieve me at once." Wolfram sighed. "I'd rather go back
to Oakhold and have nothing to do with the matter. But I can't.
Even if Prince Maurey hadn't asked, I would be going to face
the Yehillon with this. Will the captives in Dralla be handed
over to King Dugald and the Warden as well?"

"No," my father said decisively. "The common sailors,
maybe. Those who aren't Yehillon. Eventually. If their king

in Hallaland asks nicely, they might be released to Queen Eleanor's custody to pass on to her cousin of Hallaland. But the others, no, they will not be released."

Wolfram seemed to expect that, and said no more.

"Take care," I thought I heard my father say, "for Annot's sake." I drifted away, and in the morning, Wolfram was gone. So was Mannie's white stallion, though only the captain of knights asked about it, and she got no answer that satisfied her.

"We swapped. My brother's horse needs a rest and some feeding up, before she tackles the Greyrock Pass again," Mannie said.

"But that human knight can't just…"

A raised eyebrow. Mannie could radiate quiet as well as her father, the quiet of a great, vast weight of snow, hanging above you on the brow of a cliff. Taynalla'den's eyes narrowed and she went away chewing her lip, but Wolfram was not mentioned again, at least, within my hearing. What the captain's report eventually said of him I do not know. Perhaps the fact that my father had greeted Wolfram by name and shown no surprise at seeing him helped as well.

Aunt Mara's pen scritched. No one but Alabeth could read what she wrote, but she had already commandeered every scrap of paper and parchment she could lay hands on among the knights in the lodge, and had drafted Mannie into helping her with a table for transliteration, rows of Homeland syllables marching by rows of ours. She wrote in her High Court language, so that any scholar knowing the Maker's tongue would soon be able to decipher her writing phonetically, with the table to learn the old characters as they went.

Aunt Mara made faster progress when I could keep my father away from her. Romner'kiro's own pen flew as swiftly as his questions. He had carried the Hayonwey speaking-stone with him, which meant I hadn't dreamed that voice in the night before Wolfram left. The Warden had been asking questions through it as well, though his were mostly about the Great Calamity and the damage done by use of the shadow road.

For now, though, all was silent but the scratching of pens and the faint scraping as Gentalir sharpened a new quill for Mara, the click of glass game pieces as Mannie beat Crow at owls and towers once again. My father was making his own copy of the character transliteration table in the margin of a romance of the Yerku that one of the rangers had been carrying—about the last unfilled space left on any parchment. I think Aunt Mara feared a lifetime would not be enough to recreate all the lost records of her wooden chest in the Homeland, and she was already old. No time to waste. Tomorrow we would leave the hunting lodge and ride, at an easy pace, for Sennamor. My mother and Aunt Robin were to meet us there, and Aunt Mara was promised a corner of her own in the great library and all the parchment and imported paper she could dream of.

"We will bring the others through some day," Gentalir said, looking up from the pen.

I was silent. I had been enjoying the warmth of the fire in the cool evening, the feel of clean skin and clean clothes, the taste of bread and cheese, strawberries and watered wine, black cha with honey. I seemed able to eat constantly, as if making up for lost time. Now I crumbled the slice of bread in my hand, watching the pattern of white crumbs on the dark wood of the table. In its sling, my left arm lay quiet, fingers curled. It hadn't woken. It never would. Already it looked thinner, muscle wasting away.

"Ye are the rebel Kiron," Gentalir persisted, looking around. "Ye went to find a new world, and ye did. Someday, we will go back and persuade them to follow. It was too much use of the shadow road that began the damage of the world and brought about the Great Calamity. Not two openings of the road, or three, or four. We can do it. We can go back."

"They will not be willing to listen, Gentalir," Alabeth said. "Not yet."

Our eyes met. Maybe not ever, was the thought we shared. I could imagine—the Yerku send that it was only imagining and not true seeing—the stones of the Coronation Shrine falling, the headland slumping into the sea. Smoke rising from the water west of Dralla, a plume on the wind, and a dark mass beneath the surface, rising. But could we call ourselves decent people, good people, could we face Genehar's judgement or the eyes of our own children, if we did not try again to save our kinsfolk of the dying Homeland?

But where would we draw the line? One mission? Two? When was it too late? How to weigh duty to our own world, to the safety of those who came after us and all the innocent, unknowing human folk of the world, whose lands and lives we could destroy, becoming the murderous warlocks of their nightmares all unintended?

Alabeth's fingers took the battered bread away and wound through my own, stilling their restless fretting. "Perhaps," she said. "Someday."

✣ ✣ ✣

If all this is a fiction, a romance written by Nethin'kiro Rukiar, whom we know as a poet, not a historian, then, well and good. If it is not, if it is truth long hidden in the secret archives of the Freemarch of Greyrock, then we must ask ourselves, why have the princes of Greyrock allowed this history to escape now, when the Makers' guild talks of experimenting with a great spell to travel between Talverdin and the colony of Port Ancrena in a day, to end the need for long and dangerous ocean voyages? What does Greyrock fear? And are they right to fear it?

The merchants of West Overseas report there have been earthquakes south of Port Ancrena.

✤ GLOSSARY OF CHARACTERS ✤

Abner: One of the Yehillon High Circle (*Shadow Road*).

Alabeth Narran Kiron: A Nightwalker girl of the Homeland, one of the last surviving members of the Kiron caste to bear the name (*Shadow Road*).

Alberick: Prince of the Yehillon (*Warden*).

Aldis: Prince of the Yehillon. See **Wolfram**. (*Shadow Road*).

Aljess: A knight of House Keldyachi; Captain of Maurey's bodyguard; twin sister of Jessmyn.

Alun: Fenlander, hearthsworn of the Moss'avver (*Treason, Warden*).

Ancrena: Queen of Talverdin; Maurey's aunt; mother of Imurra and Korian.

Anders: Dunmorran lord, commander of Dugald's bodyguard (*Treason*).

Annot: Baroness of Oakhold; Maurey's friend and wife; mother of Mannie, Ranulf, and "the brats," Waldere, Dougal, and Laverock. She inherited the barony of Oakhold because she had no brothers. A scholar, she founded the first Dunmorran women's grammar school and college, Asta College, at Cragroyal University. She has been subject to witch-like visions and dreams since a head injury.

Arromna: A mountain ranger, later in the employ of the Queen's Office of Inquiry in Talverdin (*Warden, Shadow Road*).

Arvol: Former Master of Fowler College and Dunmorran traitor; cousin of Annot's father (*Nightwalker, Treason, Warden*).

Blaze: Annot's dog, faithful companion of her youth (*Nightwalker, Treason, Warden*).

Boots: Korby's black Kordaler charger (*Treason, Warden*).

Burrage: Previous king of Dunmorra. Father of Dugald (*Nightwalker*).

Calmic: Pupil at Fowler Grammar School; a bully (*Nightwalker*).

Crow: Preferred name of Gwenllian Moss'avver, eldest child of Korby and Robin; Korby's heir. In the Fens, as in Talverdin, the eldest legitimate child, whether male or female, is the legal heir of the most important ancestral honor. Other children may inherit lesser positions from either parent (*Shadow Road*).

Dandie: Dunmorran ambassador in Hallasbourg (*Treason*).

Dellmurran: Talverdine man-at-arms of House Keldyachi (*Warden*).

'den: Talverdine honorific given to everyone "from swineherds to knights."

Drustan: Second child of Korby and Robin, regarded by them as heir to the lordship of Kanifglin because he is the second child, but under Dunmorran law, because he is the eldest son. Korby's attempt to apply Fen law to Kanifglin may become a legal controversy in future if Drustan's eldest child is a daughter.

Dugald: King of Dunmorra, husband of Eleanor, father of Lovell, half-brother of Maurey on their mother's side.

Eleanor: Queen of Eswy, Consort of Dunmorra, wife of Dugald, mother of Lovell. Also a celebrated composer and musician.

Elinda: Hallalander mother of Eleanor; adherent of the austere Penitent sect (*Treason*).

Elwinn: Talverdine knight of Maurey's bodyguard (*Warden*).

Ervin: Former Warden of Greyrock (*Warden*).

Eslin: An apothecary and member of the Homelanders (*Shadow Road*).

Eugeneas: A member of the Yehillon High Circle (*Shadow Road*).

Faa: A Moss'avver blacksmith; Korby's brother-in-law (*Warden*).

Findley: Physician to Queen Elinda (*Treason*).

Fuallia Shepherd: A mountain witch. Younger sister of Robin, wife of Romner, mother of Nethin.

Fuallia: Princess in a near-forgotten legend of the Westwood, sister of the Lady of the Kanifglin (*Warden*).

Gelskorey: Consort of Talverdin, husband of Queen Ancrena (*Nightwalker, Treason, Warden*).

Gentalir: A young boy of the Homeland (*Shadow Road*).

Gerhardt: A Yehillon renegade, uncle to Katerina, although they were nearly the same age; Wolfram's great-uncle, savior and mentor (*Treason, Warden, Shadow Road*).

Gillem: Alleged nephew of Baron Sawfield, murderer of Prince Lovell of Eswy (*Treason*).

Gregor: Eswyn peasant of the Westwood (*Treason*).

Gwenllian Moss'avver: see **Crow**.

Haidy: Korby's niece, lady-in-waiting to Queen Eleanor (*Warden*).

Hallow: "Good King" or "Bloody" Hallow, continental human conqueror of Eswiland, five centuries before these histories. See also **Miron**.

Hanna: Wife of Harl Steward (*Nightwalker*).

Harl Steward: Steward of Dame Hermengilde's manor; later steward of Oakhold's home manor (*Nightwalker, Warden*).

Harrier: Korby's gray Kordaler charger (*Treason, Warden*).

Hedenor Caste: The caste of the sacred imperial rulers of the globe-spanning empire on the one supercontinent of the Homeland (*Shadow Road*).

Hermengilde Elspeth of Greyrock: see **Mannie**.

Hermengilde: A knight's widow from near Erford in Dunmorra, who raised Maurey (*Nightwalker*).

Hestor: Companion of Eleanor's mother (*Treason*).

Hiram: King of Eswy, father of Eleanor (*Treason, Warden*).

Holden: Former Chancellor of Cragroyal University; also Dugald's Chancellor in Dunmorra. Brother of Master Arvol, murderer of Annot's mother, traitor, executed for his crimes (*Nightwalker*).

Homelanders: A Talverdine secret society which would like to see all Eswiland under Nightwalker rule once more (*Shadow Road*).

House Keldyachi: The royal House of Talverdin.

House Langen: A House (like a clan) in Talverdin.

House Rukiar: A House in Talverdin.

Hullmor: Governor of Prince Korian's household and husband of Jessmyn (*Nightwalker, Warden*).

Imurra: Crown Princess of Talverdin.

Iohn: Dunmorran knight, lieutenant of Dugald's bodyguard (*Treason*).

Jehan: Commander of the Dunmorran knights in Greyrock under Maurey; later Lieutenant Warden (*Warden, Shadow Road*).

Jessmyn: A knight of House Keldyachi, captain of Prince Korian's guard. Wife of Hullmor. (*Nightwalker, Warden*).

Katerina: Former lady-in-waiting to Queen Eleanor; mother of Wolfram (*Treason, Warden, Shadow Road*).

Kiron Caste: The mage-caste of the Homeland, warrior-warlocks dedicated to service of the sacred emperor, his family, and the entire Hedenor caste (*Shadow Road*).

'kiro: Talverdine honorific more or less meaning lord or lady; used for Heads of Houses, hereditary lords and elected royal councillors; occasionally used in a purely honorary way, as in Hermengilde'kiro.

Korby: The Moss'avver, that is, chief of the Fenlander Clan Moss'avver, equal in rank to a baron of Dunmorra and sometimes styled baron. A powerful witch, sworn man of Maurey, distant cousin of Annot, husband of Robin, father of Crow. Maurey's lieutenant in the Dunmorran secret service.

Korian: Younger child of Queen Ancrena, a noted sailor and explorer.

Labienus: A Ronish bookseller and member of the Yehillon (*Warden*).

The Lady of Kanifglin: An ancient title from the days before the continental human conquest of the island of Eswiland, recently revived when Kanifglin became of strategic importance in the defence of Talverdin. Robin is the Lady of Kanifglin, a vassal of the Warden of Greyrock, i.e., Maurey, not Dugald, is her direct overlord (*Shadow Road*).

The Lady of Kanifglin: According to near-forgotten legend, a woman of mixed Nightwalker and native Eswilander heritage who led the last resistance to King Hallow's conquest and sacrificed herself to cover the Nightwalker's final retreat; responsible for the death of Miron the burner.

'lana: Talverdine honorific meaning prince, princess. Heritable only to the second generation, that is, to grandchildren of a monarch.

Leopold: Name of a number of kings of Hallaland, including Eleanor's uncle and cousin (*Treason*).

Lighting: Maurey's warhorse, a black-maned white Talverdine (*Warden*).

Linnet: Korby's elder half-sister, and despite being Clan Kin'arret, his chosen "voice and hand" or deputy (*Warden*).

Lishon: Prince of Talverdin, younger brother of Queen Ancrena; executed in philosopher's fire in Dunmorra; Maurey's father (*Nightwalker*).

Lola: A member of the Yehillon High Circle, aunt of Orlando (*Shadow Road*).

Lorcanney: A Talverdine lord, Head of House Langen (*Shadow Road*).

Lovell: Crown Prince of Eswy-Dunmorra, only surviving child of Dugald and Eleanor (*Shadow Road*).

Lovell of Eswy: Eleanor's brother, whose murder precipitated events in *Treason in Eswy*.

Lowrison: A Dunmorran lord, Maurey's first Lieutenant Warden (*Warden*).

Luvlariana: A Gehtish sea-captain with designs on Korby (*Warden*).

Mannie: Hermengilde Elspeth of Greyrock, eldest child of Maurey and Annot. She is not her mother's heir, because Dunmorran/ Eswyn law does not let females inherit if there is a male heir, and she has four younger brothers. In Talverdin, she would be her father's heir, except that Maurey holds no Talverdine lands or heritable titles; thus the Wardency of Greyrock will not pass automatically to any of Maurey's children. However…situations change (*Shadow Road*).

Aunt Mara Hedenor: A teacher, preserver of the past and last known descendent of the emperors of the Homeland (*Shadow Road*).

Marcia: A murdered Ronish maidservant (*Warden*).

Margo: Peasant-born waiting woman of Annot (*Treason, Warden*).

Mathilda Clerk: Fenlander of Clan Moss'avver; the first Fenlander of either sex to attend university; sister of Alun (*Treason, Warden*).

Maurey: Prince of Talverdin, Dunmorran Warden of Greyrock. Illegitimate son of Queen Ancrena's younger brother Lishon |and Rhodora, the human wife of King Burrage of Dunmorra, thus King Dugald's half-brother. Husband of Annot, father of Mannie, Ranulf, and the three brats.

Miron: Magister or "Burner" Miron; inventor of philosopher's fire; companion to Conqueror Hallow; assumed to have been a prince of the Yehillon. See also **Hallow**.

Mollie: Hearthsworn of the Moss'avver (*Treason, Warden*).

Moonpearl: Talverdine mare owned by Annot, a gift of Queen Ancrena (*Nightwalker, Warden*).

The Moss'avver: see **Korby**.

Aunt Nan: A peasant of the Eswyn Westwood (*Treason*).

Nethin: Only surviving child of Romner and Fuallia, cousin of Crow (*Shadow Road*).

Oakhold: A Dunmorran barony; also the baroness herself. See **Annot**.

Oalla: The Watersmeet shepherd (*Shadow Road*).

Orlando: Member of the Homelanders. See also **Roland** (*Shadow Road*).

Owlfoot: Talverdine gelding given to Maurey, his first horse (*Nightwalker, Warden*).

Ranulf: Eldest son and second of Maurey and Annot's five children; heir of Oakhold (*Shadow Road*).

Robin Shepherd: A human witch of the mountains and onetime bandit, now Lady of Kanifglin; wife of Korby, mother of Crow, Drustan, and two other sons.

Rhodora: Late wife of King Burrage of Dunmorra, mother of King Dugald. Her elopement with the Nightwalker prince Lishon destroyed the first peace talks to take place in five centuries and resulted in Maurey's birth, Lishon's execution and her own death in childbirth. Rhodora's mother was a Fenlander of Clan Steaplow and probably a witch.

Roland: A Yehillon fanatic. See also **Orlando** (*Shadow Road*).

Romner: Lord of Hayonwey in the South Quartering of Talverdin. Belongs to House Rukiar. A scholar, Maker, alchemist and breeder of horses; husband of Fuallia, father of Nethin.

The Rose Maiden: The alias under which Eleanor originally composed her music (*Treason*).

Roshing: Romner's paternal grandfather, former elected lord— representative to the queen's council—for the upper Roshing Valley, after which he was named (*Nightwalker, Shadow Road*).

Rowena: Senior Sister of the Sanctuary of Holy Dragica, a convent of sisters of Mayn (*Warden*).

Russet: Bay Kordaler charger belonging to Lord Ranulf, lent to Wolfram (*Shadow Road*).

Sanno: Talverdine knight of Maurey's bodyguard (*Warden*).

Sarval: A cousin of the head of House Langen and a leader of the Homelanders (*Shadow Road*).

Sawfield: A baron in Eswy (*Treason*).

Sennanna: Talverdine mare belonging to Romner, lent to Eleanor, briefly stolen by Robin (*Treason*).

Serrey: A Talverdine mountain ranger (*Warden, Shadow Road*).

Sneyth: Eleanor's tutor (*Treason*).

Taddie: A bluehound stolen from Dugald by Fuallia Shepherd during her time as an outlaw (*Treason, Warden*).

Tam: Hearthsworn of the Moss'avver (*Treason, Warden*).

Taynalla: A royal knight in Talverdin, captain of the patrol sent to assist Arromna (*Shadow Road*).

Theo: Human man-at-arms of the Greyrock garrison (*Warden*).

Todd: Yehillon spy (*Warden*).

Trefor: Human man-at-arms of the Greyrock garrison (*Warden*).

Ursula: Lady-in-waiting to Annot, later to Queen Eleanor (*Treason, Warden*).

The Warden of Greyrock: Vassal of the king of Dunmorra holding Greyrock Castle, Greyrock Town and the western part of the Westwood, guardian of the Greyrock and (now) Kanifglin Passes that connect human Dunmorra to Nightwalker Talverdin. In *Warden* and *Shadow Road*, Maurey.

Wolfram: Knight of Oakhold, former Berbarani mercenary, son of Alberick and Katerina, prince of the Yehillon. See also **Aldis** (*Shadow Road*).

Yehillon: An ancient, extremely secretive human cult dedicated to purging the world of Nightwalkers.

"If one book has shaped what I think a book should do and what literature should be," K.V. Johansen says, "it is *Lord of the Rings*." As Tolkien was, she is thorough in her research as she creates other worlds for her stories. Johansen, who has a master's degree in Medieval Studies, lives in a bit of another world herself; she grows exotic trees indoors and seedling oaks and apples outdoors in what used to be the vegetable garden, and hopes some day to have her very own forest, because both the house and the yard are getting rather crowded.